# "As I recall, we're no longer married. I stopped taking orders from you years ago."

"As I recall, you never took orders from anyone, least of all me." He kneeled behind her and in one fluid motion, he was sweeping her into his arms.

"Who do you think you are, manhandling me like this! Put me down!"

"Still the same hell-bent ball of fire, all right. It's good to know that some things in life don't change."

"You have some nerve." Laura squirmed in his arms before he placed her on the couch.

"No need to thank me," he said. "I wouldn't want you to exert yourself." He lowered his gaze. Even though she now lay curled under a blanket, he could picture the curves of her shapely legs. Her rumpled black skirt had been pushed up high above her knees, exposing the smooth, creamy flesh of her thighs. It had always amazed him how quickly she could arouse him just with a turn of her leg, a flash of her eyes—that was another thing that hadn't changed.

Dear Reader,

A rewarding part of any woman's life is talking with friends about important issues. Because of this, we've developed the Readers' Ring, a book club that facilitates discussions of love, life and family. Of course, you'll find all of these topics wrapped up in each Silhouette Special Edition novel! Our featured author for this month's Readers' Ring is newcomer Elissa Ambrose. *Journey of the Heart* (#1506) is a poignant story of true love and survival when the odds are against you. This is a five-tissue story you won't be able to put down!

Susan Mallery delights us with another tale from her HOMETOWN HEARTBREAKERS series. *Good Husband Material* (#1501) begins with two star-crossed lovers and an ill-fated wedding. Years later, they realize their love is as strong as ever! Don't wait to pick up *Cattleman's Honor* (#1502), the second book in Pamela Toth's WINCHESTER BRIDES series. In this book, a divorced single mom comes to Colorado to start a new life—and winds up falling into the arms of a rugged rancher. What a way to go!

Victoria Pade begins her new series, BABY TIMES THREE, with a heartfelt look at unexpected romance, in *Her Baby Secret* (#1503)—in which an independent woman wants to have a child, and after a night of wicked passion with a handsome businessman, her wish comes true! You'll see that there's more than one way to start a family in Christine Flynn's *Suddenly Family* (#1504), in which two single parents who are wary of love find it—with each other! And you'll want to learn the facts in *What a Woman Wants* (#1505), by Tori Carrington. In this tantalizing tale, a beautiful widow discovers she's pregnant with her late husband's best friend's baby!

As you can see, we have nights of passion, reunion romances, babies and heart-thumping emotion packed into each of these special stories from Silhouette Special Edition.

Happy reading!

Karen Taylor Richman
Senior Editor

Please address questions and book requests to:
Silhouette Reader Service
U.S.: 3010 Walden Ave., P.O. Box 1325, Buffalo, NY 14269
Canadian: P.O. Box 609, Fort Erie, Ont. L2A 5X3

# Journey of the Heart

## ELISSA AMBROSE

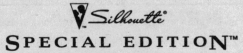

# SPECIAL EDITION™

Published by Silhouette Books

**America's Publisher of Contemporary Romance**

Dedication
To my husband, Robert, for his continual support,
and who for some strange reason likes to refer to himself as "her long-
suffering husband"; and to my daughters, Sarah and Aviva Mlynowski,
who, although they have left the nest, still keep me on my toes.
Acknowledgments:
Special thanks to my editors Karen Taylor Richman,
for taking a chance on a new kid on the block,
and Patience Smith, for her insight and guidance;
and to Anne Lind, a fine writer and editor,
and always, a friend.

 **SILHOUETTE BOOKS**

ISBN 0-373-24506-8

JOURNEY OF THE HEART

Copyright © 2002 by Elissa Harris Ambrose

## *ELISSA AMBROSE*

Originally from Montreal, Canada, Elissa Ambrose now resides in Arizona with her husband, one smart but ornery cat and one very sweet but dumb-as-a-doorknob cockatoo. When not writing, she's either editing, skating or trying out a new recipe. She was a computer programmer for too many years, and now serves as the fiction editor at *Anthology* magazine, a literary journal published in Mesa, Arizona. Currently, she is working on an inside axel, a cheese soufflé and another novel.

Dear Reader,

It is with profound pleasure I present to you my first book, *Journey of the Heart*. A few years ago, after she was diagnosed with cancer, a close friend set out to change her life. She made a vow to live the rest of her life to the fullest, no matter how much time she had left. True to her word, today she continues to search for the joy in every passing moment. Although the plot in the novel is fictional, my friend prefers to remain anonymous. She is truly the inspiration behind this story—a story that I hope you will find as emotionally satisfying to read as it was for me to write.

I am proud that *Journey of the Heart* has been selected for the Readers' Ring, and I look forward to your comments in an online discussion. Only through interaction can we make any sense of this voyage we call life, and what is life if not a journey of the heart?

*Elissa Ambrose*

## *Chapter One*

She knew he'd show up.

Face it, she told herself. She'd *hoped* he'd show up.

She'd spent five long years telling herself she had forgotten him, all the while wanting to see him once again. For closure. It was closure she desired, not the man himself. And what better place for closure than at a funeral?

Now here he was, standing directly in front of her, extending his hand, and she could think of nothing, not one single thing, to say. Take his hand, dummy, her inner voice directed. Don't be nervous. Now smile. That's it, you're doing fine!

She raised her head and looked into his eyes. They were as dark and compelling as she remembered, eyes a woman could easily get lost in. But those telltale lines around the corners were new, and so was that little scar above his right brow.

An accident at a site? A fallen crane? A minor explosion? But wouldn't Cassie have told her if something had happened to Jake? Laura had instructed her dear friend to never, absolutely never, speak his name to her again, but where Jake was concerned, Cassie never listened.

"It's good to see you, Squirt," he said, holding Laura's hand. "You look well. So do you, Cass." He nodded at the slim, dark-haired woman sitting next to Laura in the pew.

Laura *was* well. Surgery and chemotherapy had seen to that. After her recovery, she had resolved to follow a healthy lifestyle, which meant regularly working out at the gym. Now, five years later, she was in better shape than ever. She wasn't one to toot her own horn, but these days Laura Matheson knew she looked *better* than well. She had managed to keep off those extra pounds she'd lost during treatment, and after her hair had grown back in, she'd added gold highlights to her natural dark blond.

As for Jake, he looked basically the same. Laura remembered the lanky boy she had adored in high school, the cocky teenager with the dark, unruly shock of hair that kept falling in his eyes. And he still had that same little dimple on the left side of his smile, although he wasn't smiling now. The scowl on his face looked as fixed as a tattoo.

But even though he was no longer the happy-go-lucky boy from her youth, Jake Logan still looked good. Damn good, especially in that suit. Laura suppressed a smile, imagining him swearing under his breath, trying to straighten his tie. He'd always been a jeans-and-lumber-jacket kind of guy. A man's man. Strong and muscular because of so many years in construction, at six foot two he was almost a foot taller than Laura. Now, hearing him call her Squirt, her old nickname, she felt a familiar rippling in her heart.

"You look well, too," she said, trying to ignore the electricity from his touch. She pulled her hand away. Stupid, stupid, stupid. Why couldn't she think of something clever to say? Something with ginger, Cynthia might say. *Might have said,* Laura corrected herself.

Her throat tightened with remorse. Would she ever be able to think about Jake without thinking about Cynthia? But that wasn't the six-million-dollar question. It was Jake who had never stopped thinking about Cynthia, Laura's best childhood friend, and years later, Jake's first wife.

"I'm sorry about your aunt," he was saying now, his voice somber. "I know how difficult this must be for you. How are you holding up?"

Before Laura could respond, the minister arrived at the lectern, signaling that the service was about to begin. Jake abruptly turned his back and began to walk away.

"Jake, wait!" she called after him, surprising herself with her forwardness. "Will you be coming over later? People will be dropping by the house after the service, and I'd like it if you came by. Bring Cory, too. How is he? I'd love to see him."

He spun around. "How the hell do you think he is? How would any ten-year-old kid be in his situation? You have your nerve, asking about him. You may not have given a hoot about me, but don't sit there pretending that you cared about my son. You abandoned him when he was only five."

She felt the color drain from her face. "What are you talking about? My leaving had nothing to do with him. I never thought—"

"That's just it, you didn't think—which is odd, considering how you used to overanalyze everything." He exhaled slowly. "Look, I didn't come here to make a scene. No, Cory and I won't be coming by later. He doesn't remember you, and I don't want to resurrect old wounds." He gave her a curt nod of farewell. "Take care of yourself, Laura."

Tormented with conflicting emotions, she watched her ex-husband walk away. What exactly had she expected? To find that Jake had changed and wanted to start over? She had made a life for herself without him. She had a fiancé who adored her, and she was happy. She had come back to Connecticut to pay her last respects to her aunt, and that was all.

But that was *not* all. She still hadn't decided what to do with the house. The rambling two-story cottage was now hers. Legally it had been hers since the death of her parents, but after she had left home to marry Jake, she had been content to let her aunt stay on. On the one hand, Laura wanted to sell the house and get on with her life. On the other hand, part of her wanted to keep it, reluctant to let go of the past once and for all. Although she had almost no memory of the years before her parents had died, she had a vague sense that she had been happy there, before her aunt had moved in.

"Looks like Jake still has the old charm," Cassie murmured, breaking into Laura's thoughts.

Laura reached into her purse for a tissue. "I can't really blame him. I just thought he'd be over his anger by now. He's still so...bitter."

She scanned the pews, telling herself she wasn't looking for him. She took in the scene around her, noting how quickly the chapel had filled. Who were all these elderly people? Aunt Tess hadn't exactly been the sociable type. Or the motherly type, either.

Laura closed her eyes, trying to conjure up an image of her parents. If she could only remember one thing, a lingering scent of aftershave, a hairpin left on the bathroom counter, anything at all.... She had been five years old when the driver of the truck lost control and crossed the median, killing himself and her parents. Five years old. The same age as Cory when she'd left Jake. A dull ache centered inside her. Did Cory ever think about her? Or had he completely obliterated her from his mind, as Jake had said?

She opened her eyes and tried to focus on the minister.

"...generosity of spirit," he was saying. "Elizabeth Armstrong touched the hearts of all those who knew her, and will be sorely missed...."

Cassie leaned over and whispered, "'Generosity of spirit?' The only one generous here is the minister."

"Be good," Laura admonished. "Try to remember, she took me in. She raised me."

"Took you in? It was your parents' house, not hers! That woman got a free ride, living in that house. Not that she was ever there to take care of you. Raised you? I don't think so. You raised yourself."

"Shhh!"

But Cassie whispered on. "And while we're on the subject of who wronged whom, I want you to remember that it was charm-boy here who abandoned you, not the other way around. Sure, technically you left him, but he didn't try very hard to get you back, and he wasn't there for you when you needed him most."

As far as Laura was concerned, the issue regarding who left whom was still off-limits. As if sensing her friend's discomfort, Cassie relented and leaned back in the pew. But Cassie was Cassie, and couldn't stay quiet for more than a minute. "Where did you find this guy?" she snickered, motioning to the pulpit. "'Touched the hearts of all those who knew her'? Is he for real?"

"He's from Ridgefield," Laura answered in a low voice. "My mother and Aunt Tess grew up there. Honestly, Cass, can't you just sit still and listen to the sermon? The woman was my mother's sister."

But Cassie remained undaunted. "Remember when she caught me climbing through your bedroom window, trying to sneak you down the old oak tree?" She poked her friend lightly in the ribs. "I'll never forget the look on her face. But we made it! And Ellen and Cyn were waiting at the bottom, waving flashlights. Ellen was all prepared with swabs and bandages. She was so sure we'd fall. How old were we? Seven? Eight?"

Despite her resolve to keep up a solemn front, Laura smiled at the memory.

"And what a sight your aunt made," Cassie continued, "flying out the front door, trying to stop us from getting away. I can still see her running down the street, wearing that wretched old bathrobe, her face in that awful mudpack."

"Will you please stop? People are looking!"

"And what about the time she ran outside, screaming like a banshee after finding a snake in the toilet? Did you ever tell her it was Jake who put it there?"

"Cass, I'm warning you!" But it was too late. Laura had doubled over in a fit of giggles. Cassie could always make her laugh, in any place or situation, even a funeral.

What's wrong with me? she thought. This is a funeral. My aunt's funeral. It doesn't matter that she left me all day with baby-sitters. It doesn't matter that she was always so critical, scolding me for the least little thing. Control yourself! What kind of person behaves this way at a funeral? "Stop it, Cass! What will people think?"

"You mean what will Jake think, don't you?" Cassie's face turned sober. "Okay, take it easy, kiddo," she said. "Put your head on my shoulder. They'll all think you're crying."

Except that Laura *was* crying, somewhere deep inside.

From her pew in the front row, she could feel Jake's eyes on her back. Who was he to judge her? What did he know about her life? When they were growing up, he'd been her ally and her foe, her friend and her tormentor and, always, her secret love. But throughout their three-year marriage, he'd remained distant, as if he'd never really known her.

She turned in her seat and looked in his direction. Their eyes met, and for a moment she felt dizzy. He needs to keep a safe distance, she thought sadly, noting that he'd chosen to sit in the last pew.

She looked back at the minister, who was now saying, "...a beautiful soul who will be mourned by her dearly beloved niece and friends..."

One glimpse at Cassie and she fell into another fit of giggles.

Laura's feet were aching. After the service, people had been dropping by the house all afternoon and evening. Laura had been standing for hours, acting as hostess to a stream of strangers, and now she was in the hallway, bidding her guests farewell.

"What a caring, lovely person she was," Reverend Barnes was saying. Except for Cassie, he was the last to leave. "When I heard that a stroke had taken her from us, I insisted on giving the eulogy."

Laura was having difficulty concentrating on the minister's words. Her thoughts kept returning to the scene in the chapel. It had shaken her to discover that Jake was still angry, or that she even cared how he felt. She kept playing his words over in her head like a song on repeat until she was sure she'd lose her mind.

"...great childhood friends," the minister was saying. "I had a secret crush on her, but she had her eye on some other fellow...."

Angry or not, he should have come to the house. Not that she'd been expecting him. Not that she'd wanted him to come. But they had been married. It would have been the right thing, the *decent* thing, for him to do.

"...didn't work out. Poor Tess, bless her heart..."

Every time the doorbell had rung, she'd stiffened, half with anticipation, half with dread. But he hadn't shown up. This is ridiculous, she rebuked herself, glancing at the front door. What did she care?

"...would always tag along. But we never minded. Your mother was such an adorable little thing. Just like you at that age."

Laura's attention was riveted back to the minister. "You knew my mother?"

"Of course I did! Even though she was six years younger, Elizabeth used to take her everywhere. I can still picture little Caroline, her golden-brown pigtails, those shining turquoise eyes. And those freckles! She couldn't say the word 'sun' without twenty new dots popping up all over her face. And she had a cute little bump on her nose, just like yours."

Automatically Laura raised her hand to the bridge of her nose. As a teenager, she'd wanted to have it fixed, but all her friends had been against it. "It gives you character," Jake had said, "not that you lack any." Later, she decided that the bump she had inherited from her mother was too small for her to even consider having it removed.

Why can't I remember what my mother looked like? Laura thought now. I wasn't that young when she died. I should be able to remember *something*. For years after the crash Laura had searched for her mother in the park, at school, at the doctor's office. Even to this day she still caught herself looking around corners in department stores, in the supermarket, in the library. It's no wonder, she told herself, considering I've never seen pictures of my parents. Where are the mementos of our lives? Where are the family albums? These were questions Aunt Tess had never answered.

"My mother looked like me." The statement had been meant as a question.

"My stars, yes! And how your aunt doted on her! Until the day I performed the wedding ceremony for your parents, Tess was always there, looking out for her. Always sewing something special for her to wear or fixing her hair or baking a special treat. That girl was more like a mother than a sister."

It was as if Reverend Barnes were describing some other person. Aunt Tess, so it seemed, had worn two faces, one at home, the other for the outside world.

A honking outside jolted Laura back to the moment.

"My taxi must be here," the minister said, taking her hands in his. "Don't be a stranger, Laura. Come visit our church in Ridgefield. You might find comfort there."

She watched as he shuffled down the front walk, leaning heavily on his cane. The taxi drove away and she closed the door.

Her thoughts returned to Jake. She remained in the hallway for several minutes, her eyes fixed on the door as though she could will the bell to ring.


"Weren't they a nice bunch? Who would have figured she knew so many people?"

Laura sat on the couch next to Cassie, her feet propped up on the coffee table. They had just finished rounding up plates and coffee cups and were relaxing in the living room, going over the events of the day.

"Just be grateful that everyone from the chapel didn't show up," Cassie answered, yawning. "These walls would have burst wide open. It would have been a geriatric nightmare. Speaking of absenteeism, why wasn't Steady Eddy at the service?"

"I told you, Edward couldn't get away. His surgery schedule is set weeks in advance." In truth, Laura was relieved. Somehow she couldn't picture her fiancé here in Middlewood, Connecticut, as she went on with her everyday life. She burst out laughing, trying to imagine the prominent heart surgeon wearing one of her aunt's prissy smocks, helping her clean the house.

"No fair," Cassie said. "You've got to share your private jokes."

There was no stopping Cassie once she got started on the defectiveness of the male species, and Laura had no desire to discuss Edward's flaws. "I was thinking about Ellen with all those bandages, the night we climbed down the tree. I wish she could have been here today. But you know Ellen, busy saving the world."

"How is our little Florence Nightingale? It must be months since she last called me. Any man in her life?"

"*Dr.* Ellen Gavin is fine," Laura said with affection. "And the phone works both ways. To answer your question, yes, there *is* a man. Although I don't know how she makes time for any kind of personal life, with the schedule she keeps."

"There's always time for a personal life. Trust me, I know."

Laura didn't know how Cassie did it, flitting from relationship to relationship without getting involved—or hurt. When it came to men, Cassie claimed she knew exactly what she wanted; the problem was that what she wanted changed from week to week. When it came to business, however, she was as sharp as a razor. Cassie was one of the town's most successful real estate brokers. Her rise to the top of her field was a result of hard work and shrewd planning, but to Laura it was nothing short of amazing.

Ellen Gavin, too, amazed Laura. Even as a child, Ellen had known exactly what she wanted to do with her life, letting nothing stand in her way. Years later, it was that same will, that same determination, that had helped save Laura's life. When Laura first became sick and decided to leave Jake, it was Ellen who had convinced her that life was worth living. Even though Ellen had just become a resident in internal medicine, she was the one who had made sure that Laura had the best team on staff—the oncologist, the anesthesiologist, the surgeon, the chemotherapist. And despite her heavy schedule, it was Ellen who had been there for her day and night throughout the entire ordeal.

"It was Ellen who introduced me to Edward," Laura said to Cassie. "She has a lot of friends at the hospital. Maybe if you're nice to her, she could set you up with someone who just might convince you to settle down. Didn't your mother always want you to marry a doctor? How about a psychiatrist?"

"Are you insinuating that I'm not nice, I have bad taste in men *and* I need therapy?" Feigning indignation, Cassie reached behind her and picked up a throw pillow.

"No, don't!" Laura squealed. But it was too late. Feathers were flying everywhere. "I tried to warn you," she rebuked her friend lightly, "but as usual, you just ignored me."

"Did you say something?" Cassie said, and Laura laughed. Cassie rose from the couch. "I guess this means you want me to sweep up. What a mess!"

"It's nothing compared to the mess before I cleaned up for the gathering. This place was like a warehouse. Aunt Tess had put everything into boxes and stacked them all in here. It was as if she had known she would be leaving this house."

"Spooky," Cassie said. "Where are the boxes now?"

"Forget the broom, and come with me."

Cassie raised an inquisitive eyebrow, and followed Laura through the archway. "I'd forgotten how dismal this place was," she said with a shudder. "You should probably renovate before putting it on the market. You could make a tidy profit. What about adding a breakfast nook at the back of the kitchen? And a skylight would do wonders."

"I don't want to spend the time, not to mention money I don't have. Edward keeps asking when I'm coming home." She pulled open the door to the pantry off the kitchen. "Voilà!" she sang out.

The pantry had been intended as a maid's room when the

house was built in the early 1900s. Layers of wallpaper and different markings on the walls indicated that at one time the room might have been used as a den, a guest room or even a sewing room. As a child, Laura would sneak in there to daydream, and in her fantasies, her mother would be sewing something special—a Halloween costume, a new party dress, Laura's wedding gown....

Piled up in the middle of the room were dozens of boxes. "You should have seen what I threw out," Laura said. "There were hundreds of rusty tins on the shelves, and over there—" she pointed to the far wall "—barrels of flour had turned black. I had to disinfect before moving in the boxes. These boxes, by the way, are my next project. I can't just throw them away without first checking what's inside."

"You sure have your work cut out for you," Cassie said. "I'll be glad to help—but not tonight. This puppy is off to bed, and I suggest you do the same. It's been a long day."

Laura turned to her friend and hugged her. "Thanks so much for being here for me, Cass. I don't know what I would have done without you."

"You always say that, but the truth is, you're the strong one here. You're the fighter, the survivor." Laura opened her mouth to protest, but Cassie cut her off with a quick peck on the cheek. "You don't have to walk me to the door. I'll let myself out. If I know you as well as I think I do, you won't call it a night until you've gone through every box with a magnifying glass."

Sometimes it seemed as if Cassie knew Laura better than Laura knew herself. But on one particular point, Cassie was wrong. Laura was *not* strong. There were times when she felt she couldn't go on, times when she didn't *want* to go on. Whenever she thought about going through life without having children...

She waited for the click of the front door before reaching

for one of the smaller boxes in the middle of the room. Wrapped in silver cellophane, it was tied with a faded crimson bow. It was one of her own old memory boxes, she realized, one of the many she had not taken with her after she had married Jake and moved into his house. I wanted us to have a fresh start, she thought as she removed the bow.

She tore away the wrapping and hesitated. Weren't some memories better left buried? As if taunting her to take that scary trip down memory lane, the box lay there, unadorned on the pantry floor. She took a deep breath and lifted the lid.

The first thing she pulled out was a snapshot of her and Cassie proudly dressed in full Girl Scout garb, marching down Saw Mill Road in the Veterans' Day Parade. She smiled. Going down memory lane wasn't so bad, after all. Next, she picked up a picture of Jake in his gold-tasseled uniform, playing the trumpet. That is, *trying* to play the trumpet. His cheeks were puffed out, his eyes bulging out of their sockets.

Then she picked up a photo of Cynthia.

Cynthia was wearing a white satin gown she had designed and made herself. With its deep décolleté, and a side slit that ended at the hip, it was so risqué that Cynthia's mother had forbidden her to wear it. But Cynthia had been determined, and what Cyn wanted, Cyn got. The night of the Sweetheart Dance, she told her mother that Jake would be picking her up at Laura's house. She put on a plain, high-neck dress, then drove over to Laura's, where the girls spent hours on their makeup and fixing their hair. Laura had always felt awkward next to her chic, lithe friend, but she had to admit, by the time Cynthia had finished working on her, she looked good. In fact, for the first time in her life, Laura felt beautiful. She slipped into her gown, a fairylike creation of dawn-tinted crepe, and twirled around and around, feeling wonderful and weightless.

Cynthia then wriggled her body into her sleek, tight dress. She was not only sensuous, she was majestic, and wore her confidence like a crown. Laura looked at her with awe. "After you, Your Royal Highness," she said, curtsying.

"You're the one who looks like a princess," Cynthia said, then added jokingly, "I'll be watching you tonight, so don't get any notions about my prince!"

Laura studied the photo, trying to recall the name of the boy who had taken her to the dance. That night, all she had thought about was that he *wasn't* Jake. David? Donald? I guess some things aren't worth remembering, she thought now with a twinge of regret.

But there were some things a person *couldn't* forget.

An old pain came hurtling back. Cynthia had told her mother that she'd be spending the night at Laura's.

Laura pulled out more snapshots. Here was Cyn waving goodbye after spring break. Laura remembered how she, Ellen, Cassie and Cynthia had huddled together at the station, as though New York was a thousand miles away. And here was Cyn walking down the aisle, wearing a stunning gown of silk and lace, which she had designed and sewn herself. And here was Cyn, hair and blouse drenched, holding her pink, naked one-year-old son after giving him a bath.

She fingered the photograph of Cynthia with Cory. It might have been the last one ever taken of her once-best friend.

She thought back to that final day, that final hour, that final moment in the hospital when Cynthia had opened her eyes for the last time.

"Take care of my men," she'd said.

And Laura had. Eight months later she and Jake were married.

What was it Rhett Butler had said to Scarlett? It must be convenient having the first wife's permission.

*Oh, Cyn, I certainly made a mess of things, didn't I?*

Maybe resurrecting old memories wasn't such a good idea. With each recollection came a fresh wave of pain.

Laura's thoughts strayed back to her childhood. Aunt Tess had been a cold and stern caretaker. Yet in spite of the resentment Laura felt, she was filled with pity. Poor Aunt Tess. The woman had never known the meaning of happiness.

Before Laura could stop herself, she started to cry. Not the low, broken whimpering that, as a child, she used to smother by burying her head under her pillow, but deep, loud, heartwrenching sobs that threatened to tear her body into pieces. Whether it was because of her reminiscing or because she was exhausted made no difference; her anguish was an acute physical pain that wouldn't ease. She crossed her arms tightly over her chest, rocking herself to and fro as if her spirit were the mother, her body the child. Through a small window in the kitchen, the late night's moon cast its rays over the boxes. Outside, the wind had picked up, and she could hear the insistent tinkling of the chimes hanging from the eaves. She sat there for what seemed like hours, weeping for all the losses she and those she had known had endured, until finally her sobs dwindled into whimpers, and exhausted, she lay down and fell asleep.

## Chapter Two

Morning was bright and crisp. Last night's lusty wind had waned to a breeze, its cool breath lingering in the air. In the margins of the roads, sunlight streamed through the trees, exposing hints of autumn's palette dappling the leaves. Summer was coming to an end.

Jake stood under the overhang outside the front door, pressing the bell. When no one answered, he tried the large brass knocker. He knew she was home. A Ford Taurus was parked in the driveway leading to the garage behind the house. On the rear bumper, a sticker indicated that it was a rental. "What normal person in New York City owns a car?" he imagined her saying.

He stepped back from under the overhang and glanced around. To Jake, the charming Colonial reproduction was a dignified testament to days gone by. He'd always been drawn to this style of architecture, with its direct outlines and sturdy proportions. Especially pleasing to his eye was the way the chimney jutted out from the center of the roof into the sky, majestically uniting hearth and heaven. He'd always believed there was beauty in this kind of design, and that in this kind of beauty lay truth.

Unfortunately, years of neglect had caused both aesthetic and structural damage. Alongside the house, pieces of clap-board had broken off, exposing wood studs. He looked at the broken fence and frowned. Laura hadn't lived here in a long time, but the house still belonged to her, and she should have seen to its upkeep.

He walked down the pathway and rested his gaze on the window of Laura's old bedroom. Was that where she was sleeping these nights? Or had she moved into one of the larger rooms? He couldn't imagine her spending one hour, let alone one night, in her aunt's room, even though it had once belonged to her parents.

He made his way around to the back of the house. The steeply pitched roof, which covered a lean-to and sloped down almost to the ground, was in need of repair. Several of the shingles had flipped over, and many were missing altogether. The yard here was as unkempt as it was out front. Weeds had overgrown any signs of healthy plant life, and the once trimmed bushes now resembled a forest. He vaguely remembered a garden, and for a moment he could have sworn he smelled roses. But the memory slipped away like a dream, and the scent was gone.

After completing a circle of the entire property, he found himself back at the front door. Where could she be at eight in the morning? Wanting to apologize for his outburst at the chapel, he'd come by early to make sure he'd catch her at home.

A movement at the living room window caught his eye.

Suspended from a swag of faded green velvet, white lace curtains flapped in the breeze like laundry on a line. He cut across the lawn, crashing his way through the overgrown grass and weeds.

What was wrong with that woman? Maybe this wasn't New York, but she just couldn't go around leaving her windows open! He pushed aside the fabric and peeked inside. Why was there a light on? He knew she liked it bright, but drawing the curtains would have supplied all the light she needed. She must have left it on all night. His concern mushroomed, and he sprinted back to the front door to try the bell again.

This time if she doesn't answer, he told himself, I'm going to climb in through the open window.

He knew he was being irrational—she could be asleep, or in the shower—but still, he had the unsettling feeling that something was wrong. It was that radar again, the radar she'd always said was between them. Normally he didn't go in for all that psycho mumbo jumbo, but it was weird how she used to finish his sentences or tell him what was bothering him when he tried to keep it all inside. Maybe now the radar was working the other way. How else could he explain the nagging in his gut?

Maybe I can pick the lock, he thought, not thrilled with the prospect of climbing onto the splintered wood ledge of the living room window. He pulled out the Swiss Army knife from his back pocket. Rattling the knob to test its give, he was surprised when it turned in his hand. It didn't make any sense. Laura had always been too trusting and a little naive, but she would never have left the door unlocked all night.

He entered the hallway and scrambled up the steep staircase, his footsteps thumping loudly on the threadbare carpet. "Laura!" he called, convinced she was lying unconscious somewhere in the house. "Laura!"

Once inside her childhood bedroom, he allowed himself a moment to think. On the nightstand was a photograph in an expensive-looking frame. His eyes lingered on the couple in the picture. Laura looked exquisite, in a long black-pearl satin gown that slid off her right shoulder, her hair swept back into an elegant knot. The man standing next to her was dressed in full tux, his arm resting familiarly on her exposed shoulder. On the window behind them, a heavy brocaded green curtain served as a backdrop.

In a flash Jake recalled the green velvet swag in the living room. What if she *hadn't* left the window open? What if someone had broken in? What if...?

He ran out of the room and down the stairs, taking them three at a time. But she wasn't in the living room, or anywhere else, as far as he could see. And then, standing in the hallway, just outside the kitchen, he heard a faint, low moan coming from the pantry, no louder than the mew of a kitten.

He rushed into the small room and for a moment his heart stopped beating. She was lying on the floor, motionless. He bent low and nudged her gently.

She blinked her eyes open and stared at him blankly. "What are you doing here?" she sputtered, her blue-green eyes coming to life. "How did you get in?"

"The question is," he began, "what are *you* doing here?" A small naked bulb hanging from the ceiling, and a haze of sunlight from the kitchen window provided the only light. Looking at the boxes, he tried to assess the situation. Dozens of photographs were piled in a heap, and in a far corner, a stool lay overturned. "Are you all right? When I saw you lying there, I was afraid...I thought..."

"Of course I'm all right!" She pulled herself to a sitting position. "What's the matter with you? Don't I look all right?"

"Don't move. You may have a concussion, or a broken bone—"

"As I recall, we're no longer married. I stopped taking orders from you years ago."

"As *I* recall, you never took orders from anyone, least of all me." He had intended his remark to be as caustic as hers, but the relief flooding through him had washed away the sting. She wasn't hurt. A little irritable and a whole lot rumpled, but she was okay. He eyed her critically. She was still wearing the black linen suit she'd worn at the service, only now it was dusty and wrinkled. Her hair was a mass of stringy tangles, her complexion pale and pasty. Under reddened eyes were large puffy bags, a sure sign that she had been crying. "Actually, you don't look so hot," he said matter-of-factly. "What did you do, spend the night here?" When she didn't answer, he reached out and touched her cheek. "My God, you're like ice! You *did* sleep here. Here, let me help you up." He kneeled behind her and placed his arms around her belly, just above her hips.

"Why are you doing the Heimlich maneuver?" she snapped. "I'm not choking." She tried to stand, but her legs gave way, and she fell back against him.

In one fluid motion, he was standing again, sweeping her into his arms.

"Who do you think you are, coming in here and manhandling me like this! Put me down!"

"I see you're feeling better. Back to your old self again." He rotated the front of her body into his chest, pinning her arms between them. "Still the same hell-bent ball of fire, all right. It's good to know that some things in life don't change."

"You have some nerve," she hissed, squirming in his arms. "Where are you taking me?"

"No need to thank me," he said, releasing his grip and dumping her onto the living room couch. "I wouldn't want you to exert yourself." He felt her eyes burning on his back as he walked over to the window and banged it shut.

"Now what are you doing?" she called as he retreated into the hallway.

He returned with a bright red afghan. "To answer your question, I'm taking care of you. Apparently, you have forgotten how. Now, are you going to cover yourself or do I have that honor?"

"My fingers..." A look of pain flashed across her face, stripping away the veil of her defiance. "These pins and needles feel more like knives."

He pulled the blanket over her legs and sat down at the foot of the couch. "Serves you right for leaving the door unlocked." He reached over and began kneading the life back into her fingers. "It's payback time. Instant karma."

"Ouch! That hurts! I suppose you're enjoying this."

"Keep still."

"I thought you didn't go in for all that stuff."

"What stuff?"

"Karma and all the other mystical forces of the universe. And for your information, karma is about ethical consequences, not stupid mistakes. And it's never instant. Although sometimes I think that nothing ever changes, at least not in one lifetime. You even said so yourself. But don't worry, maybe there's truth to this reincarnation theory. Maybe next time around, you'll finally get it right.... Am I babbling?"

"If you're going to quote me, do it right. My exact phrase was 'Some things in life don't change.' And yeah, you're babbling."

"All better," she said, pulling her hands away. "You missed your calling, Jake. You should have been a doctor. Tell me, Dr. Logan, will I be able to play the piano now that you've saved my hands?"

On the coffee table, several charcoal pencils were neatly lined up next to a sketchbook. He leaned forward and picked up the book. "And they're such talented hands," he said, leafing through her drawings. "I see you haven't given up your art."

"I did give it up, when we got married. I started again after the divorce. Remember my dream? To make a living from my painting? I never gave *that* up."

The way she talked, you'd think their marriage had been one long exercise in sacrifice—on her part. He picked up one of the pencils and rotated it in his fingers. Laura had always been quick to delegate blame. That, apparently, hadn't changed. He studied her carefully. Maybe some things in life never changed, but some things sure as hell did. This new Laura, well, he hadn't completely figured her out yet, but something was different. She was still headstrong and stubborn, with a quick, hot temper, but he saw something else, something he'd never seen before. The old Laura wouldn't have wasted a minute feeling sorry for herself, as her puffy red eyes and the splotches on her cheeks clearly indicated.

He lowered his gaze. Even though she lay curled under the blanket, he could picture the curves of her shapely legs. He couldn't erase from his mind the sight of her when he'd dropped her onto the couch. Her rumpled black skirt had been pushed up high above her knees, exposing the smooth, creamy flesh of her thighs. It had always amazed him how quickly she could arouse him with just a turn of her leg, a flash of her eyes—that was another thing that hadn't changed.

He thought back to the night he had proposed, when she had come to him so eagerly, so ready. They had always been friends, good friends, and Cory had adored her. It was only natural that they would drift closer and eventually marry. He would have been content with just companionship, and Cory needed a mother, but what she brought to the marriage was an added bonus.

No, they'd never had problems in *that* department.

In the hallway, the grandfather clock rang out four short

chimes, indicating that it was a quarter past the hour. "Doesn't that thing bother you?" he asked, replacing the pencil in its ordered, straight row. "It would drive me crazy, ringing out like that every fifteen minutes."

"You get used to it. A person can get used to anything.... Jake?"

"What?"

"I'm sorry I yelled at you. I know you were only trying to help. It was a stupid thing to do, falling asleep in the pantry. Cassie was here, and after she left, I forgot to lock the front door. I was so tired, and it was such a long day—"

"Forget it. I'm just glad you're all right."

She sat up and wrapped her arms around her bent knees. "Jake?"

"What?"

"Do you remember this afghan?"

He grinned. She must be a mind reader. Once again, he recalled the night he had proposed, when he had said he wanted to spend the rest of his life with her, when he had said he wanted her to be a mother to Cory. They had taken the blanket out to Freeman's Pond and lain under the stars, talking, dreaming, planning. "Yeah, I remember."

"We had some good times, didn't we?" she asked, her eyes meeting his. "I mean, they weren't all bad, were they?" Without warning, two plump tears rolled down her cheeks.

"Laura..."

"I don't know what's the matter with me," she said, her lips twisting down. "Ever since I've been back, I've been crazy. Maybe it's remembering how my aunt treated me. Maybe it's just being here in Middlewood after so many years. Either I'm laughing or crying, or doing both at the same time."

He pulled her toward him, closing the distance between them. Stifling a sob, she slipped into his arms and buried her face against his neck. Her tears flowed easily. He held her in his embrace, feeling the last of her defenses melting away like a late-spring snow. The scent of her natural perfume floated in the air, and he inhaled deeply. And then, ever so slowly, his hands traveled a wavy path down to the small of her back.

"Oh, no." She stiffened in his arms. "I can't do this."

"You can't do what?" he asked, feigning ignorance. He knew what she was thinking. Was it his fault she had misinterpreted his intentions? "Let someone take care of you? You act as if it were a sign of weakness."

She wriggled out of his hold. "What do you want from me? Why did you come here?"

He looked at her coolly. "You know what your problem is? You don't need anyone. You like playing the martyr." He teased her lips with his fingers. "Tell me, doesn't it get lonely up there, alone in your ivory tower?"

"Stop it," she said, recoiling from his touch. "Answer me, Jake. Why are you here?"

He leaned back into one of the sofa pillows and sighed heavily. "You probably won't believe me, but I came to apologize."

"You, apologize? For what?" she asked, narrowing her eyes.

"For yesterday. I shouldn't have said the things I said. You had your reasons for walking out of the marriage, even if I don't agree with them."

"So, we're back to that again. Your apology makes me sound like the bad guy."

"Come on, Laura. This isn't easy for me. Don't make me grovel."

"Now that would be interesting." She stared at him, and then shrugged. "Apology accepted. I'm still not sure what you're up to, but I have to admit, humility becomes you."

This was the Laura he remembered, all right, all spit and vinegar. But he was willing to overlook her attitude. For the sake of peace, he told himself. It had nothing to do with how her lips had felt under his touch, as soft as a whisper. "Truce?"

"Truce." She picked up a stray goose feather and blew it into the air. It spiraled to the floor, landing in the same spot where it had been lying. "Last night Cassie had a fight with a pillow—the pillow lost. I should probably clean up these feathers before I start tracking them through the house."

He made a motion to rise. "Sit. I'll take care of it."

"No, leave it. Given the condition of this place, getting rid of a few feathers would be a drop in the bucket. Cassie says I should renovate before I put it on the market, but I think I should just clean it up as best I can and sell it the way it is."

"So that's it? You've decided to sell?" Although he hadn't spent much time in the house, he felt a sense of loss. It had been his father's first restoration project, long before Jake was born.

Dotted with old Colonial-style homes, Middlewood had once been a sleepy little New England town. Charles Logan, Jake's father, was going to restore these old homes to their original beauty and make his fortune in the doing, but the business had never become the success he had envisioned. Eventually Jake's parents grew tired of the harsh northeast winters and retired to Florida, leaving the business to Jake. Under his adept management, restoration gradually gave way to construction, and the business flourished.

"I haven't decided anything," Laura said. "I've even been considering keeping the house, but the thought of living here, in these conditions..."

Jake looked around with a keen eye, but it didn't take someone in construction to see that the interior had gone downhill. The wallpaper was peeling, its pattern of white roses now yellow with age. All the baseboards were scuffed and splintered, and on the far wall, the window panes were cracked, their wooden frames damaged by water. But the builder in Jake knew that it would take more than cosmetic repairs to whip the house into shape. "You should probably open the place up," he said. "Maybe knock down that wall in the hallway."

"That costs money. If I do decide to keep it, I'm going to do only what's absolutely necessary. The rest can wait. Not that I'd move back permanently, but it might be nice to have a hideaway. A home away from home." A frown crossed her brow.

"And the problem is...?"

"You know what my childhood was like. This house doesn't exactly evoke pleasant memories."

In spite of her gloomy expression, he grinned. "They can't all be bad. What about all those get-togethers you had, the ones you didn't invite me to? What did you girls do at those hen parties, anyway? Besides man bashing, or at our age, boy bashing."

"Correction. I did invite you, and a lot of other boys from school, but Aunt Tess wouldn't let any of you into the house." She sighed. "But I suppose this place will always feel like home, regardless of its condition *or* Aunt Tess. And you're right. I did have some good times here, with Cass and Ellen...and Cynthia." She averted her eyes when she spoke his first wife's name. "But I feel my aunt's presence everywhere. Home or not, this place can be downright eerie."

"Maybe it's haunted," he said, trying to appear serious.

"This from the man who defines paranormal as 'indefinable hogwash'? Am I to believe that your definition of reality now includes ghosts?"

"That's why I'm in this line of work," he joked. "I enjoy digging up ancient burial grounds for new homes, and all that sort of thing."

Even though her eyes were laughing, she looked at him reprovingly. "Speaking of work, don't you have a job to go to?"

"That," he said, "is one of the perks in running your own business. I make my own priorities." If only that were true. Although it was still early, he knew that his secretary would be frantic. Mary liked knowing where to reach him in case of an emergency. "And my first priority today is making sure you're all right."

"I'm fine, really." She lay back and pulled the blanket up to her chin. "I'm just a little cold."

"Do you want me to make a fire? What about some brandy?"

"A fire in September? As for the brandy, it's not even eight-thirty! I have to meet the lawyer today, and that's all I need, for him to think I'm some kind of lush. Not that there's any brandy in the house, anyway. You know how Aunt Tess felt about alcohol. But seriously, I would think you have something more important to do than baby-sit me. In the old days nothing could have torn you away from your work."

"Well, the old days are gone," he said.

His words hung in the air like fog, and an uncomfortable silence fell. The only thing that could be heard was the *tick, tick* of the seven-foot grandfather clock in the hallway, which had marked time for over a century, punctuating the lives of previous generations.

Jake rose from the couch. "Like I told you," he said with forced brightness, "I get to set my own priorities. And right now, I intend to get something hot into you." He headed off to the kitchen before she could even think about responding to what sounded like a double entendre. If she had never been married to him, she might have blushed.

"Do you still take cream?" he called from the kitchen.

"Yes!" she called back. "But I don't have any!"

"What about sugar?"

"No sugar!"

"Where's the coffeemaker?"

"There isn't one! Make instant!"

"Where are the mugs?"

"In the cabinet next to the sink!"

Good grief, she thought, if he calls out one more time, I'm getting off this couch and taking over. She smiled to herself. He'd always been such a klutz in the kitchen. Like the time she'd been confined to bed with the flu and he'd insisted on making dinner. At first she'd protested, saying she couldn't eat a thing, and that he should order a pizza for himself. No, he was going to take care of her, he said. A half hour later he returned to the bedroom, carrying a bowl filled with what looked suspiciously like canned soup. "Ta-da!" his voice rang out. The next morning when she ventured into the kitchen, she found pots and pans, bowls and dishes, knives, forks and spoons all over counter, in the sink and on the stove.

In spite of being sick, in spite of having to clean up the mess, she'd seen this as one of the good times. It was one of those rare times when he'd been there for her. And here he was again, fussing about in the kitchen, when she was feeling under the weather.

Here he was again, telling her what to do.

The phone rang on the side table next to the sofa. "Don't move!" he called from the kitchen. "I'll get it!"

"No, I've got it!... Edward! How are you?... I don't know, at least another few days, maybe a week.... I have three weeks' vacation, remember? Don't worry, we'll have plenty of time for a honeymoon. My vacation time starts all over in January.... What do you mean I'm a bum! You're just jealous because you can't take that much time off, as if you could tear yourself away from your practice for even a week.... Look, I'm a little busy at the moment. Why don't I call you tonight?... Yes, the meeting with the lawyer, and afterward, lunch with Cassandra.... No, I haven't forgotten the hospital dinner next Saturday. I'll be back before then, Friday at the latest.... Yes, I know it's a whole week away, but you'll just have to survive without me for a little while longer. I've got to go now, darling. I'll talk to you later." She hung up the phone.

"The guy in the picture, I presume," Jake said formally, standing under the archway. He was carrying a tray with two cups of black coffee. "Sorry, I didn't mean to eavesdrop."

"And I *presume* you didn't mean to snoop, either," she replied tersely. "What were you doing, snooping around in my bedroom? You had no right to go in there."

"I was looking for your body," he answered dryly. He set the tray onto the coffee table, next to the sketchbook. "It's ready, *darling.* But there was no cream, *darling.* You'll have to take it black, *darling.* Where do you think you are? In a 1940s movie? When did Cassie become *Cassandra?*"

Good grief, he was acting like a jealous lover. It was almost comical—and ironic. He had always been so sure of her; it had never been the other way around.

He sat down beside her. "Look, I was worried about you. I thought you'd been hurt. But you're right, I shouldn't have snooped. And I'm glad you've found someone, really I am. It's time you got on with your life. It's time you forgave yourself."

A warning bell went off in her head. "Excuse me?"

He held out his hand as if to ward her off. "Hear me out. I'm trying to bury the hatchet."

She eyed him suspiciously. "Go on..."

"Sometimes when I think about the past, I still get angry. I know it'll take me a while before I can get to where you are now, but I want you to know, I forgive you."

Their three years together came hurtling back, resurrecting resentment. "You forgive *me?* Just who do you think you are? If you got down on your hands and knees, I wouldn't for-give *you*." She took a deep, slow breath. "Tell me something, were we ever really married? Where were you all that time? I don't mean *physically*. You were always there physically, that is, when you weren't working—which was most of the time. But when you were home, it was as if you were look-ing right through me. The only time I ever had your attention was when you were telling me what to do and how to run my life."

His gaze slid from her face, downward. "You have my at-tention now," he replied, his eyes raking her boldly. "My *full* attention."

Laura knew that there was something about her when she got angry, something that either sent his libido into overdrive or made him want to throttle her. His libido, so it seemed, had won.

He reached across the couch, encircling her with his arms. Every instinct told her to push him away, every nerve in her body screaming, *Run, Laura, run!* She let out a gasp as he pressed his mouth on her throat, his breath warm and moist on her skin, his scent reminding her of timber and grass. "Jake, no," she whispered into the air, not sure if she'd even said the words aloud. He ran his tongue along the side of her neck, up to the coil of her ear, sending little shivers down her spine. Her pulse throbbed wildly.

She jerked herself free. "I said no."

"Could have fooled me." His voice was dripping with mockery. "Like I said, some things in life don't change."

In an instant she was on her feet, her face hot with humil-iation. She wanted to lash out, yell, throw something. On his lips he wore that awful, smug smile, but it was his cool, know-ing eyes that sobered her. "In case you haven't noticed," she spoke in a dull, flat voice, "I'm not your plaything anymore. That's all you ever wanted, anyway. A plaything for you, and a nanny for Cory. Poor, sweet Cory. I wish he had been mine. I wish to God I could have taken him with me. Not that you would have noticed."

"What's that supposed to mean?"

Something in her snapped. Words she'd kept locked up for years started pouring out in a furious torrent, and she couldn't have stopped them if she'd tried. "Tell me something, did you ever really see him? Did you ever really see *me?* Well, I've got news for you. Some things *do* change. I have a full life now, which includes an attentive, caring man who knows I exist. And let me tell you something else, Mr. Macho, you made the same mistake with Cyn you made with me."

"Be careful, Laura...."

She ignored his warning and continued her tirade. "Did she ever tell you she gave up going to college to become your wife? Ever since we were kids, she'd wanted to study design. Do you have any idea of the sacrifice she made? And speaking of Cynthia, it would have been nice if once in a blue moon, you hadn't taken her to bed with us. I'm not talking about sex, lover-boy. Get your mind out of the gutter. I just wish that you had remembered it was me you were sleeping next to. Just once I wish you had known I was even there."

Afraid her legs would buckle under her, she stepped back to lean against the credenza. "I loved her, too," she said in a tired voice. "She was my best friend. Not a day goes by when I don't think of her. But she's dead, Jake. She's gone."

He gave her a hostile glare. "What are you talking about? What does Cynthia have to do with us? Let me remind you that you were the one who left me. Where do you get off thinking you were blameless?"

"Go home," she said without expression. "I have a life to get on with."

He stared past her for a long moment and finally stood up.

With hands clenched stiffly at his sides, he turned on his heels and left the room.

She slumped down on the couch, listening to his footsteps thundering in the hallway. The front door opened with a creak, then slammed shut. From the living room she could hear the squeal of his tires as he pulled out of her driveway.

In the hallway the grandfather clock erupted in a series of chimes. She sat in the living room a little while longer, and when she finally reached for her coffee, she wasn't surprised to find that it had grown cold.

## Chapter Three

It was close to nine-thirty by the time Laura finally found the energy to rise from the couch. On the way to the kitchen, she caught her reflection in the antique mirror hanging next to the clock. Her face was ashen and smeared with mascara, her hair damp and tangled like a fallen nest after a storm.

Good Lord, had Jake seen her like this? She thought of Cinderella before the ball. Except in Laura's version of the story, there was no fairy godmother, and the prince got to see Cinderella at her worst.

After downing a glass of juice and some dry toast, she climbed the stairs sluggishly, her body still aching from sleeping on the floor. Inside her room she glanced in the mirror over the bureau. Her linen suit was a rumpled mess, her panty hose twisted at the ankles. This is what she had worn at the ball, except there hadn't been a ball; she'd gone to her aunt's funeral, and there her prince had rebuked her.

He had no right to talk to me that way, she thought. Who does he think he is? And why should I care that he saw me looking so disheveled? For that matter, why should I care that he didn't bother to show up at the house yesterday after the service? Not that it makes any difference, but he did come by this morning. Except he forgot to bring the glass slipper.

She recalled the way he'd pulled her onto his lap, teasing her, mocking her, expecting her to react exactly as she had, and once again her anger rose. She was angry with herself for having responded. Angry with him for being a jerk.

This was *no* Cinderella story. The man was no prince.

She watched herself in the full-length mirror on the bedroom door as she stripped off her wrinkled suit. Here I am again, she thought. I seem to follow me everywhere. Her eyes swept over the reflection of her petite frame, stopping to appraise her toned legs, her flat stomach, her narrow waist. Her gaze continued upward to her firm breasts, visible through a sheer rose-pink bra. Not bad, she admitted reluctantly, remembering when she'd been heavier. She'd always been self-conscious about her body. Even now, she focused on what displeased her, noting the lines of fatigue on her forehead and the dark circles under her eyes. Maybe I should get rid of all the mirrors in the house, she thought.

She pulled her green fleece robe from the closet and went into the bathroom. Still wearing her bra and panty hose, she reached into the shower and turned on the faucet, wincing as a brown liquid trickled out. She knew she would have to wait five minutes before the water started running hot and clear. The plumbing was shot. Coronary artery disease, she imagined Edward saying. Eroded arteries caused by fatty streaks along the inner walls.

What would the meticulous Dr. Palmer's reaction have

been to her appearance this morning? He could never acknowledge that she could be anything less than perfect. The prestigious heart surgeon probably would have had a coronary himself.

Be fair, she reprimanded herself. Isn't this what you always wanted? To be perfect in someone's eyes? To sit up there, high on that proverbial pedestal?

*Tell me, doesn't it get lonely up there, alone in your ivory tower?*

Be quiet, she imagined herself telling Jake. I'm happy now. Edward and I are perfect for each other. You shouldn't put him down; he's a lot like you—handsome, bright, driven by his career. Oh yes, there's one more thing. Like you, he doesn't want children. Except there's one small difference. You don't want more children, and he doesn't want any. But any way you look at it, it comes down to no children in my life, now that I no longer have Cory or the ability to conceive. So you see? Edward and I are made for each other. What's that, Jake? Why did I leave you, only to hook up with someone who's a lot like you? The difference between the two of you is that he knows I'm around. He adores me. In his eyes I'm perfect.

She ran her fingers along the bridge of her nose. Well, *almost* perfect. Edward was always urging her to get that little bump removed. He didn't see it as an addition to her character, as Jake always had.

Maybe she would have her nose fixed, after all.

Looking in the vanity mirror over the sink—oh, those damn, cruel mirrors!—she rubbed her hand against the side of her neck. With clarity she remembered the sick feeling she'd had when she'd first discovered the swelling. She'd tried to ignore it, hoping it was only a sign of another cold—the third in two months. But the swelling didn't go away, and she was exhausted all the time, often waking up in the middle of the night in a sweat. It was Ellen who had insisted that she undergo tests, and it was Ellen who had diagnosed her with Hodgkin's disease.

A chill spread through Laura's body as she recalled her friend's words. She remembered how the air in the room had been suddenly sucked away. This is what drowning must feel like, she'd thought with cold detachment. Even though Ellen had insisted that the prognosis was excellent, Laura had felt as though she'd been given a death sentence. It was then she realized that whether she lived for fifty more years or only one, she didn't want to spend whatever time she had left in a one-sided relationship. She deserved more. It was then she had decided to leave Jake.

Her fingers left the base of her neck, slowly moving down between her breasts, to the left side of her upper abdomen. After the diagnosis, her spleen had been removed and she had undergone a regimen of chemotherapy. The scar from the surgery was gone, only a long telltale line remaining. The first time she'd spent the night with Edward, two years ago, he'd remarked that the surgeons had done an excellent job, that Laura was a good healer. She was a lucky woman, he'd added jokingly, telling her she'd be a good candidate for a facelift when the time came. She'd punched him playfully in the shoulder.

Her incision may have healed, but the wound from the chemotherapy would never go away. She recalled the oncologist's words, that dark day a lifetime ago. Dr. Waring had told her, as gently as possible, that as a result of the treatment, Laura would likely never be able to have children.

*A lucky woman.* Lucky? She supposed she was. She was alive, wasn't she? She had been in remission for almost five years, which according to many was the magic yardstick for being considered cured.

She pressed her hand across the flatness of her belly. Edward was always complimenting her on her slim, youthful shape. She was well preserved for an old lady of thirty-three, he liked to say in jest. Slowly, she inched her hand down to the satiny expanse of her firm thighs, trying to remember the last time she and Edward had made love. Sex was no longer an important part of her life, hadn't been for a long time. Trying to conjure up the image of Edward's face, she told herself she was lucky to have found someone who felt the same way she did.

*A lucky woman.* She frowned. When had she put sex on the back burner? When she left Jake, she admitted to herself. She'd once read that sex was often the last thing to go in a relationship; she now questioned if it had been the only thing, outside of being a mother to Cory, that had kept her in the marriage. If it hadn't been for the sex, would she have left a lot sooner? She considered what her life might have been like. She might have met someone else and had a child of her own, before the cure for her terrible disease had left her sterile.

Tell the truth, Laura. It wasn't only the sex that kept you and Jake together. At least not on your part. After he had proposed to her that night at Freeman's Pond, they had lain under the stars for hours, talking about the future. Her happiness had been complete, and she had believed with all her heart that it would endure.

She removed her bra and rolled down her panty hose, every muscle in her body screaming in protest. She stepped into the shower. For a long while she just stood there, immobile under the rusty showerhead, allowing the steamy, now clear stream to beat against her face. After she had arrived at the house two days ago, she had immediately gone to work scrubbing down the upstairs bathroom, and afterward, replacing her aunt's face and body soaps with her own special preferences. She'd always had a penchant for expensive toiletries—it was her one personal luxury, she liked to tell herself. But she found herself wondering why she had brought so many of her things here in the first place.

Just how long was she planning to stay?

Still lingering in the air, the smell of cleaning disinfectant assaulted her nostrils, taking her back to that Saturday in December at the indoor community pool. It was the winter she turned twelve, and she had just finished her first period. Jake had accidentally-on-purpose bumped into her under the water. Pressing his body against hers, he dragged her poolside as if he were rescuing her from drowning. Big hero. All he wanted was to cop a feel off her newly budding breasts. But as angry as she was, she also felt a tingling in her stomach, although at the time she couldn't identify the sensation. "I think she needs artificial respiration," Jake announced to all their friends. She pushed him away and ran off to the lockers, Cassie and Cynthia following closely behind.

*Like I said, some things in life don't change.*

It's true, Laura thought now—some things never change. Jake was still the same cocky adolescent. Every time she thought about what had happened earlier that morning, she felt her blood churning.

There you go again, Laura. Can't you ever tell the truth? Sure, you loved him and for you it wasn't just the sex that kept you in the marriage, but let's be honest here—the sex *was* good. Once again she caught herself thinking about the night he had proposed. Admit it, Laura, it wasn't just the talking you remember so well. And speaking of sex, didn't it feel nice, that day at the community pool so long ago, when he pushed his cool, bare chest against the thin layer of your bathing suit top? Haven't you always regretted, one little bit, running off to the lockers before he had a chance to perform mouth-to-mouth?

She picked up her favorite soap, My Secret Sin, and her body sponge from the caddy over the faucet, and began washing her arms and legs. Gradually, the cleansing gave way to a slow massage, the nylon both fleecy and scratchy against her skin. The aroma of the scented suds merged with the memory of Jake's woodsy scent, blotting out the last traces of disinfectant. She closed her eyes. Once again she tried to picture Edward's face, and once again she failed. "Go away, Jake," she moaned into the vapor. "Some things in life *do* change." Oblivious to the groaning in the pipes behind the wall, she stood under the slow, hot flow, and then, dropping the sponge, slid her hand down her soap-streaked belly, seeking the softness below.

She was thinking of him three hours later as she sat at a table outside the Café St. Gabriel in Ridgefield, sipping a glass of chardonnay. Although Jake had always preferred to dine at what he called less "artsy" places like Joe's Burger Hut or Mama Rosa's Pizza Pub, he had taken her here from time to time to please her. A neighbor to Middlewood, Ridgefield was acclaimed for its restaurants, and the café was one of Laura's favorites.

The trendy French restaurant hadn't changed in the time she'd been away. Inside, heavy wooden beams lined the ceiling, and the far wall boasted a floor-to-ceiling stone fireplace. The décor outside, with its provincial blue-and-yellow tablecloths, accentuated a French country motif and was as welcoming as it was inside. The day had warmed up unexpectedly, and the patio was filled with patrons enjoying what remained of summer.

A voice drifted into her consciousness. "Would you like something with your wine, Madame Logan?"

"Uh, no thank you," Laura answered, startled out of her reverie by the sound of her married name. She'd taken back her maiden name, Matheson, when she'd left Jake. "I'm waiting for a friend." She glanced down at her watch, a gift from Edward on her last birthday. The polished stainless steel case

of the Cartier gleamed in the sunshine, the numbers on the
mother-of-pearl dial showing that Cassie was fifteen minutes
late.

"What about an appetizer in the meantime? May I suggest
our house smoked salmon? Or perhaps you'd prefer the
steamed mussels?"

She looked up at the stocky, well-dressed man hovering
over her. They sure pay their waiters well, she thought, taking note of his Armani suit. "I'd like to wait for my friend, if
you don't mind," she said, growing impatient with his per-
sistence.

"Forgive my impudence," he said, as if sensing her dis-
pleasure. "I was hoping you'd recognize me. You and Mon-
sieur Logan used to come here sometimes. If memory serves
me, he always ordered the sixteen-ounce sirloin with fries on
the side." Disapproval flashed in his eyes. "But you," he continued, now smiling, "preferred our finer selections. As I recall, your favorite was the coq au vin."

"Michel! Michel Dubois! I'm sorry, I didn't recognize
you." She flushed, embarrassed that she'd mistaken him, the
proprietor, for a waiter.

"It's the goatee," he said, fingering a sparse spread of
whispers on his chin. "It even confuses my wife. *Bien,*
here's your friend now." He pulled out the chair for Cassie.
"Will you be having your regular?" he asked as she sat
down next to Laura.

Cassie was as chic as ever, in a high-neck jade shell and a
knee-length black skirt, her outfit complementing her lively
green eyes and bobbed dark hair. Next to her Laura felt dowdy.
In her shower that morning, it was as if Jake had sneaked in
beside her, and afterward she had wanted to cover up as much
of her flesh as possible, as though to compensate for having
exposed herself to his eyes—and touch. Now, sitting in the
golden September sun, she was uncomfortably warm in her

gray cashmere turtleneck and black wool slacks. She should have reserved a table inside.

"Yes, I'll have the regular," Cassie said. "How are you, Michel? And how is Madame Dubois?"

"I'm fine," he answered. "Madame is well, too. She's in her last month, big as a bathtub and still growing. The doctor says twins for sure." Laura's back stiffened in her chair. As though he had taken her gesture as a personal rebuke, Michel took on a more formal demeanor. "It's nice to see you again, Madame Logan. I'll send a waiter over with the menus shortly. I hope you enjoy your meal." He nodded at the two women, and after bowing his head, walked off to another table.

There's something wrong with me, Laura thought. Other than not being able to have children. Other than I'm having wild fantasies about the most wretched man in the world, even though I'm engaged to the most wonderful man in the world. Why is it that everywhere I go, I seem to tick some-one off? I can't go through life alienating people this way. I can't go through life pretending that people don't have chil-dren.

Cassie instantly picked up on Laura's frame of mind. "Did you see him bow?" she said, lowering her head as Michel had done, trying to make her friend laugh. "Give me a break! How pretentious can one get? Let me tell you, the man is as French as an English muffin."

Leave it to Cassie. That woman could probably cheer up a turkey the week before Thanksgiving. "Tell me, is your reg-ular still a gin-vermouth martini, straight up with an olive?" Laura asked, smiling in spite of her mood. "No, make that two olives. Not very French, either, I must say."

"As if there's anything French at all about this restaurant. Michel Dubois, my foot! His real name is Mike Dunbar and he's from New Jersey."

"Shhh! What if he hears you?"

Cassie waved her hand dismissively. "As if his day could be worse than mine. Last night, after I left your house, I got an offer on an estate for a smooth ten million, and this morning I found out that the mortgage company won't finance. The whole deal fell through. That commission would have put a guest house, gazebo and pool in my backyard."

"But you don't own a house," Laura said, laughing out loud at her friend's outrageous fabrication.

"So I'll buy one. I'll buy *your* house"

"My backyard's not that large, and you hate yard work."

Eventually the joking settled down. Cassie sat back in her chair, her legs crossed at the knees, while Laura leaned forward, her elbows on the table.

"So tell me," Cassie said. "How was the meeting with John this morning? Any surprises?" She stared across the table. "Laura?"

"What? Oh, John Collins. The lawyer. It went just as I suspected. No surprises. The money's all gone. Every red cent."

A server arrived with the martini, and Cassie took a healthy swig. "If it's just as you expected," she said after he left, "what's got you so down?"

"It's like you said. My aunt got a free ride, living in the house. I can't believe she spent all the money from my parents' insurance! The will stipulated that the money was to be used for expenses, which to me includes the upkeep of the house. It's obvious she never made any repairs. What did she do with it all?"

"You already knew there was nothing left. John only confirmed it." Cassie reached across the table and took her friend's hand. "What's really going on here? This is me you're talking to."

Two doves flew into the courtyard and landed near the next table. "I've decided to keep the house," Laura said, watching the birds as they pecked at crumbs. "I know it's a mess right now, and it's dark and gloomy. But it's not hopeless. I could make it into a kind of retreat. I could spend my spare time there, painting, gardening, relaxing..."

Cassie nodded her approval. "I was hoping you'd sell so I could make a big fat commission, but hey, this is much better. I'd love to have you back again, but what does Steady Eddy say? He doesn't strike me as a small-town kind of guy."

"It's not like I'd be asking him to commute. We wouldn't actually be living here. And if we change our minds, we can always sell."

"You mean you haven't consulted him?" Cassie narrowed her eyes. "Exactly when did you make this decision?"

"When you threatened to buy it," Laura kidded. In truth, although she'd been mulling over the idea, only now had it crystallized into something tangible, something attainable. It had something to do with the sound of the cicadas in the yard, and the smell of the night air when the temperature dropped. She belonged in Middlewood, where she had grown up, and if she couldn't move back permanently—Edward was a New Yorker through and through—at least she could visit. And she would paint, on weekends, over the holidays, on her vacations.

"Actually, I just decided now," she said. "So tell me, what do you think?"

Cassie smiled broadly. "I think it's a wonderful idea! So why the blues?"

"Repairs aren't cheap. And don't forget the property taxes."

Cassie let out a derisive laugh. "You can't be serious. Steady Eddy would lend you the money in a heartbeat. He'd even give it to you, no strings attached. What kind of marriage are you entering into? Don't tell me he's making you sign a prenup!"

"I suggested it, but he wouldn't hear of it. One thing about Edward, he's very generous. But the house is my responsibility, not his."

"He's going to be your husband. Why not let him help? You said it yourself, repairs aren't cheap. You'll need to completely revamp the plumbing, not to mention the roof. And I imagine you'll want to paint and redecorate."

"I don't want Edward's money," Laura said firmly. "Besides, I'm not helpless." Ideas were forming in her head faster than she could speak. "I could do a lot of the work myself. Like painting the rooms and tiling the kitchen floor. I could do it over time. As for the immediate problems, like the plumbing and the roof, I could take out a loan. It's not as if I have a mortgage to pay. Aunt Tess's room is the largest, so I'll use that as my studio, once I figure out how to bring in more light. I wonder how much it would cost to double—no, triple—the size of the window. You're in the business, Cass. You could probably refer me to someone who would cut me a good deal."

"Oh." Cassie's eyes went cold. "You don't need *me* to cut you a deal with *him*."

"Don't 'oh' me. I have no intention of going to Jake for help. But even if I did, it would be strictly business."

"Right. Strictly business. I should have known. Your glum mood has nothing to do with Michel's wife being pregnant, and it has nothing to do with money."

"Don't give me that look," Laura warned. "I know what you're thinking."

Cassie raised her hand defensively. "I know you don't want to hear my opinions about Jake, but I have to tell you, I'm worried. You finally have your life in order, and there's a great guy waiting for you in New York. I'd hate to see you screw it up."

"If you think Edward is so great," Laura said testily, "why do you always refer to him as Steady Eddy?"

"You know I'm only teasing. I think Edward's perfect for you. You're both so...organized. It's a match made in spic-and-span heaven. And you're always saying he has your best interest at heart, which is something Jake never did." Cassie studied her friend's face. "Trouble in paradise?"

"No, of course not. Edward and I are fine. Look, I'm sorry I snapped at you. I know I'm being ornery. It's just that coming back here has revived old feelings as well as old hurts. But don't worry, it's just a momentary lapse into the past. Call it a momentary lapse of sanity, if you want. Forget I ever mentioned Jake. I'll bring in a team from New York to work on the house."

"Can you?"

Laughter suddenly erupted from the table next to theirs. "Can I what?" Laura asked, studying the man seated there. With his classically handsome profile and short-cropped dark hair, he bore a striking resemblance to Edward.

"Can you forget you ever mentioned him?"

Laura's gaze left the scene at the next table and fell back on the two doves. They were now less than a foot away, squabbling over a crust of bread.

She didn't answer.

Laura knew what Cassie had been thinking.

She picked up another carton. She was planning to spend the afternoon going through the boxes in the pantry, keeping the good memories, discarding the rest.

Her thoughts returned to the conversation at lunch. Cassie was wrong. Laura had no intention of jeopardizing her relationship with Edward.

Steady Eddy, Cassie called him.

So what if he liked things just so? So what if he was...fastidious? So was Laura. They were completely compatible. There were no ups and downs, no roller coasters in *this* relationship.

And no surprises, either. She sat down on the faded

linoleum floor, imagining what the meticulous doctor would say about the way she was dressed now. She knew *exactly* what he would say—in a breezy but disapproving tone—about her old gray sweats and bunny rabbit slippers.

She debated calling him. She wanted to talk to him about keeping the house, certain he'd agree it was a good idea. A home in Connecticut would make a wonderful place for entertaining. A wonderful place to schmooze with the bigwigs who worked at the hospital—as long as he didn't have to mingle with neighbors.

She decided she would call him later.

She sliced open the top of the box with a knife. Inside was a bundle of envelopes bound together with a stretched-out rubber band. With a start she realized that these were the letters Cynthia had given to her for safekeeping. Letters written to Cynthia by a man whose existence Jake had never suspected. Letters given to me so that Jake wouldn't find them, Laura recalled with hostility. She'd always felt like an accomplice in her friend's deception, and had resented Cynthia for involving her.

After the accident, there had been no reason for Laura to keep the letters, but she hadn't been able to bring herself to dispose of them. They were a part of Cynthia, and Laura hadn't been ready to relinquish any part of her friend, as if preserving a memory, even a shameful one, could somehow bring her back.

No, that wasn't it at all. She had kept them because she was angry. Angry with Cynthia for deceiving Jake. As long as I held on to my anger, Laura rationalized, I could justify loving my best friend's husband. I kept them to remind me of her guilt, hoping to dispel my own. *I would not have married Jake if Cynthia had lived.*

Cynthia had also asked her to keep a few mementos as well, but no matter how curious Laura had been, she had never once considered going through her friend's things or reading her letters. She carried the small carton into the kitchen, without further examining what was inside.

The garbage trucks would be coming by on Monday. Several of her aunt's cartons were already lined up next to the door, to be taken out to the curb for removal. Why on earth had Aunt Tess kept all this stuff? Why would anyone hang on to torn curtains and linen? Who would keep old shoes and hats? These cartons were Aunt Tess's links to the past, Laura realized, thinking about her own memory boxes. Laura hadn't thrown those out, either, when she'd left home.

She picked up another box. Inside was a child's tea service, complete with cups and saucers, sugar bowl, creamer and teapot. Had the set belonged to her mother? She tried to picture her aunt and mother as children sitting at their kitchen table in Ridgefield, hosting a tea party for themselves and their dolls. But Tess had been six years older than Laura's mother. Would she have been interested in a child's tea party? Maybe what Reverend Barnes had said was true. Maybe Aunt Tess had been a warm and doting sister, Caroline's true caretaker.

Laura remembered another child sitting at a different kitchen table, passing a cup and saucer to a fair-haired woman. The child, wearing a brightly colored party dress, could not have been more than three years old. I was that child, Laura realized. Fingering the delicate bone china, she tried to bring the memory into focus.

The sound of the doorbell broke into her daydream. She wiped her hands on her sweatpants. Back in New York, she never would have answered the door dressed like this, but this was Middlewood. *Pretentious* was not a word in the town's dictionary.

The doorbell was ringing insistently, and Laura hurried through the hallway, calling "I'm coming! I'm coming!" She threw open the front door without asking who was there—

something else she would never have done in New York. Under the overhang outside the front door stood a tall, thin boy. Laura hadn't seen him in five years, but she recognized him immediately. Although he wore a frown, and his cheeks were smudged with dirt, his face was still the mirror image of Cynthia's, and like Cynthia's eyes in her final year, his were filled with sadness.

# Chapter Four

"I heard you were back and I was wondering if you wanted to be on my paper route."

Cory's shoulders were almost level with hers. He's so tall, Laura thought. Tall like his father. But it was Cynthia's face she was looking at, her high exotic cheekbones, her gold-flecked hazel eyes, her smooth olive skin. "I think we should talk about this," Laura said, trying to imitate the serious tone in Cory's voice. "Come on in."

He glanced inside. Shrugging, he stepped into the hallway.

She motioned for him to follow her into the kitchen. "Are you hungry? I have peanut butter cookies and cake. Marble cake with vanilla frosting. Why don't you wash up at the kitchen sink while I fix you a snack?" she suggested, glancing at his muddy hands. "So, tell me. Are you still in Peewee? No, of course not. You'd be in Little League by now."

"Nah, baseball's dumb. All they do is swing a stupid bat

and run around a field." He turned on the faucet. Underneath the sink, a pipe rattled. "How come the water's brown?"

"Give it a few seconds. It'll run clear." She filled a plate with cookies and squares of cake from yesterday's gathering and placed it on the table. "I won't be needing the paper during the week, but maybe you have a weekend deal?"

"Sure, no problem. Lots of people only get the paper on the weekend. You know, for the comics." The clanking of the pipes suddenly stopped, and clear water began gushing from the tap. "Tommy's grandmother saw you at the funeral. I'm sorry about your aunt. She said you looked different, skinnier. I mean, Tommy's grandmother said it, not your aunt. She's dead. I don't mean Tommy's grandmother. She's alive. Anyway, I'm sorry. I mean, about your aunt."

"Thank you, Cory," she said, suppressing a smile. She searched through her memory. Tommy? Tommy Pritchard? Wasn't he that short, frail-looking kid who'd been in Cory's kindergarten glass? "And how is Tommy these days?"

"He's okay." Cory turned off the faucet and wiped his hands on a dishcloth, leaving a dirty stain in the floral pattern. Eyeing the cookies hungrily, he sat down.

"Go ahead, take one," Laura said, pouring him a glass of milk. She sat down across from him. "Take two, if you want."

"Dad says my teeth will rot."

"You'll brush when you get home. Go ahead, eat."

He reached for a cookie and started munching. "Dad said that you were sick and that's why you went away. Are you better now?"

Seeing him again, sitting across from him, listening to him speak, was almost more than Laura could bear. "What else did your father say?" she asked, suppressing the urge to jump up and hug him.

"He said you were never coming back. Can I have some cake, too?"

"Help yourself. That's what it's here for."

He picked up a square and popped the entire piece into his mouth. Traces of frosting dotted the sides of his face. "He lied. You came back."

Gingerly, she reached across the table and wiped away the icing. He didn't pull away. "Your dad didn't lie," she said in a thick voice. "He didn't know I was coming back."

"But you're here. So what he said wasn't true. How come you left, anyway?"

What could she say that he could understand? She thought for a moment, and then spoke slowly. "Sometimes married people, even though they still love each other, can't live together. I got sick, and we thought the best thing I could do was go to New York. They have good doctors there. I got better, but the problems between your father and me didn't go away." It wasn't the complete truth, but it was all he needed to know.

"This is where you tell me that your going away had nothing to do with me. You still love me and all that crap."

She ignored the crass word—for now. Apparently, Cory had been given this lecture before.

He took a big swallow of milk. "Tommy's parents got divorced. His father takes him every second weekend and buys him neat stuff. He bought him a computer. How come you never bought me a computer?"

She knew that Cory wasn't talking about electronics. "You aren't my natural child," she said plainly and honestly. "If you were, I would have taken you with me to New York after I got better. I wanted to come back and see you a million times, but I thought...your father and I thought...it would be better if I didn't."

"You made a mistake," Cory said, his face solemn. "You should have come." He wiped his mouth with the back of his hand. "But that's okay. No one's perfect. Dad says even grown-ups make mistakes."

"Your father is right. No one's perfect." *Especially* grown-ups.

He reached for another piece of cake. "Tommy heard his grandmother say that you stole my father from my real mother. Tommy said that's why you got sick. Because God punished you."

Laura gasped. "That's a load of...crap. What did you say? You didn't believe him, did you?"

"Nah, he's crazy." Cory grinned. "Hey, you're okay, Lulu. Dad always yells at me when I say that word. He says it sounds like hell. Oops, I mean heck."

"He's right." She tried to keep her face stern, but inwardly she was smiling. He had called her Lulu. Lulu had been the first word he had ever spoken, at fourteen months, two months after Cynthia had died, and it had remained his name for her.

"I beat him up."

"Who?"

"Tommy. I told you, he's crazy. And he has a lot of uncles. You know, guys who stay over and pretend to like him. They buy him stuff, too. But nothing like a computer. Stupid stuff. Yesterday this short guy with a big head and no neck bought him a yo-yo. How stupid is that? But I told Tommy it was the perfect present, seeing how Tommy is a yo-yo himself. He said I probably have a lot of uncles in New York. He said you probably brought me back a dozen yo-yos. So I hit him."

"Sorry, no yo-yos."

"What about uncles?"

"Nope. No uncles." Would he consider Edward an uncle?

"No uncles," he repeated. "That's good. I hate yo-yos."

She regarded him closely, remembering how he had towered over all his friends at school. "Do you think it's fair beating up on guys who are smaller than you?"

"Who, Tommy?" Cory's eyes widened. "I'm a midget next to him! He's a whole head taller!"

They sure grow up big in Middlewood, she mused. Must be the brown water. She looked at the torn pocket at the front of Cory's backpack. "I can mend that for you, if you'd like. How did it happen?"

"Last week Tommy called me a geek. So I punched him. He got mad and threw my backpack across the schoolyard."

"You punched him because he called you a geek?" She shook her head. "What does your father say about all this fighting?"

"He yells a lot. Says I'm a problem child. Maybe he'll send me to correction school. You know, jail for kids? I hear New York's full of those schools. And you don't have to sleep there. You go there in the daytime and you sleep at home, or wherever. I mean, you could stay at somebody's house, if you knew someone in New York. I used to hope he'd send me to one of them. I mean, when I was little."

"I don't think you need correction at all," she said, tears welling up behind her eyelids. Maybe a little attention, she thought. No, make that a lot of attention. An idea began to take hold in her mind. "I could sure use some help around this place," she said, wiping the moisture from her eyes. "Look at this pigsty! I know you're busy with homework and friends and your paper route, but maybe you could come over once in a while and give me a hand. I'd even pay you."

"Like a real job?"

"Exactly."

"I'd have to ask my dad. I can't do anything without asking him first."

She looked at him with squinted eyes. "Does he know you're here?" She dreaded the thought of calling Jake, dreaded hearing his voice.

"Oh, yeah, sure. I told Rose. She must have called him. But she's really old. Maybe she forgot. Dad says I have to tell her where I'm going. He treats me like a baby. He thinks I'm going to have an accident and die like my real mother."

"Fathers worry," she said, trying not to appear shocked a Cory's words. Stepmothers worry, too, she thought. As a par ent, she had been just as protective as Jake. She remembere how she had felt after moving in. What did she know abou being a mother? Even though Rose Halligan, Jake's longtim housekeeper, had been there to guide her, Laura had beer plagued with anxiety.

"Where have you been all this time?" she said, frowning The elementary school was only two blocks from her house and school had let out an hour ago.

"I went to the park. You know, to mess around." He stare down at his hands. "So is it true what Tommy's grandmothe said? Did you steal my father from my mother?"

"No. Tommy's grandmother was wrong." A thought sud denly occurred to her, and she added, "Your father must hav told you that your mother and I were friends when we wer kids. Would you like to see some pictures?"

"You have pictures of my mother?" he said, his face light ing up. "Dad doesn't keep any around the house."

Laura wasn't surprised. Jake had never wanted mementos o his first wife. You'd think I would have been happy, she though A second wife doesn't need constant reminders of the firs one—a face on the mantel in the living room, next to the book case, on the desk in the den.... But the lack of *any* pictures ha had a reverse effect. It had confirmed what Laura had alway feared, and apparently, nothing had changed. After all this time Jake still hadn't recovered from the pain of losing Cynthia.

"You don't have *any* pictures of your mother?" she asked thinking about her own parents. It had been terrible growin up not knowing what they looked liked. It was still terrible not knowing.

"I have some in my room, but she was all grown-up whe they were taken. It would be cool to see what she looked lik when she was a kid."

"Come on, Cory, you're in for a treat," she said, taking his hand. "I have loads of pictures. Your mother and I weren't just friends, we were *best* friends."

"I guess it's not true then. I mean, best friends don't steal from each other, do they?"

"No, Cory. Best friends don't steal."


Jake sat at his large rectangular desk, surveying his office. On the wall to his right hung a watercolor of the town center, painted by Laura before they were married. The painting showed five young children building a snowman in the town square. It reminded him of when he was young, and he often imagined he'd been one of those kids. He liked to stare at the painting for long stretches of time. It gave him inspiration.

The folder containing the plans for the new community center lay unopened on his desk. But no matter how long Jake stared at the watercolor, inspiration evaded him. He couldn't seem to summon up any enthusiasm for work.

The board had accepted his proposal only last week. This was more than a coup on his part; it not only added another supporting column in the structure of his financial security, it also served as a concrete affirmation of his integrity. Jake's bid had not been the lowest, as he had been unwilling to compromise his standards in any way to secure the contract. He'd always taken pride in his work, refusing to sacrifice quality and safety by cutting corners. Having lived in Middlewood all his life, he was interested in more than just profit; he'd invested his heart.

Other matters, however, now clouded his concentration. He had behaved badly at Laura's that morning, and he couldn't stop chastising himself. But even more pressing was this latest episode regarding his son. Rose had called to tell him that Cory had not come home on the school bus.

So, it was starting again. The summer had been only a brief reprieve. Cory had attended day camp and had been happy—at least he had seemed happy. There had been no incidences of fighting or rebelliousness, no sudden disappearances, no mood swings. Jake had believed that the bad times were finally behind them. Now he saw it was only wishful thinking. School had just started and Cory was already in trouble.

Was it Laura's return that had triggered this latest episode? He didn't think so. Cory wasn't even aware that she was back. Or was he? Jake had lied when he'd told Laura that Cory didn't remember her. What if Cory had learned she was back? Middlewood was a small town. Word was bound to get around. The more Jake thought about it, the more certain he was that his son knew of her return, and because of this, because of *her,* Cory had suffered an emotional setback. Taking off without telling anyone where he was going, causing everyone grief, was so like Cory when something was bothering him.

Jake got up from his chair, and with nervous energy began to pace the room. He wasn't too worried about Cory; *protective* would be a better description. Cory had taken off several times before and had always returned home safely. But even though Middlewood was relatively safe, Jake knew that anything could happen. No matter how many times he warned his son, no matter how many lectures and groundings he administered, Cory always reverted to his old behavior, offering only, "What's the big deal?"

Jake knew he was overly cautious, but he believed he had good cause. Look what had happened to Cynthia—a stupid, senseless accident. If she'd been wearing boots that day, she might not have fallen on the steps outside the front door. If she'd listened to him, she would not have even gone out. But she *had* gone out, insisting that it was only a mild flurry, not a major snowstorm.

"What's the big deal?" she had said.

The big deal was that she had died.

The big deal now was that Cory was a mixed-up kid, and Jake didn't have a clue how to help him.

Oh, he'd spoken to the counselors at school. He'd even read a few of those silly psychology books, but nothing had helped him get through to his son. Before this summer, not a day had passed without an incident—a black eye, a torn shirt, a failing grade in school. Jake cringed, recalling that day last spring when the school principal had informed him that Cory had been caught smoking in the bathroom. Smoking, at ten years old!

Jake walked back to his desk and retrieved a pack of cigarettes and a lighter from a side drawer. Disgusting habit, he told himself, lighting up and inhaling. He'd stopped smoking years ago, but the events of the past two days had led him to start up again. Laura was to blame for this, too. All the pressures of his work had never once tempted him to begin again, but just seeing her sitting in the chapel, looking so cool and collected, had turned him back into a human chimney.

He drew hard on the cigarette and exhaled. Was it so hard for Cory to call, to let Jake know where he was going? Jake was now fully convinced that Laura was responsible for his son's latest act of defiance. Just when the balance in life was finally restored, she had to come along and upset it. Jake had begun smoking again, and after a whole summer of compliance, his son was back to his old tricks.

Was it possible that Cory had gone to see her? She was the only mother he'd ever known. Jake held his hand in midair, his cigarette halfway to his mouth. Wouldn't Cory be curious to see her? Or would he be too angry with her? Jake had no idea. And that was the crux of the problem. He had no idea what his son was feeling.

He picked up the phone but stopped himself before he

began dialing. It would be better to go over there in person, he decided, not bothering to ask himself why. The image of Laura lying on the couch appeared before his eyes. Using his empty coffee mug as an ashtray, he stubbed out his cigarette with force, as though hoping to extinguish the picture of her pushed-up skirt, which burned in his mind like a flame.

He failed.

"Mary," he spoke into the intercom. "I'm going out."

Mary Johnson was more than just his secretary. She had been with the company ever since Jake's father had started it, and Jake never made a move regarding the business without first consulting her. "Are you going to the site?" she asked brightly.

"No" was all he offered.

"When will you be back?"

"Monday. I'm starting the weekend early."


Fifteen minutes later Jake was standing in Laura's doorway, demanding to see his son.

"I'm fine, thank you," Laura said. "And how are you?"

"Sorry for the intrusion, but Cory didn't show up at home after school. I had a hunch he might turn up here."

"Your hunch was correct. Come in. He's in the kitchen."

He stormed past her through the hallway and stood in the entranceway to the kitchen, his lips pulled into a thin, tight line.

"Dad!" Cory called out, jumping to his feet. "Have you seen these pictures?"

"Why didn't you call? You know you're not supposed to go anywhere without first checking with me or Rose."

"What's the big deal?" Cory's eyes were shining. "Lulu's been showing me all these cool shots of when you guys were kids. I never knew there was a toboggan hill behind your old school! Now I can't wait for winter. Hey, Lulu, who's this other kid with you?"

"Don't get any ideas about tobogganing," Jake said before Laura could answer. "I broke my leg coming down that hill."

Cory's face fell. "Oh, right. Too dangerous. See what I mean, Lulu? He never lets me do anything."

"I don't want any back talk from you," Jake said. "You're already in trouble." He glared at Laura. "What's the matter with you? Why didn't you let me know he was here?"

She and Cory exchanged a quick look. Just this once. Just this once she would cover for him. "I—I'm sorry. We were so engrossed in these old pictures, I completely forgot. The time just got away."

Cory had lied when he'd told her that Rose knew he was here, and Laura resolved to talk to him later. But right now she wanted to talk to Jake about Cory's coming over to do chores. "Come into the living room," she said. "There's something I'd like to discuss with you."

A muscle flicked in his jaw. "There's nothing to talk about. Cory knows the rules. He should have called."

Standing there with that scowl on his face, Jake looked more like a spoiled child than an irate parent. A spoiled child who was used to getting his own way.

She turned her attention back to Cory. "The other girl in the picture is my friend, Ellen, when she was a kid. She's been living in New York for a long time now. She's one of those great doctors I told you about." Motioning to a small carton near the pantry door, she said, "Why don't you look in that box? I have a lot more photos of your dad when he was young." When Cory didn't answer, she added, "Go ahead, it'll be all right. Your father and I need to talk."

She saw the way Jake had been looking at her, his gaze taking in her old sweats and furry slippers. She was convinced that her unruly appearance somehow diminished her authority. "On second thought, Jake, our talk can wait. I'd like to freshen up. I've been cleaning all afternoon, and I need a few minutes to pull myself together. You can look at old photos with Cory, or you can make yourself busy and put on the kettle while I'm changing." She paused in the doorway. "By the way, I like herbal, particularly the apple cinnamon."

He looked at her as if she were speaking a foreign language.

"Tea, Jake. I'm talking about tea."

Once upstairs Laura took the time to marvel at her composure. She realized that her calmness stemmed from the knowledge that she had the edge in the situation. Jake could have called her from the office, but he had chosen to come over in person. He had made the move, not she. The ball was in her court.

Made a move? *What* move?

The ball? *What* ball?

What kind of game was she playing?

She turned on the faucet at the bathroom sink and waited patiently for the water to run clear. There was no time for a shower. I can't keep the opponent waiting too long, she thought, washing her hands with a bar of her perfumed soap. She imagined Edward saying in his teasing way, "Nice hands for an old lady." He'd once told her that the hands were often the first part of the body to show the signs of aging.

She went to her room and changed into a short denim skirt and a burgundy scoop-necked sweater. She quickly brushed her hair and tied it back in a ponytail. Jake had always liked simplicity. She examined her nails and frowned. Edward liked them this way, long and red, and she had to admit, the length didn't interfere with her painting. But Jake had always preferred a more natural look, which meant short and no polish. Natural also meant no makeup.

Hold on a second. What did she care what Jake thought?

It was time she stopped making herself over for any man. If she wanted to wear makeup, she would. So there.

Recognizing the irony of her actions, she laughed. She was doing herself over, in a reverse kind of way.

She opened the side drawer of her nightstand and pulled out her favorite shade of lipstick, Blushing Petals. A little powder wouldn't hurt, either, she decided, defiantly digging back into the drawer for her compact. Why stop there? Humming a romantic tune from an old movie, she applied mascara to her already naturally thick lashes. She couldn't remember the movie's title, but she did recall that Cary Grant had starred in it, and an actress named Deborah...Deborah what? The last name evaded her.

Back downstairs she found Jake and Cory sitting at the kitchen table, sorting through the photographs. Cory noticed her first. "Lulu, come and look at these!" he said. He picked up a snapshot of his father. "Hey, Dad, you never said anything about playing the trumpet!"

Jake laughed wholeheartedly, a sound long forgotten in Laura's ears. Something inside her fluttered, deep and warm. "Your father played in the high school band," she said, trying to keep her voice steady.

Cory looked at his father as if seeing him for the first time. "That's so cool! Do you still have it? Can I play it sometime?"

"Maybe I'll dig it up someday," Jake said. "Who knows? Maybe I'll even start playing again."

"He was wonderful," Laura added. "He played at all the games."

"Don't listen to her," Jake said. "I was terrible."

Laura joined them at the table. "No, you weren't. They made you the lead trumpet, didn't they?" She picked up another photograph. "Cory, here's one of your mother in her cheerleader's outfit. She sure could twirl that baton. She never dropped it. Not once."

Cory barely glanced at the picture. "So how come you didn't play football?" he asked his father. "You were big enough. Did Grandma think it was too dangerous?"

Jake took the picture from Laura and ran his fingers across its glossy surface. "No, my parents would have let me. It was because of my leg. After the toboggan accident, it was never the same. But you're right," he said, tossing the photo back into the pile. "Football is too dangerous, so don't even think about it.... Laura, you said you wanted to talk?"

"Let's go into the living room," she said. "I'll bring the tea." Jake had set a steaming pot and two cups onto an ornate silver tray. She glanced over at Cory, who had discovered her high school yearbook and was busy leafing through the pages.

"So fancy," she remarked, once she and Jake were seated on the sofa. "I didn't even know this tray existed. Where did you find it?"

Ignoring her question, he stared past her, studying the blue-and-green prism in the lamp on the side table, an original Tiffany that had belonged to her grandmother.

Okay, what did I do now? Laura thought.

"You shouldn't let him eat junk food," he said, as though she had spoken her question out loud. "All that sugar makes him hyper."

"And rots his teeth."

"Don't make fun of me. I'm being serious."

"He's not hyperactive, is he?" she said, suddenly alarmed. "Have you been to a doctor? Is he on some kind of medication?"

"No, I haven't been to a doctor." He rose to his feet and then sat down again as though he couldn't decide what to do with himself. "But you've seen him. He can't sit still for an instant."

"Are you talking about Cory or yourself? Sit still, Jake, you're making me crazy. Anyway, Cory seems like a perfectly normal ten-year-old boy to me." That wasn't exactly true. Cory was a normal, *troubled* ten-year-old boy.

"Normal? You call lying and fighting and mouthing off normal? And he's always pulling these disappearing acts, staying away for hours at a time. This, in my book, is not what I'd call normal behavior. I don't mind telling you, I'm scared. He's even run away from home, and I'm terrified that one day he won't come back."

"He's unhappy, Jake. Anyone can see that."

"Why should he be unhappy? I give him practically anything he wants, within limits. I admit I'm a little too protective, but it's not as if I lock him in his room, or anything like that."

She reached for the teapot and began to pour. "Have you talked to anyone at his school? Someone in the guidance department, or even his teacher might be able to help."

"I've already been down that route. It was a waste of time. After a whole week of counseling, what does he go and do? Smoke! He was found lighting up in the bathroom!" He reached into his shirt pocket and took out a pack of cigarettes. "Speaking of which, do you mind?"

"As a matter of fact, I do," she answered curtly. "When I was in treatment, half the people in the waiting room were there because of that vile habit. I thought you gave it up."

"Sorry, I wasn't thinking." He was about to return the pack to his pocket, but stopped himself. He tossed it onto the tray instead. "There. I've just quit. Again."

"I certainly hope so." She chose her next words carefully. She knew how Jake felt about psychotherapy. After Cynthia's accident, he had refused to seek professional help, insisting that he was perfectly all right and that he had no intention of letting outsiders pry into his private life. "There are people out there trained to handle these kinds of problems. I could get a name through Ellen, if you want."

His eyes hardened. "You mean a shrink. Cory may have a few problems, but he's not crazy."

"No, of course he's not. But he does need help."

"I have to admit," Jake said, taking a sip of his tea, "I was surprised he came here. But you always did have a way with him. I haven't heard him speak so much in a long time. Usually, he just grunts at my questions."

"Maybe that's part of the problem."

"What is?"

"Your questions. And your orders, too. Maybe all you need to do is sit down and talk with him. And listen."

"I talk to him all the time. I talk to him until I'm blue in the face."

Laura shook her head. "Not *to* him. *With* him. Listen to your son. He talks to you all the time, but you refuse to hear. When he disobeys you, he's telling you he's unhappy. Can't you see? He's begging you to listen to him."

"By fighting? By smoking?"

"That's his way of getting your attention. 'A waste of time,' I believe were your exact words. He probably feels that *he's* a waste of time. A waste of *your* time."

"You got all this from only one meeting with him?"

"No, I got all this by talking with you, just now."

He stared blankly through the archway. The grandfather clock in the hallway chimed five times, and he looked back at her. "Am I that bad?" he said quietly. "Have I always been such a coldhearted clod?"

"He loves you, Jake. Anyone can see that. Did you notice the way his face lit up when you told him you used to play the trumpet? He idolizes you, and you won't give him the time of day."

"I spend time with him," he protested, although his eyes

told her differently. "But you know how demanding my work is. Besides, what's so special about the trumpet?"

"What's so special is that it was *your* trumpet. Why do you think he asked you if he could play it sometime? He wants to be part of your life, not a waste of your time."

"All this you got in just a few minutes. Amazing."

"Don't mock me," she said.

His mouth curled into a small, sad smile. "I'm not mocking you, I'm praising you. In just a few minutes you managed to open him up and see inside him. I wish I had one ounce of your insight." He put down his cup. "You look nice, by the way. I like your lipstick. It's soft and warm, just like you."

His comment took her by surprise. This from the man who had always been adamantly opposed to makeup? Maybe it wasn't the most original of lines, but she felt as if she'd been caressed. He continued to stare at her, his gaze lapping her like a tongue.

*No.* She wasn't going to go where he was obviously headed. This was so like him, reading sex into everything, ignoring the problem at hand. She turned her head away, hoping to dispel the heat that had risen in her cheeks. "About yesterday..."

"I made an ass of myself," he said, surprising her again. "I was way out of line and I'm sorry. Seems like every time I see you, I'm apologizing for something."

"I said some pretty nasty things," she found herself saying. "I'm sorry, too."

Awkwardly he cleared his throat. "Look, I have an idea. More of a favor, really. You have such a good rapport with Cory, would you mind talking to him again? He relates to you, always has. Maybe you can get to the bottom of what's bothering him. I need to know what's going on in his head."

"Talking to him just one more time won't give you answers." She set her cup onto the tray, next to Jake's. "I want to spend time with him, don't get me wrong. In fact, that's why I wanted to talk to you in the first place. I've decided to keep the house, which means I'll coming back on weekends. I'd love to see Cory, if you'll let me. But I'm not a psychologist, Jake. Won't you at least think about getting him professional help?"

"I told you, he's not crazy. Spending a Saturday with you now and then is all the doctoring he needs. That is, if you're willing."

Suddenly, Laura wasn't so sure. She leaned back into the sofa, gathering her thoughts. What if Cory became too attached? It wasn't as if she and Jake were still married. She had another life, other commitments. It was possible she could cause more damage than good, and judging from the lost look in Cory's eyes, he'd had more than his share of damage.

On the other hand, he could use all the love he could get. Laura knew how lonely it was, living in a single-parent home with no extended family to speak of. Even if she couldn't spend much time with him, wasn't some love better than none? Not that Jake didn't love his son; he just had trouble showing it. He'd never been good at relationships. Look at us, she thought wryly. If there had been a contest for dismal marriages, ours would have won first prize. It had been a mistake from the start.

*You made a mistake,* Cory had said. Yes, she had. And she was terrified of making another one.

She thought back to her own childhood. Like Jake, she had been an only child, but unlike him, she had never felt wanted. If her aunt had only given her a kind word now and then, if she had shown her just one gesture of affection, a touch on the arm, a kiss on the cheek...

Laura had much more to give than a gesture or a word.

Cory, too, was an only child, and loneliness was written all over his face.

Her decision was made. "I would love to be part of Cory's life again," she began. "We were going to ask you if it would be all right if he came over once in a while to do a few chores. This way I can get to know him again. But to him it'll be a part-time job, to supplement any allowance you give him and what he earns from his paper route."

"His paper route?"

"I thought...he said...oh, never mind."

"I think it's a great idea," he said. "It'll also teach him a sense of responsibility, something, it seems, I haven't been able to do. But I'd like to do something for you in return, like maybe some of the repairs. For one thing, your roof is about ready to collapse."

She didn't miss the gleam in his eyes. Was he glad she had agreed to help Cory, or was he thinking about spending time with her? "I'll be paying Cory," she reminded him. "In any case, you're far too busy to concern yourself with all *this*." She gestured expansively around the room.

"Getting my son back on track means everything to me. But I want to repay you in some way. I just landed the contract for the community center, and it'll be a few weeks before we start on the legalese. It's a good time to take a little time off. My crew can handle what's on my plate, and Mary can handle the paperwork."

Laura recalled the sweet but efficient gray-haired secretary and smiled. What would Mary say if she knew her boss was planning to work pro bono?

"Think of it as a business arrangement," he said. "I get my son back, you get your house fixed. Strictly business. Deal?"

*Strictly business.* She had used these same two innocuous words only a few hours ago, in an attempt to convince

Cassie—as well as herself—that there was nothing between Jake and her.

Cassie's knowing look flashed before her eyes. In spite of Laura's reservations, in spite of her earlier resolve to manage the repairs on her own, Laura answered, "Deal."

## Chapter Five

Someone was pounding at the door. On the roof, the rain was coming down like pellets. Somewhere in the distance thunder was rumbling, and in the recesses of her mind she heard a child cry out, "Mama! Mama! Let me in!" Muted in her ears, the words pushed their way into her consciousness, waking her up with a start. She looked around the room. Although the bureau and mirror seemed vaguely familiar, she couldn't find a logical place for them in her mind.

Shaken, she rose from the bed and went to the window. Drawing aside the flower-patterned drapes, she saw that the sun was shining, the sky tranquil and blue. A white van was parked on the street. Was that one of Jake's company vans? Why was he here?

Where was *she?*

Suddenly it all came back. Relief flooded through her as

the memory of the dream faded and reality took hold. She was back in Connecticut, in her old room. She was home.

What was that banging?

Coming from somewhere above, a rhythmic thumping echoed in the room. She threw on her robe and slid into her slippers, then made her way downstairs. In the hallway, the clock rang out seven chimes. She opened the front door and stepped outside under the overhang. Jake's car was in the driveway, one of his company vans parked on the street. Shielding her eyes from the sun with her hands, she walked down the pathway and peered up at the roof.

"Morning, Squirt!" Jake called down. "You remember Farley, don't you?" A man wearing a bright-orange baseball cap raised his head. He saluted her with his hammer and then resumed banging.

"What are you doing?" she shouted at Jake. "Do you have any idea what time it is?"

Taking the rungs two at a time, he clambered down the ladder at the side of the doorway. "You know what they say," he said, bypassing the last few steps and swinging himself to the ground. "The early bird and all that stuff about the worm."

She groaned. "What normal person wakes up before seven on a Saturday morning?"

"Most of the real world, Squirt." His face split into a teasing grin. "Nice to see you all dolled up. Did you dress especially for me?"

What did he expect her to be wearing at this hour? A sequined gown? "You don't look as if you're off to the prom yourself," she said, taking in his worn overalls and faded denim shirt. "Where did you spend the night, in a barn?"

"Now don't get all testy on me. Then again, you've always been cranky before your first cup of coffee. Speaking of which, I brought you a present." He picked up a box at the bottom of the ladder. "I know a man's not supposed to give a woman anything attached to an electrical cord, but I thought you'd appreciate this." Grinning, he tore open the lid and removed a new coffeemaker from inside the box. "So how about it? I could sure use a cup of your special brew. That jar of instant has got to go. And I'm not crazy about that apple-cinnamon concoction, either. Come to think of it, a couple of eggs would be nice. Bacon, too. Extra crispy. And while you're at it, don't forget the toast."

She rolled her eyes. "How could I forget the toast?"

"Thanks for the gift, Jake," he said, mimicking her voice. "It was so thoughtful of you." He climbed back up to the roof.

She stomped back into the house, her bunny rabbit slippers slapping on the stone walkway. In spite of her irritation, she smiled, remembering how he used to tease her about her coffee. Thick and bitter, just the way he liked it. Strong enough to put hair on a young boy's chest, he used to say. She pictured him at thirteen, no longer a young boy but far from a man, and once again, she caught herself thinking back to that day at the community center when he'd pulled her out of the water and eased her down by the side of the pool. Even back then, his chest had been hard and muscular, and except for a few dark hairs here and there, his skin had been as smooth as hers. In spite of her anger, in spite of her embarrassment, she'd wanted to touch him. She'd been curious to know whether his few chest hairs felt anything like the thin and wiry growth that had recently sprouted between her legs.

*Now, now. There'll be none of* that *kind of thinking.*

After a quick shower, she dressed in jeans and a turquoise cotton sweater—Jake always said the color set off the tone in her eyes just right—and hurried back downstairs to the kitchen. She threw open the refrigerator door. What a sorry sight. She'd stopped at a convenience store on her first night back to pick up a few supplies, but she was nearly out of everything.

"I told you to keep the door locked," Jake said, startling her. "I could have been a prowler, or worse."

"I wish you wouldn't do that! You know I hate it when you sneak up on me."

"I remember you never liked surprises," he said, reaching into the refrigerator and pulling out the juice. He peered into the carton. "There's only enough for one person. Don't make anything for Farley, by the way. *His* wife gets up early to fix him breakfast."

"In case you've forgotten, I'm not your wife," she said, remembering the conversation they'd had yesterday, after he'd found her in the pantry. She'd had to remind him of their marital status then, too.

"And in case *you've* forgotten, you and Cory would still be in bed when I left for work. I used to make my own breakfast."

"And the kitchen would be a mess." She handed him a glass. "Go ahead, take the rest of the juice."

"Thanks, but I wouldn't dream of taking away your last bit of sunshine." He sat down at the table. "I guess all this must be driving you crazy," he said, glancing over at the boxes on the floor. "You always liked things in order. Neat. Clean. Everything in its place. Makes things...predictable. Like you."

She pulled out a bowl and slammed it down on the counter. "You know what your problem is? You always wait for things to...*happen*. And then you complain when things get out of your control. I may like things in place, but you go ballistic when something doesn't go your way."

"Hey, I'm not the one who's complaining now. It's not my fault you overslept."

"I'm not complaining. Do you hear me complaining?" She yanked open a drawer and rummaged for a fork. "But you should have called before coming over."

"You forgot the mugs. For the coffee."

She glared at him. "I don't see any casts on your arms.

Don't just sit there. Set the table. Make the coffee, which will have to be instant, by the way. What good is a coffeemaker without real coffee? Do *something,* will you? I could use a hand."

"Since when? As I recall, you always preferred to do everything by yourself. And it used to drive me crazy."

Laura was fuming. Oh, she knew what he was thinking, all right. As far as he was concerned, her independence had been the wedge that had driven them apart. *She* was the reason their marriage had failed.

"I'm letting you help me with the house, aren't I?" she retorted. "I certainly don't know how to fix a roof." She stirred the eggs furiously with the fork, as if punishing them for her lack of skill in roof repair. "Although," she added, ramming two slices of bread into the toaster, "this is a business deal. You said it yourself. Strictly business."

He got up and took two plates from the cupboard. "Look, I didn't come here to fight. I'm here to work on the house. The sooner you feed me, the sooner I'll be out of your hair."

"I don't remember feeding you as being part of the arrangement." She turned on the burner and emptied the eggs into the frying pan. "Speaking about our arrangement, why didn't you bring Cory? He's feeling okay, isn't he?"

"He's still asleep. Rose will be driving him over later. It's Saturday, remember? What normal person wakes up before seven on a Saturday morning?"

She stared at him for a long moment, and then, shaking her head, swatted him lightly with a dishcloth. He let out a deep, resonant laugh, and she laughed right along with him.

As quickly as it had erupted, their laughter broke off. Tenderly, he wiped away a loose tendril of hair from her cheek. "It's nice to hear you laugh," he said, his voice wistful. "I've missed that."

Although touches of merriment remained around his

mouth, his eyes shone with a yearning she hadn't seen before. A familiar sensation came over her, similar to what she had experienced after awakening from her dream that morning. Not the initial dizzying disorientation, but the acute relief that had followed when she'd realized where she was.

Once again she felt as if she were home.

Her heart throbbed with a longing she had managed to suppress for years. Missing *his* laughter, missing *him,* was how she had felt yesterday, when they were looking at old photos, and it was how she felt now, after hearing him laugh again.

She could still feel his touch on her cheek as she turned away from him and attended to the pan on the stove. The eggs were ready. She filled the plates and brought them to the table. "I'll pick up Cory," she said easily, as if they were a married couple discussing the everyday events of their everyday life. "I have to go out and get groceries, anyway."

The toaster popped and Laura jumped, not at the sudden clunk but at the unexpected sight of Farley, who was standing outside the open window. "'Scuse me, ma'am," he said, removing his baseball cap. "I didn't mean to scare you. Say, Jake, are you coming back out or what? I need a hand up there. I think I might have busted a few shingles."

"No rest for the wicked," Jake said. "I'll have to take a rain check on the coffee, as much as I love that instant stuff. Can you call Rose and let her know of the change of plans? And while you're out, can you pick up some sodas? A six-pack of beer wouldn't be a bad idea, either." He dumped the eggs between the two pieces of toast and, wolfing down the sandwich, darted out through the back door.

She sighed. Talk about being taken for granted.

Yup, once again, she felt as if she were home.

Jake was wrong.

It wasn't true that she hated accepting help from anyone.

What about when she was diagnosed with Hodgkin's? She'd had no qualms about letting her friends help her then. Or had she? She remembered feeling helpless. She'd hated having to depend on others.

She sat at the table, nursing her second cup of coffee. Plates and cups were stacked in the sink. She looked at the dishwasher and sighed. What a relic. Why even bother using it? She knew she would have to rinse everything by hand before loading up the machine.

Her thoughts returned to Jake. Maybe he hadn't been so off the mark, after all. But what was wrong with wanting to do things by yourself? She had learned at a young age to be independent, and it had made her strong. If Jake couldn't accept her the way she was, it was his problem, and it had been his loss. Edward, on the other hand, found independence in a woman attractive. In fact, her ambition to paint full-time was a major topic of discussion at the many cocktail parties they attended—although at times, she had to admit, it bothered her when he talked about her lifelong dream in such a detached, analytical manner. Still, his admiration and respect meant a great deal to her, and before going to bed last night, she finally called him to tell him of her plans to keep the house. He hadn't been as excited as she had expected, but he hadn't been against the idea, either. And, yes, he'd offered to pay for the repairs, but to her relief he hadn't pushed the point. But that was just like Edward. He never argued. If there was one thing she could depend on, it was his even temperament.

Sitting at the table, she tried to remember why she had been so excited about keeping the house in the first place. The repairs seemed overwhelming. She glanced down at the floor. More than half the tiles had gouges, and next to the broom closet, entire pieces had broken off. It was hard to believe that the linoleum had once been powder blue with a distinct daisy design.

Aunt Tess sure had a fondness for flowers, she thought, picturing the rose-patterned wallpaper in the living room. She shifted uneasily in her chair, an unsettling notion taking hold in her mind. What if her aunt hadn't changed a thing after moving in? What if all those tacky flowers had been her mother's taste? No way, Laura thought, immediately dismissing the idea. Her mother and her aunt had been totally different. Her mother had loved her.

She looked over at the old-fashioned cabinets. The paint was chipped and two of the doors were missing knobs. The entire kitchen was a mess—why bother cleaning the breakfast dishes? But she couldn't just leave them rotting in the sink, could she? Jake's words came back to her: neat, clean, everything in its place. "Is that so?" she spoke to the tarnished faucet. "Maybe he doesn't know me as well as he thinks he does." She carried her coffee to the pantry. The dishes could wait.

She put her cup onto the concrete floor and picked up a small box. Inside, a yellowed corsage was stapled to a pale blue bow. She lifted the flower, flakes of the petals breaking off in her hands. "A little bit of sunlight to match the smile on your face," the attached card read. "Yours forever, Peter." Corny but touching, she thought. It was difficult imagining her aunt in a romantic light.

She picked up a second, larger box. Across the top, the word "Navy" was scrawled in small faded letters. Inside was a stack of papers. Leafing through them, she realized they were letters that had been written over the course of three years, the first one in the pile dated thirty-seven years ago. I shouldn't do this, she told herself. It was an invasion of privacy. She hadn't read the letters addressed to Cynthia, so why consider reading these? Staring out the pantry doorway, she debated what to do. Maybe these letters would help her understand her aunt. Maybe understanding her aunt would help her remember her mother. She began reading.

*Dear Elizabeth,*

*What an exciting time to be alive! I can't think of a better way to spend my life than as an aviator. All I've ever wanted to do was fly. I'm convinced that the Navy was the right decision. The program here is topnotch.*

*You can't imagine the sense of freedom! When I'm in the air, time ceases to exist. The only thing that jars me back to the present and roots me to reality is the sound of the engine purring like a kitten. (Maybe I should have been a poet. You always did accuse me of having my head in the clouds.)*

*But even lofty fliers like myself—I should say would-be fliers, as it will be a while before I complete my training—need to feel part of the real world, and you give me that feeling, Tess. Still, I appreciate that you're not trying to "clip my wings," as you assured me before I left, and that you're not trying to make me commit to a future which at this time is so up in the air (excuse my lousy punning).*

*I'm proud of you for not quitting your job. Working in that dress shop, going to school and helping take care of your family was a heavy load, but now it's time to move on. I know that going to Western Connecticut State was the only way you could go to college and still live at home, but now that you've graduated, you should think about moving out. At twenty-two, you're more than ready to make the break. Caroline is now sixteen, old enough to take care of herself. In fact, I just finished reading a letter from her in which she asked me to re-*

*mind you that she's no longer a child, that she's old
enough to make her own choices. In any case, it's time
you thought about yourself. I know how much you love
Ridgefield, but get out of town for a while—travel, enjoy,
find a lover! Now don't get offended. I mean these words
with the best intentions. Over the next few years, we'll
both be doing a lot of growing, a lot of changing. And
with any luck, we'll find each other again. In the meantime, keep those letters coming. I can't tell you how
much I enjoy hearing from you and your sister.*

*Angel*

Travel? Enjoy? Find a lover? Laura almost laughed, thinking about the joyless, prudish woman who had raised her. She
picked up another letter and another until she had read them
all. They had all been signed "Angel," and except for the last
one in the pile, they all described a young man's love of flying.

She examined the handwriting of the last letter. Angel's
earlier style had been looser, freer, full of hope and expectation; the loops in this letter looked emaciated. She ran her finger across the words as though she could feel the difference,
and then, with sudden realization, she pulled it away. This last
letter had been written after a full year's lapse. What had happened in that time? Where were the other letters?

Short and concise, the final letter had hinted at a crisis, and
Laura was intrigued. Hoping to catch something she might
have missed, she read it a second time.

*Dear Elizabeth,
This is just a short note to tell you that it is now official.
I have resigned my commission and I will be com-
ing home.*

*What a strange turn fate has taken. It's too bad life doesn't come equipped with a crystal ball. But maybe this has been a blessing in disguise—I might have been sent overseas, and who knows when I would see you again. The support of your family has been un-failing, and because of this continuing faith, I still have hope for the future.*

*I'm pleased that you and Peter Barnes have be-come such good friends. I'm not surprised. The two of you have a lot in common, having grown up in Ridge-field. I'm sure you realize he's in love with you and is probably thinking about marriage. Be careful not to hurt him when you turn him down. Remember, good friends are hard to come by.*

*Enough philosophizing. The next words from me will be delivered in person. I want to make Ridgefield, the town you love so much, my home, too. You've always known I would never go back to Hartford. But then again, you've always known me better than I know my-self.*

*Angel*

Peter Barnes? Was that Reverend Barnes he was referring to? The minister who had spoken at the service? "I had a se-cret crush on her," he'd said at the gathering at her house, "but she had her eye on some other fellow." That other fellow must have been Angel, the author of the letters.

So, Aunt Tess hadn't been a wallflower. She'd had at least two suitors in her life. But had there actually been a romance between her and the man who called himself Angel? In the letters, although he had hinted at a future, he had never re-ferred to their relationship in terms of anything but friendship. Laura was about to reach into the box for more memorabilia, anything that might shed more light on the mysterious Angel, but the sound of the clock chiming in the hallway reminded her that it was time to get going.

She went back to the kitchen to grab her grocery list. If Cory's appetite was anything like his father's—and given the height of the boy, she didn't doubt it for a moment—come lunchtime, Cory would be bellowing like a hungry grizzly.

After she had shopped for groceries and picked up Cory, the two of them worked together cleaning out the garage. Cory, however, hardly said two words to her. Yesterday he'd been so cheerful, but today he was almost hostile. Laura was almost relieved when noon came around. She told him she was going inside to prepare lunch.

She prepared a stack of sandwiches, then placed a tray of unbaked cinnamon rolls into the oven. What male could resist a hearty home-cooked meal? Not that fixing pastrami and turkey sandwiches required a degree in the culinary arts. Fifteen minutes later a whiff of cinnamon floated across the kitchen. If the sandwiches didn't do it, these fresh-baked rolls would turn him around.

Was she thinking about Cory or his father?

"Hey, Squirt, what smells so good?"

She whirled around. "Don't you ever knock?"

"Don't you ever lock your door?"

"I have a doorbell, too, in case you haven't noticed. A marvelous invention. You should try it sometime."

"We can avoid having this conversation in the future, if you remember to lock up. I'll need a key, by the way, in case you go out."

That's all she needed, Jake coming in and out as he pleased. She pulled the pan from the oven, and he reached for a roll. "You'll have to wait," she said, swatting him lightly with her free hand. "They're too hot. Besides, they're for dessert. Now go get Cory. What about Farley? I've made enough for everyone."

"Farley left. His wife makes him go home for lunch."

Laura found it hard to believe that Sarah McLaughton could budge her husband even an inch, let alone make him come home for lunch. Farley, Jake's right-hand man, was a robust six foot four, whereas his wife, Sarah, was a thin and frail four foot ten. Laura set the pan on the counter and looked up at Jake. "What is it?" she asked, noting the frown that had crossed his brow. "Has something happened to Farley? Did he drop the hammer on his foot again?" She'd always questioned whether Farley was in the right business. He might be Jake's top worker, but he was accident-prone.

"Those cinnamon rolls...all that sugar..."

She let out her breath, relieved that Farley was okay. But for some reason Jake was back to that sugar issue. "I bought coffee," she said. "Real coffee so I can make that lethal concoction you like so much. Can't be too good for a person, either, but I don't hear you complaining about *that*."

"I told you, Cory—"

"You told me nothing. No doctor, no diagnosis. No hyperactivity going on here, as far as I can tell."

A shuffling noise caught her attention. Cory was standing in the doorway, watching them closely.

"Be realistic," Laura continued. "A little sweet once in a while can't hurt. You know that old saying, everything in moderation. Now go wash up, you two, so we can eat."

She wondered what price she would have to pay for arguing with Jake on the subject of child-rearing—and for disagreeing with him in front of Cory. But the discussion had been started before she'd noticed Cory, and she hadn't wanted to let it go.

Jake turned to his son and winked. "We'd better do what

she tells us," he said, surprising her. "She gets awfully bossy when she means business."

After Jake and Cory had sat down at the table, she pulled out a deck of cards from her pocket. Predictable, was she? I'll bet Jake never knew I was a card shark, she thought. I'll bet he never expected me to pull out a deck right in the middle of lunch. She cut the deck in half. "So, do you want to play crazy eights? You guys have been working so hard, I figured it was time for a little—" she shuffled the two parts into each other, producing a crisp, crackling noise "—relaxation."

"But we're eating!" Cory muttered, chewing noisily.

"Don't eat and talk at the same time," Jake admonished.

"But we can eat and *play* at the same time." If ever there was a kid who needed more fun, it was Cory. "Now who wants to deal? Or do I have to do that, too?"

Cory looked at his father with uncertainty. "What about germs? Aren't you always telling me to be careful of germs?"

"What germs?" Laura said innocently. "Up to now these cards have never been touched by human hands. This is a brand-new pack. I go through a lot of packs, seeing how much I like to play solitaire."

Jake gave her one of his smug smiles. "You must not get a lot of excitement. Now if I were Edward..."

"For your information, I happen to like solitaire," she said stiffly. "I find it relaxing. And you'd better not go where you're thinking, Jake Logan. There's a minor here. Now are we going to play this game or not?"

Cory looked at Laura, then back at Jake. "Huh? What's going on?" He shook his head in mock disgust. "Grown-ups. And you think *I* have problems."

"Problems? No problems here," Jake said, now grinning broadly. "And no germs, either. They wouldn't dare come around, not with Dragon Lady guarding the castle."

"You finally get the picture," Laura said. "Now listen carefully. We're not going to play your regular, everyday crazy eights. We're going to play the Spanish version. In Mexico, they call it *ocho locos*."

Cory and Jake exchanged a look, one that suggested to Laura they thought *she* was loco. "What's ocho?" Cory asked.

"It means eight in Spanish," she said.

"When were you in Mexico?" Jake asked, reaching for a turkey on rye. "By the way, thanks for the spread. I didn't expect you to make us lunch. I appreciate it."

"You sound surprised," she said.

"No, really. I was planning to take you and Cory out for pizza."

"I wasn't referring to lunch. I was referring to Mexico. That's where I learned to play Ocho Locos, even though the game comes from Puerto Rico. Cassie, Ellen and I went to Cancún after graduating from college. It was a present we gave to ourselves. I'm surprised you don't remember."

Cory looked at Laura. "My mother didn't go?"

"She had other commitments." At first Laura wasn't sure if Cory was asking about college or the trip to Mexico, but that was silly—why wouldn't he know that his mother hadn't gone to college? What he probably didn't know was that Cynthia had given up not only her education, but also her dreams.

Laura started dealing. "Now pay attention. Here's how it goes. It's just like crazy eights, except we play eight hands. In the first round, we each get eight cards, seven cards in the second round, and so on. The person who wins the most rounds wins the game. Although we may have to have a tiebreaker—"

"But that's not how it's played!" Cory burst out. "Each person gets five cards, and when the first person gets a hundred penalty points, the game is over. You don't know anything! This is so dumb!" He shoved back his chair and stormed out of the kitchen.

Laura's mouth dropped open. "What did I say? What did I do?"

"Nothing, Squirt," Jake said, his face glum. "Believe me, it's nothing you did. He just gets this way sometimes."

She turned her head in the direction Cory had gone. "I don't know," she said slowly. "Maybe he does need professional help."

"What he needs is *you*," Jake said. "Please, Laura, don't give up on him."

She looked back at her ex-husband. His shoulders were hunched over as if in defeat, his hands palms up on the table as if beseeching her to help him. Without speaking, she reached across the table and closed her hands over his.

In his eyes she read, "Don't give up on *me*."

## *Chapter Six*

Jake looked so vulnerable that for one dizzy moment Laura forgot that anything had ever come between them. "You need to talk to Cory," she said, forcing herself back to the matter at hand. "You need to talk to him about Cynthia."

He jerked his hands from her grasp. "I fail to see how Cynthia fits in with his little tantrum. She has nothing to do with his life anymore. You said it yourself, she's gone."

Laura felt Jake's withdrawal as acutely as if she had been stung by a wasp. "Cynthia has *everything* to do with his life," she said. "Cory is one confused little boy, in case you haven't noticed. He wants to know about his mother. He wants to feel connected. Isn't that a word you always use? Isn't that why you like these old homes? You always say they give you a sense of belonging. Don't you see? Cory needs to feel as if he belongs. He's not sure what he's feeling, and what's more, he's not sure what he's supposed to be feeling. You've got to talk to him—and you've got to listen."

"I won't talk to him about Cynthia."

"He's probably in the garage," she pressed on. "There's no time like the present."

"No. After he's had one of his outbursts, he likes to be alone. It helps him calm down." He rose from his chair. "Thanks for the grub. Don't forget to lock the door behind me. Which reminds me, where's the key you promised me?"

She didn't answer. Two could play at this game. He didn't have the corner on avoiding issues.

"Now don't go and get your feathers all ruffled," he said. "You're angry, right?"

She reached for another cinnamon roll. So much for my you-can-eat-anything-you-want-as-long-as-it's-in-moderation rule, she thought, taking a large bite.

"Come on, Squirt, talk to me." He bent over to wipe a crumb from her face, but she pushed his hand away. "Look, I'm sorry," he said. "If it makes you feel better, I'll talk to him. Later...soon...today..."

"About Cynthia?"

"No...maybe...what the heck, okay. If you think it'll help."

"It'll help."

He smiled at her in a little-boy way and handed her a napkin. "Still friends?"

It was strange the way his lips curled. Why hadn't she ever noticed this before? They stayed in a straight line as though they couldn't decide which way to turn, and then, as if they had a will of their own, the corners suddenly turned up and twisted. "Still friends."

"And the key?"

"I don't recall promising you a key."

"But you'll think about it?"

"I'll think about it."

He grabbed two cinnamon rolls and headed back outside. She sat at the kitchen table, trying to figure out what had just happened. Jake had been so bullheaded about not talking to Cory about Cynthia, and then just like that, he changed his mind. The man was as stable as a pendulum.

She carried a tray of sandwiches, cinnamon rolls and lemonade out to the garage. There was no way she was going to let that little boy stay out there, alone and stewing.

Cory was huddled in a corner on the floor, holding his knees to his chest. She wanted to gather him up as if he were a baby. "I brought you something to eat," she said softly. She put the tray down next to him. "You ran out without finishing your lunch."

He looked at her with large, doleful eyes and reached for the food. Pretending to examine a set of rusty garden tools, she waited patiently for him to finish eating. Three sandwiches and a cinnamon roll later, he wiped his mouth with his sleeve. "Thanks, Lulu," he said. "I guess you're pretty mad at me, huh?"

She picked up a broken spade. "It looks like I need to do some shopping, if I ever want a garden again. I need to get the soil ready before winter comes. That's another thing I'll need help with. What do you think? Is this something you'd like to do?"

He shrugged. "I suppose."

She sat down next to him. "So I guess you don't like crazy eights too much."

"It's okay. I just don't understand why we couldn't play it the normal way. You know, with five cards."

"I thought it might be fun to do something different." She studied his face. He looked as though he wanted to say something, but was debating whether or not to speak. Debating whether or not to trust her. "Level with me, Cory," she coerced gently. "What's really bothering you?" Other than the fact that the only mother he had ever known had left him and now, after a five-year absence, was suddenly back in his life. Something clicked in her mind. It was no wonder he had a hard time playing a new game. Like most people, he didn't like it when out of the blue someone came along and changed the rules.

"Nothing," he said glumly, "but if you ask me, I think it stinks."

If he hadn't looked so glum, she might have laughed. He certainly had a unique way of zeroing in on a topic. "What stinks?" she asked.

"I told you, nothing. Except how come my mother didn't go with you? To Mexico, I mean. It was because of me, wasn't it? She had to stay home to take care of me."

"No, Cory, you weren't even born yet." She tilted up his chin and looked into his eyes. "Do you know how much your mother wanted you? And when you finally came along, she loved staying home and taking care of you."

It was a half truth. Cynthia and Jake hadn't wanted children, although once Cory came along, they were thrilled. But before that, Jake had been too busy building up the business, and Cynthia had been involved with her home-decorating venture—not a thoroughly satisfying substitute for being the designer she'd always wanted to be, but it had kept her busy and, for a while, content.

Life sure played funny tricks. Laura was willing to give her right arm for a baby, while Cynthia and Jake, who had made a conscious decision to go childless, were given Cory, this wonderful gift of life.

"He shouldn't have come here without me!" he suddenly burst out. "I told him I wanted to come with him this morning, but did he listen? Does he ever listen?"

So, Jake had been right. Cory's mood had nothing to do with Cynthia. But Laura suspected it wasn't totally about Jake's listening habits; it was also a matter of territory. Was

Cory jealous of his father? Did he see him as a kind of rival? Or more likely, did he blame his father for Laura's going away?

She could hardly ask Cory these questions. "Maybe he just wanted to let you sleep a little longer," she said, "but you're right, he should have listened."

"I told you, he never listens to me."

"I have an idea," she said. "You guys will stay for dinner and we'll talk. You and I will talk to him right through the night, if that's what it takes to get him to open up his ears. But remember, if you want him to listen to you, you're going to have to listen to him, too. If you want him to trust you, that means no more taking off without telling anyone, and no more lying. Do you know what I'm saying?"

"Yeah, I know. This is where you tell me it's a two-way street. Give and take. Do unto others. All that cra—stuff." He looked up at her and burst into a grin. "Hey, Lulu?"

He may have inherited his mother's eyes, but that dimple in his left cheek was definitely Jake's. "What?" she asked, suspiciously.

"Could I have another cinnamon roll?"

She handed Cory another roll and took one for herself.

So much for moderation.

It was close to five when Jake finally knocked off for the day. Laura asked him to stay for a potluck supper, but he said he was planning to surprise Cory with an evening out. Bonding time, he called it, time alone with his son. They were going to grab a quick burger, then catch the game over at the high school. She laughed when he'd said the word *bonding*—he must have read some of those psychology books he always made fun of. She told him she thought it was wonderful he was spending time with Cory, wonderful he was bonding. It shouldn't have mattered to her that he hadn't included her in their plans. She wasn't all that interested in basketball, anyway.

So why was she feeling so let-down?

Never mind. She would stay home tonight and take it easy. The past few days had been hectic, and she needed some time for herself. The problem was, being alone would probably start her thinking about things she didn't want to think about. Like the way Jake had looked when he'd asked her not to give up on him. Or the way he had smiled at her when he had agreed to talk to Cory about Cynthia. Or the way his eyes had gleamed when she had given him a key to the house, just before he and Cory left. "In case I go out," she'd said. "Use it only if you have to."

*Stop it,* she told herself. Stop thinking about him. But she might as well have told herself to stop breathing.

Maybe being alone tonight wasn't such a good idea. She knew she would sit there all evening, brooding about Jake. Maybe she should call Cassie. They could see a movie or take a walk down Copper Hill, anything to prevent her head from going into overdrive. She picked up the phone, but immediately put it down. She didn't want to have to rehash the day, knowing exactly how Cassie would react. She pictured her friend sitting across from her at the Café St. Gabriel, clucking her tongue and saying, "There's a great guy waiting for you in New York. I'd hate to see you screw it up."

Laura had no intention of screwing up her relationship with Edward. Sure, she'd been disappointed when Jake had refused her invitation to stay for dinner, but they were friends, and friends disappointed each other from time to time, didn't they? If she'd ever had a notion about the two of them getting back together, she now saw how ridiculous it was. The two of them were like oil and water, cats and dogs...she searched through her mind for every possible cliché to back up her thinking. Sure, she was still attracted to him, but so what? It didn't mean a thing. Jake was a good-looking man, and that was all there was to it. With those broad shoulders and dark liquid eyes, he could turn any woman's head.

Yes, she had definitely moved on. She and Jake were friends. Good friends. Their marriage had been a mistake, but they were over that. Over the hurdle and past the hurt. Back to being pals, as when they were kids. They had come full circle.

*Enough,* she told herself. Introspection was exactly what she wanted to avoid. She decided to call Cassie after all, but after six rings, she got the answering machine and hung up without leaving a message. It was stupid to think that Cassie would be home on a Saturday—Cassie who was always in motion, Cassie who went through men the way some people went through chocolate. But wouldn't she have mentioned having a date? The chimes in the hallway announced that it was only five o'clock.

Laura, stop obsessing *right now.* Cassie has a right to her own life, just as Jake has a right to his. So what if he'd rather go to a basketball game than stay here with me?

She changed into a plain cotton housecoat and curled up on the couch, planning to spend the evening reading. But she couldn't concentrate. Her thoughts kept returning to that afternoon. She covered her legs with the red afghan and, closing her eyes, allowed her mind to drift.

A flood of memories came back to him as he sat in the bleachers of Middlewood High School's gymnasium, watching the game. He used to like to come by to watch Cynthia practice with the other cheerleaders. She always knew when he was watching, and would flash him one of her wide, glorious smiles. He could almost hear one of her cheers now. *Bop,*

*bim-bam, grind and go! Middlewood High will take the show!*
But when he tried to picture her prancing around in her gold-
and-blue costume, all he could come up with was the sight of
Laura in her wrinkled linen suit, lying on the couch. When he
tried to picture Cynthia smiling at him from the gymnasium
floor, he saw Laura's clear and knowing eyes.

Damn, she had looked cute in those funny rabbit slippers.
Some men liked short teddies on women, others liked garter
belts and spiked, high-heeled shoes, but it seemed that no matter what Laura wore, he found himself, well, interested. She'd
always had the power to heat up his blood. His behavior yesterday morning, when he had pulled her into his arms and
teased her, had been inexcusable, but it was as if he couldn't
help himself, as if he were a puppet. It was almost funny, the
way she had always accused him of trying to dictate her every
move. *She* was the one pulling the strings, without even knowing she was doing it.

The home team scored a point, and a loud cheer erupted from
the crowd, but Jake couldn't concentrate on the game. He thought
back to their marriage. She'd always had this effect on him, even
when she was angry. Sometimes it seemed as though the only
time she *wasn't* angry with him was when she was unconscious.
But even asleep, she could jangle his insides. Yesterday, seeing
her lying on the pantry floor, looking so small and defenseless,
he'd felt like Prince Charming waking up his Sleeping Beauty—
except that the kiss he'd had in mind, after assuring himself that
she was all right, was intended for her fully awake body, and was
unlike any kiss he'd ever heard about in fairy tales.

But she hadn't been angry or asleep when she'd agreed to
help him with Cory. He'd wanted to cover every inch of her
body with grateful kisses. Grateful? No, not grateful, unless
someone had recently renamed what it was he was feeling.
Laura Matheson still had the power to get his engine revving
and probably always would.

Another roar erupted in the auditorium. "Did you see that shot?" Cory shouted, jumping to his feet. "I can't believe he made it, and just under the wire! What a game!"

Cory. That was another thing about Laura. Every time he thought about how easily she related to his son, he felt his heart grow warm. With a pang he realized how much he had missed Cory's excited, cheerful voice. If it hadn't been for Laura, Jake wouldn't be here tonight, spending time with him.

Relate. Now there was a word he found himself using more and more. Laura would be proud of him. He was turning into a real softie. Maybe he'd stop by the florist and pick up a bouquet to show her just how sensitive he could be. No, that was too hokey. He'd buy her some tea. Yeah, tea. More of that cinnamon-apple stuff, and other kinds, too. He'd stop at the import store and pick up an assortment.

"It was a great game, huh?" Cory said. "Maybe you were right. Maybe football is the wrong sport for me. Basketball starts at my school in two weeks, and the coach asked me to try out. I mean, with my height, it makes sense, right? Hey, Dad, why don't we get a hoop and put it up on the side of the house? Dad?"

"What? Oh, good idea. We'll wrap it up real pretty. Get some fancy paper, too. And a big red bow."

"Huh?" Cory looked at his father as if Jake's body had been taken over by aliens. "What are you talking about? I want to shoot hoops with you, not wrap Christmas presents."

Jake looked at his son's baffled face and burst out laughing. "I think shooting hoops with you would be great," he said. "We'll stop at the sporting goods store on Monday to check out equipment. But right now," he continued, "I have another idea. What do you say we get out of here and stop for ice cream on the way home?"

"What about the sugar?" Cory asked warily. "What about my teeth?"

"You'll brush when you get home," Jake said, remembering Laura's words about moderation.

Cory smiled. "Let's stop by Lulu's," he suggested. "Did you know that her favorite flavor is pistachio? How weird is that? I mean, who likes green ice cream?"

Jake smiled. When they were kids, he'd thought it was strange that she wasn't a chocoholic like most of her friends. Like most females. He recalled reading somewhere that chocolate released endorphins, causing the same effect as romantic arousal. But Laura hadn't been boy crazy the way so many of her friends had been. She'd been more interested in getting good grades in school, more interested in painting and drawing. No, Laura hadn't craved chocolate. She was sweet enough the way she was—when she didn't let her temper get in the way. He'd had a crush on her, but she hadn't given him the time of day. And then he had started dating Cynthia, who had been so open and full of life—and to be frank, willing. She'd liked the bad-boy image he projected. It was as if he had been hit on the head with a sledgehammer, the way he had been drawn to her, and almost overnight his fantasies about Laura had vanished.

Sometimes he thought about how different things might have been if Laura hadn't been so shy. He could now see how he might have scared her off. He had to admit, at times he'd been a little too forward, a little too aggressive. He'd always regretted the way he'd acted that day at the community pool. But she'd been so darn cute in that bathing suit with the short frilly skirt. So young, so innocent…and it was an innocence she'd never lost.

Later he was to learn that, combined with unbridled passion, her innocence was a lethal combination, as addictive as a drug.

But there was something else about Laura, something he'd never been able to erase from his mind, even when he was married to Cynthia. He'd never been able to define it, but it had something to do with the way she saw the world. She always said that to be an artist, a person had to consider the other senses as well as sight. Like this thing she had for pistachio. She used to say that it was cool and refreshing, that she liked the way the taste would linger on her tongue long after she finished eating. Chocolate, on the other hand, offered only a fast fix, and minutes later you found yourself craving more.

Like pistachio, the taste of Laura had always lingered on his tongue, but like chocolate, she had been rich and sweet, and after they had been together, he'd always found himself wanting more.

"Dad, you're not listening again."

"I'm listening," Jake said, tousling Cory's hair. "Green ice cream, huh? So when did she tell you she liked pistachio?"

"She didn't tell me. I remembered. I remember a lot of stuff."

Jake looked at Cory, and with a stitch in his heart, answered, "So do I, son. So do I."

It was after ten when Jake drove by Laura's. Except for a dim light peeking through the partly drawn curtains, the house was sheathed in darkness. "Sorry, sport," he said to his son. "It looks like she's already gone to bed. Do you still want to go for ice cream?"

"Nah, I just thought it would be fun if we all went." Cory's words were tinged with disappointment. "But we're coming by tomorrow, aren't we?"

"You know it."

"And you'll wake me? I mean, you won't go without me?"

"Scout's honor," Jake said. "What do you say we stop for bagels before going over?" he added, remembering that the import store was closed on Sundays.

Minutes later he pulled into their driveway, whistling under his breath. "Why don't you read for a while before going to bed?" he suggested as they made their way up the walkway. "You didn't get to do any homework today, and if we're going to be out all day tomorrow, you might not have time. Now that you're a working man."

"Uh...I can't. I left my backpack at Laura's."

Jake unlocked the front door, and they entered the foyer. Moonlight trickled in through the stained-glass windows, barely lighting the room. "Why did you take it to Laura's in the first place?" he asked, clapping his hands loudly to activate the lighting in the hallway. Right after he'd bought the house, he'd redone the wiring so that almost everything inside responded to a command. For instance, Rose would prepare the coffee at night before she retired, and in the morning, all Jake needed to do was say the word *drip* to get the coffee started. Although he liked things simple and straightforward, he'd always been a sucker for technology.

"I left it there on Friday, after school," Cory was saying, a sheepish look written across his face. "You're not mad, are you?"

"No, but you'll have to take out time from your work tomorrow to hit the books."

"I'm kind of bushed now, anyway. I guess it was all that hard work." Cory puffed out his chest. "But we're men. We can handle hard work. I guess Lulu really needs us, huh?"

"She sure does," Jake answered, grinning. "You go on up. But first knock on Rose's door to let her know we're back." He was still smiling, although Cory's words had left him with an unsettled feeling. Just what kind of values was he teaching his son?

"I heard the car roll up." A tiny wisp of a woman wearing a gold kimono appeared in the hallway. "How is the missus? I saw her at the funeral, and I thought she looked a little peaked."

"Laura's fine," Jake answered. Rose was a strange bird. He looked at her latest costume, trying to conceal his amusement. So, now it was Japan. Each month, a different country topped her growing list of "must-see" places. She claimed that traveling was her great passion in life—although, as far as he knew, she'd never even been out of Connecticut.

Rose Halligan had moved in after Cynthia's death, and had stayed on after Jake had remarried. At sixty-plus she was a godsend with an endless supply of energy. Even though she was bossy and nosy, Jake and Cory adored her and would have been lost without her. Although Jake wished only the best for her, he was afraid that one day she would leave them to marry Fred Moulder, her gentleman friend, as she liked to call him. But Rose, a widow since forty, swore she would never remarry. "These days I get paid for the cooking and ironing," she liked to say. "Why should I do it for free?"

"You taking good care of her?" she asked Jake, her eyes filled with accusation.

"Now don't go worrying your curly mop." He waved his finger, pretending to scold her. "And I'll thank you to remember, she's not my missus."

"If you ask me, she's better off keeping it that way," she said with a snort.

"Go to bed, Nosy Rosy. If you don't get your beauty rest, you'll scare off poor Fred all the way into the next county."

"And you wonder where Cory gets his mouth from," she answered back. "I'm not one to meddle, but if you ask me—"

"Good night, Rose. You, too, Cory."

She retreated to her suite off the dining room, and Cory went upstairs. The usual sounds of a household winding down—footsteps creaking, water running, doors closing—drifted downstairs, and eventually, the tranquility of late evening settled over the house. These were the moments Jake savored, when the house lay in stillness and he had some time to himself. When he wasn't out at a site, he was usually at the office, and someone was always bursting in with one crisis or another. Sometimes he worked at home, catching up on paperwork, but staying home didn't mean relaxing.

And, of course, there was Cory. Sometimes Jake felt overwhelmed. Sometimes being a single father took the wind right out of him.

In the family room, he sat back in his recliner and closed his eyes. Laura used to tell him that he should try meditation, but he couldn't imagine himself sitting there, mumbling the same word over and over. A mantra, she called it. What if Rose walked in while he was chanting? She'd have him committed, if he didn't have her committed first. What a pair they'd make, Jake in a straightjacket, his housekeeper in a kimono.

And then, of course, there was Laura, flapping around in those silly rabbit slippers.

Laura. His eyes shot open. Damn. Why did his thoughts always go back to Laura? This was *his* time, and he was determined to clear his head of everything, including her, *especially* her. He picked up a magazine from the end table, then put it down. He reached into his pocket for a cigarette, and remembered that he had quit—again. He said the words, "Idiot tube," and the TV came to life. He then said, "Tube off," and it immediately died. This is crazy, he told himself. He finally had some time to himself and he'd forgotten how to relax.

He went to the kitchen to get a beer. "The missus," he repeated out loud, rummaging through a drawer for the opener. The word "missus" had a strange ring to it. Laura would have had a good laugh. There I go again, he thought. Why couldn't he get her out of his mind?

Laura. Now there was an enigma for you. One minute she was pushing him away, the next minute inviting him to stay.

And speaking of enigmas, why did Rose always feel the need to rearrange everything in the whole darn place just when he was getting used to the way things were? Think, Jake, where would an eccentric housekeeper in a Japanese robe hide a bottle opener? Finally he found it on top of the refrigerator, next to a set of plastic chopsticks. Makes sense, he thought, scratching his head. Laura would have had a good laugh over this, too.

Laura. He began to hum the tune he'd been whistling in the driveway. Where was it from? *An Affair to Remember.* Yeah, that was it. The movie had been a little too soppy for his taste, but Laura had loved it. She used to enjoy watching all those old movies—the soppier the better—and he hadn't minded kissing away her tears when the movie was over.

Wasn't that just like a woman? he'd thought at the time. He hadn't been alluding to Laura, whose tears had been as predictable as the story; he'd been referring to the woman in the movie—who was it again? Maureen O'Hara? No, Deborah Kerr. She gets hit by a taxi on the way to the Empire State Building and doesn't tell Rock Hudson—no, Cary Grant—that she can't walk. He learns the truth when he sees her wheelchair in the back room of her apartment. The same thing Laura would have done, if she'd been in the same situation. What was it about women? Laura hadn't wanted him around when she was sick, and look at the way she had tried to push him away when he had found her in the pantry.

*The pantry.* Yesterday morning when he had discovered the living room window wide open, he'd been certain that something was wrong. Now that he thought about it, the window had been open when he'd driven by her house only minutes ago. And why had she left the living room light on?

Something was wrong.

He had to go over there.

He started to write a note, in case either Rose or Cory

came looking for him, but then hesitated. Cory would be upset that Jake had gone to Laura's without him. "Out for a drive," he scribbled, knowing that Rose would figure out where he'd gone. She knew him like a book. He left the beer unopened on the counter, and headed out the front door.

He reached into his pocket and took out the key that Laura had given him. Just in case. Just in case she didn't answer the door. He attached it to his key ring, which at his touch lit up like a pumpkin on Halloween.

She was all right, he told himself. He knew she hadn't had an accident—but still, he had to make sure. He would never forgive himself if he didn't go over there and something had happened.

After pulling into her driveway, he sat in the car, thinking. He realized he was acting crazy. He would ring the bell and she would answer, and when he told her why he had come, she would be furious. If he had any brains, he'd go home and avoid the aggravation.

But Cory had left his backpack here. What if for some reason they couldn't come here tomorrow to work on the house? There could be a break-in at one of the sites. It wasn't common in Middlewood, but it happened from time to time. Actually, it had happened only once, and the site had been in Danbury. But it could happen again, and Jake would have to go out there. How would Cory get his backpack?

Jake knew his logic was faulty. Cory would still expect to go to Laura's, and Jake would drop him there on the way to the site.

Cory had sneezed twice tonight. If he were coming down with a cold, it wouldn't be advisable for him to exert himself doing chores at Laura's. Jake sincerely hoped that Cory wasn't getting sick, but if he were, Jake would have to stay home tomorrow to make sure his son stayed put, Sunday being Rose's day off.

Cory had reading to do for homework. It was the perfect activity for someone confined in bed with a cold. Jake had to get the backpack *tonight.*

He turned off the ignition. On the ring, Laura's key burned against the palm of his hand, like a hot ember. If she didn't answer, he could always let himself in.

# Chapter Seven

She walked along the brick footpath, which started at the front door and ended in the rose-and-lily garden in the backyard. Pointing a skeletal finger, a hooded figure leaned out through the kitchen window. It called out to her in a laughing voice—*There she is!*—and beckoned her to approach. She ran across the yard to the kitchen door, seeking the safety of her room at the top of the stairs, but the door was gone, and, grotesquely twisted in the shape of the figure she had seen at the window, thick black vapors coiled out from the opening. She backed away in fear and, breathless, ran alongside the house, down the narrow footpath to the overhang outside the front door.

She was certain she had seen Death.

She didn't know what Death looked like, or even what it meant, but she was sure it was something awful, something grim. She rang the bell, once, twice, three times, and when no one answered, she pounded on the door. The brightness of day faded, as if a dark storm cloud were passing overhead, and in the receding light, she looked up and saw a figure leaning out her bedroom window. Billowing and transparent, the way she had always imagined a ghost would be, the figure stared down at her from her bedroom window, swaying in the dimness.

*Mama! Mama! Let me in!*

Laura was shaking. Once again the dream had locked her in its hold of terror, twisting its tentacles of fear around her heart, and once again she saw herself standing under the overhang, alone. The front door was locked, as it always was in the dream.

Jake tried to be quiet, but the door squeaked loudly as it swung open and then slammed shut behind him. He muttered a curse. He crept through the hallway on tiptoe, as though the muting of sound could make up for the disturbance he had caused upon entering.

He stopped in his tracks. From where he stood next to the antique mirror, he could hear her whimpering. Less than two seconds later he was in the living room, where he found her lying on the sofa, moaning in her sleep.

Immediately he realized that she wasn't hurt, and heaved a sigh of relief. "Déjù vu," he said aloud. The red afghan lay in a bundled heap on the floor, her housecoat riding high above her knees. He thought of the other day when he had carried her into the living room and set her down on the couch, her firm, smooth thighs peeking out from under her skirt. Then, too, she had looked pale and helpless. Now her face was contorted with fear, and she was clutching a cushion as if it were a shield.

He sat down on the edge of the sofa and pulled her to an upright position. "Wake up, Laura," he said gently. "It's only a dream."

She opened her eyes. "Jake," she said simply.

"Yeah, it's me. Not the bogeyman." He held his breath, waiting for the bomb to detonate. Waiting for the anger he knew he deserved for letting himself into the house.

Instead, she laid her head on his chest. "It was coming after me. I…I couldn't get away. I wanted to go to my room and pull the covers over my head, but no one would let me into the house."

He wrapped her in the safety of his embrace, feeling the tension slip from her body. "The same old dream," he said. "After all this time, you're still having that same old dream." He laced his fingers through her hair, tendrils the color of wheat and gold springing to life as if they, too, had been asleep.

In the hallway the clock suddenly rang out. She lifted her head and stared into his face. The realization that he was sitting next to her, fondling her, finally took hold in her mind. Maybe there were no bogeymen in the real world—but there *was* Jake.

She yanked herself from his hold. "What are you doing here?"

"Here it comes. The explosion."

"You didn't answer my question."

"Uh, Cory left his backpack here and he has homework?"

"You said you were coming by in the morning. What's the rush?" She looked at him the way an impatient teacher might regard a wayward pupil. "Pick another explanation. I'm sure you have a million of them."

"I saw a light on in the living room and I was worried you might have fallen?"

"I can see how you might have come to that conclusion,"

she said sarcastically. "People fall all the time while turning on lights. You get one more shot at this, Jake."

"I heard you cry out in your sleep and I came to rescue you from the evil grasp of the dark unknown?"

"Right. You heard me all the way from the high school gymnasium."

He burst into a smile. "No, I passed by earlier to invite you out for ice cream and I picked up a signal. It's that radar you used to talk about, the radar you said was between us."

What was wrong with him, thinking he could let himself into the house for no apparent reason? Giving him a key was like asking a child to hold a lollipop and telling him not to lick it. But what had she expected, given his track record? He had always done as he pleased. "That's three strikes," she said. "You're out. Game over."

"Come on, Laura. I was worried about you. I knocked on the front door, but you didn't answer."

"I didn't hear you. Why didn't you ring the bell?"

"I didn't want to wake you."

"Let me get this straight. The car is in the driveway, so you knew I was home. You wanted to come in, although whether to spy on me or to get Cory's backpack you still haven't made clear. Yet you wouldn't ring the bell, because you thought I was asleep—"

"I thought you *might* be asleep," he corrected. "I knew that if you were awake, you would hear my knocking. But when you didn't answer, I figured you had already gone up to bed. I was being considerate."

"Considerate! Why would you consider coming inside if you thought I was asleep? Abusing the privilege I gave you and invading my privacy is what you call considerate?"

"Wait one moment, Madam Prosecutor," he said, anger rising in his tone. "Let me remind you that I'm the one granting privileges around here. You're the one who's benefiting from this deal. Do you think it's easy, trying to put this house back together?"

"This is supposed to be a trade, remember? Or have you forgotten the details of the arrangement?"

"So spending time with my son is just business to you. And here I thought you wanted to be with him."

The conversation was taking a nasty twist. "Don't you dare turn this around to make me feel guilty," she said, glaring at him. "You know what Cory means to me. And I appreciate what you're doing for me, but that doesn't give you the right to come barging in here anytime you feel like it. Do you understand what I'm saying? Read my lips, Jake. This coming and going as you please has got to stop."

He hung his head as if he were a five-year-old who had been caught with his fingers in the frosting of a cake. "I was acting out of concern," he said, almost pouting. "Sure, I know I get a little too carried away sometimes. I know I'm a little too protective, but I'm working on it. I didn't call 911, did I? Or the fire department, or the AAA, or the CIA, or—"

"You call breaking and entering a 'little carried away'? This isn't funny." He was something else, refusing to acknowledge the seriousness of the situation, trying to joke himself out of the blame. "What if I'd had a gun? I could have mistaken you for an intruder—no, make that an ax murderer."

"You with a gun? You won't even swat a mosquito. Tell you what, I'll give you a key to my house and you can let yourself in, anytime, day or night, to even the score. You can even come barging into the bathroom while I'm in the shower, just to teach me a lesson." He rose from the sofa and got down on his knees. "Forgive me? Please?"

She looked into his wide, earnest eyes and shook her head slowly. "You're completely hopeless," she said, sighing. His words might have been funny, but she wasn't ready to let him off the hook. Not until she had made a few things clear.

"Repeat after me," she said in her no-monkey-business tone. "I, Jake Logan…"

"Funny, I thought *I* was Jake Logan."

She tapped him lightly on his nose. "Pay attention."

"Okay, okay." He placed his right hand across his heart. "I, Jake Logan…"

"…do solemnly swear to use this key to gain entrance to said domicile only when the proprietor—that's me—is absent, and for reasons related only to the repair of said establishment, as dictated in the aforementioned agreement."

"…do solemnly swear to use this key."

"Jake!"

He looked at her innocently. "I forgot the rest."

"Sure you did," she said, rolling her eyes. "Get off the floor. You look ridiculous."

"You always said you liked a man on his knees."

"Jake…"

He pulled himself back onto the couch and leaned close to her, his forehead almost touching hers. "Look, I'm sorry. It's just that caring about you is something I've never been able to unlearn. Old habits die hard, so give me a little time, will you? You've only been back a short while. You have to admit, I *am* trying."

She started to say something, but then stopped herself. There was no reasoning with him, once he got into one of his bad-boy moods. And how could she concentrate when he kept looking at her that way? She knew she should have been angrier, but mixed feelings swirled through her like waves. If he had let himself in because he'd honestly been worried, what was so wrong with that? After all, he had a reason for being concerned, after finding her on the pantry floor. She reminded herself that he shouldn't have let himself into the house that day, either. True, she had left the door unlocked all night, and he claimed he had been worried, but how could he have known she hadn't locked it, without first trying the knob in an attempt to enter?

Because he had let his imagination get away with him, she told herself. She looked at the lines knotted in his brow. He couldn't help himself. Jake was a compulsive worrier who wore his obsession like a favorite, worn-out sweater. It had been with him so long, he probably felt undressed without it.

Really, Laura. Just who was the real compulsive? Obsessing about Jake was something she'd done since she was a child. He'd been a part of her life for as long as she could remember, and in spite of his bullheaded tactics, she liked knowing that he cared.

Her heart skipped a beat. He'd said that caring about her was something he'd never been able to unlearn. "Don't try too hard," she whispered, the words escaping her lips before she could stop them.

His gaze traveled downward, then back up again. "It's never been an effort on my part."

Knowing how lethal his eyes could be, she looked away. Why did he always have to confuse caring with sex? For that matter why did he confuse everything with sex? I won't go there, she resolved, her legs shaking, her pulse racing. She had to tell him to leave *now,* or she might never find the strength. "You know that radar you mentioned? That radar is telling me that you should go."

"Actually, it was more like a thunderstorm," he said, his voice husky. "That day I saw you sitting in the chapel, I felt as though I had been struck by lightning. And yeah, that radar also told me to go, to run like hell as far away from you as possible."

"You should have listened," she said, still refusing to meet his eyes. "It would have saved you the trip over here. As for that lightning," she continued, determined to protect herself any way she could, "after the excuses you gave me for breaking into my house, I'm surprised you couldn't think of something more original. Or have you exhausted all the lines in your limited repertoire?"

His eyes flickered with a strange light, and for one small moment she thought she had seen something she had never seen in him before. Instinct told her it was an old scar, a wound from the past that had never fully healed.

Something also told her it had nothing to do with her, and it had nothing to do with Cynthia's death, either.

She bit her lip, immediately regretting her scornful words. Jake was finally opening up to her and here she was, making fun of him. Maybe he *had* changed.

The hurt in his eyes vanished as quickly as it had appeared, almost as if it had never even surfaced. "Hey, I never claimed to be Shakespeare," he said in his cocky voice, "but don't punish me just because I don't have the right words." He reached out to stroke her cheek. "'Fess up, sweetness. You know you don't want me to leave."

So much for thinking he had changed. He had never been able to see past his libido, and tonight was no exception. "There's no radar," she said, pushing his hand away. "And no storms. No thunder, no lightning. Nothing. And as you can see, I'm fine."

He smiled at her crookedly. "We seem to be at odds here, because that radar, which you claim doesn't exist, is telling me something different. It's telling me that you want me to stay." He cupped her chin with his hand, tipping her head upward. "Look at me, Squirt," he said, his voice suddenly quiet. "I know you're afraid, but I've got news for you. I'm scared, too. At least I'm honest enough to admit there's still something between us." Ignoring the warning look she shot him, he added, "I know what you're thinking, but you're wrong. I'm not just talking about sex. It's a lot more than that, and that's what's scaring you. You're afraid of everything else, of everything that goes with it." He traced the line of her jaw to her ear, making little sprinkling strokes with his fingers. "Poor Laura," he murmured, "how long can you keep running?"

His fingers were like a drizzle of tiny raindrops on her face, and she tried to ignore the tingling sensation. "Where do you get off preaching to me about commitment?" she said, once again brushing his hand away. "You were the who was never there. You were the one who preferred to be married to a ghost."

His face dropped as if it had been slapped, and for the second time in minutes, she found herself regretting her harsh words. "Please, Jake," she said, her tone thawing. "I want you to understand. I can't...won't...risk everything I've worked for. Things have changed. *I've* changed. I have a good life, and that includes someone I can depend on. I don't want lightning—I've had enough storms to last a lifetime." She smiled sadly. "For me, just staying alive has been a battle. Now, for the first time in years, I feel as though I can look over my shoulder without seeing the Grim Reaper in every corner. For the first time in a long time, I feel...safe." She spoke the word *safe* as if it were sacred, something that might vanish into the air if spoken too loudly. A single tear trickled out of the corner of her eye. "I'm not running, I'm just trying to hold on to what I have. I don't want to do something we're going to regret later. I don't want to risk losing Cory—or you, as my friend—a second time."

Without hesitating, he drew her into his full embrace. "Cory and I are not going anywhere," he whispered into her hair. "*I'm* not going anywhere."

"Jake, please," she said, struggling to hold on to the last of her resolve. "Let's not be stupid. We're friends now. Can't we leave things the way they are?"

"I can't do that," he said, his finger making tiny circles on her earlobe. "Not unless you tell me you don't want me. Not unless you tell me that you don't feel the same way I do. You know what I'm talking about. It's that radar again. Actually, lightning *is* a better word. If it were more intense, I would be lit up brighter than a Christmas tree. From the moment I saw you in the chapel, I wanted to grab you, to scoop you up—"

Her body stiffened. "Is that why you let yourself in? Did you think I would fall helplessly into your arms the minute I saw you?" She realized that falling into his arms was precisely what she had done. "Damn it, did you think you could just come here and—"

His mouth crashed down on hers as though attempting to silence her, his tongue insistently parting her lips. She knew it wasn't her silence he was after, but she didn't try to stop the kiss from happening, didn't question it further, didn't want to think at all.

It was what she had been thinking about all evening. It was what she had been thinking about ever since she'd arrived in Middlewood.

She sat with her arms at her side, her fingers spread wide open as though at a loss as to what to do. "Lust in a funeral chapel," she quipped nervously as he lowered his lips to nuzzle the base of her throat.

"A funeral chapel…under the stars at Freeman's Pond… right here in your living room…it makes no difference where. I won't lie. This is why I let myself in. I was sitting outside, not knowing what to do, trying to decide whether to go home and take a cold shower or just wait in the car. I was hoping you'd come out…hoping for…I don't know exactly *what* I was thinking. All I knew was that I couldn't go home without first finding out if there was a chance that we…that you… Just looking at you makes me crazy. I want to hold you, feel you. I want to be inside you. I *need* to be inside you."

She stifled a moan. "It's wrong," she said, not trusting the sound of her own voice.

He gathered her back to him and lowered her head against his shoulder. "Tell me you don't want me, and I'll go," he said, burying his face in the thickness of her hair. "Tell me, Laura. *Tell me.*"

She had sworn she wouldn't let it happen, but something inside her had been released, something she had kept locked up for years, and ignoring the voice of caution, she felt herself hurtling into the danger zone, past the point of no return.

You have no willpower, she chided herself.

She raised her head and opened her mouth to speak, but once again he silenced her with his lips.

*Some things in life don't change.*

With an urgency that surprised her, she threw her arms around him. One hand groping at his neck, the other clutching the back of his shirt, she kissed him in return, her tongue eagerly seeking the depths of his mouth. Having him lie next to her again, touching her, kissing her, was all she could think about. The last five years faded like an early-autumn mist, Edward disappearing from her mind as if he'd never existed.

She broke away from the kiss, and with deliberate slowness inched her lips along the side of his face. "Stay," she said, her mouth grazing the skin beneath his ear. "I want you to stay."

She didn't have to ask him a third time.

With thumb and forefinger, he deftly undid the top two buttons of her housecoat and slid his hand inside. "Just as I thought. No bra."

"You remember. It was our little secret. Our sexy little secret."

She'd always dressed for comfort, a simple skirt and blouse or sweater when going out, jeans or sweats at home, and once Cory was put to bed, she'd change into something even more comfortable—which meant no bra or panties. Whenever Jake saw her in a housecoat, he'd know what she *wasn't* wearing.

"Dance with me," he said, brushing his thumb across the crest of her nipple.

"Wh-what?" she asked. "Here? Now? With no music?"

"Yes. Here. Now." He rose from the sofa and extended his hand, and curious, she took it. He began to hum the tune from *An Affair to Remember.*

The only time they had ever danced was at their wedding. Although the reception had been simple with only a few guests attending, the small party had insisted that Jake and Laura dance the traditional bride-and-groom first waltz. Cassie and Ellen had decorated the smaller banquet room of the Colonial Inn with red Chinese lanterns, the sacred vermilion symbolizing long life and good luck, and in the cheery hue the newly wedded couple had glided into the first moments of their married life. Jake had been clumsy and awkward, but Laura had felt as if she were floating. She had waited all her life for that minute, to dance with him as his wife, and he had never appeared so elegant, so dashing, formally attired in a tuxedo, as they moved across the floor.

For the first time that evening, she noticed how he was dressed. His beige pleated trousers and blue oxford shirt gave him a sophisticated air, which she was not accustomed to seeing in him. Not only had he changed his clothes, he'd also shaved before going to the game. He lowered his head and brushed his cheek against hers. Was that aftershave? Funny, she hadn't noticed it earlier. A throb of musk underscored with traces of amber and sandalwood mingled with his own woody scent, creating a heady elixir. Yes, Jake Logan was full of surprises. Apparently, she was not the only one whose lifestyle had changed.

"You must have taken a few singing lessons," she said as they moved to the tempo of his melodic humming. "You could never carry a tune. Dancing lessons, too. You always had two left feet."

"I guess there's more to me than you thought." He turned her around in a sudden, full pirouette and, wrapping his arms around her waist, pressed himself against her.

"If there were any more of you," she said teasingly, feeling the proof of his desire hard against her stomach, "it would be a crime."

"Oh, lady, you are wicked."

With a bent knee, he smoothly pushed between her legs, parting them with his thigh. Instinctively she tilted her head backward and arched her back, her hair tumbling down her neck. No longer humming, he clasped his hands around her, and they swayed to the music of an invisible orchestra, their entwined bodies moving in a ritual dance of love.

Lost in the reverie of their rhythmic movements, she closed her eyes. For a moment she was back at Freeman's Pond, on the night he had proposed. They hadn't danced, and she had been shy rather than forward, but the way she had felt was similar to what she felt now. That night she had been caught up in the newness of their intimacy, allowing herself to succumb to its wine. Now, being with him in this way again, she found herself reliving the discovery, intoxicated with the wonder.

"Open your eyes, Laura. I want you to see everything I do to you."

He twirled her again, this time slowly, stopping halfway in the turn to crush his chest against her back. Encircling her from behind, he undid two more buttons. "Are you watching?" he whispered, his long, nimble fingers making their way to her breasts.

Still swaying, she shimmied out of his arms and turned to face him. Her housecoat had slipped off one shoulder, allowing one full breast to peek out. He reached out to touch her, his eyes riveted on the erect, pink nipple.

She undid another button. "No touching. Not yet. First I want *you* to see everything *I* do."

\* \* \*

The garment slipped off her other shoulder, the full expanse of her cleavage unveiled, shimmering in the glow from the lamp on the table. "Are you paying attention?" she said tauntingly, and as if in slow motion began to undo the remaining buttons.

He watched steadily as she moved her hand down the front of her housecoat. She freed each button with an exaggerated twist, her fingers traveling downward in little circular motions between each maneuver. Against all reason he found himself jealous of the housecoat, until finally, after what seemed like forever, it fell in a puddle at her feet.

Her breasts were now fully exposed, but Jake was looking somewhere else.

Just as he had thought, she wasn't wearing panties.

No panties. Almost driven to the brink with his desire, he reached out to touch her most secret place, but she backed away. "First things first," she said, smiling seductively. She placed her hands underneath the arcs of her breasts, as though inviting him to taste.

He stood there, unmoving.

"What is it? I thought...you wanted..."

"I'm mesmerized, can't you tell?" he said, a hot ache burning in his throat. "You're more beautiful than ever. I want to run my tongue along every inch of your body, savoring every part of you, your neck, your chin, the hollow between your breasts, the bud between your legs. I want to take you right here, right now, and after you've cried out my name, I want to start all over. And then over again, until you beg me to stop."

She laughed with delight, the peal of her joy awakening something in him he had long thought gone. It wasn't his own pleasure he was thinking of—it was the thrill of making her happy.

"You have it all wrong," she said, her eyes sparkling.

"Tonight you're going to cry out *my* name. Tonight you're going to beg me *not* to stop."

A little sassy, wasn't she? This new confidence of hers was unexpected—and titillating. "Exactly what do you have in mind?" he asked, avidly watching her every movement as she methodically peeled his shirt from his body. If that's what it took to make her happy...

"First I'm going to touch you," she said almost clinically. "All over." She moved her hands down to his belt. "And then I'm going to taste you. All over." The starkness of her words only added to his arousal. He reached down to help her undo his buckle.

She shoved his hand away. "No, I get to do that. Your job is to watch."

With an adroitness that matched his own, in one quick maneuver she undid the clasp and unzipped his pants. She reached inside his briefs, cupping him below with one hand, stroking him with the other. He groaned, burying his hands in her hair. "Oh, you are one wicked lady," he said hoarsely. "One wicked lady with two wicked hands."

"And don't forget, one wicked tongue." She sat down on the edge of the couch, and slid his pants and briefs down the length of his thighs while he stood before her, motionless with expectation.

Was this his ex-wife? She was still the Laura he remembered, but oh, she was so much more. She had always been adventurous and full of life, and the sex had always been good—no, make that *great*—but this new aggressiveness sent his blood surging from the top of his head to the tips of his toes.

She planted her mouth on his belly, sending sparks of fire racing through his veins. Lazily traveling down from his belly-button, she flicked her tongue against the moistness of his skin, tantalizing him with the promise of what was to come. She drew him deep inside her mouth, his moistness mingling with hers, moving her lips in a dance of her own making.

Liquid heat spread rapidly through his legs, threatening to burn him up alive. He held on for as long as he could, and then, not wanting to let go until she was ready to receive him, placed his hands on her head and delicately pushed her aside. "I have a wonderful talent," he said, his words almost slurred with the drunkenness he felt. "Did you know I can watch and enjoy you at the same time?"

"Prove it," she said.

He was more than happy to oblige.


With eyes locked on her face, he knelt before her, imploring her to meet his gaze. His hands slid between her legs and eased them apart. His eyes never left hers. His fingers trickled up her inner thighs, his feathery massage sending waves of pleasure cascading through her body. She placed her hands on his shoulders, then down his muscular arms to his hard, smooth chest. Tilting forward, she attempted to lick away the drops of sweat that glistened on his neck.

"My turn," he said lightly, removing her hands. "Behave."

She leaned back on the couch and closed her eyes, giving in to the gentle probing of his knowing fingers. The only thought that seeped into her consciousness was the certainty that she was slowly dissolving.

She quivered under his touch, a low moan escaping her. He pulled his hand away and replaced it with his mouth, driving her to an even higher plateau as she drifted deeper into her own pleasure. He locked his hands around her wrists, holding them immovable above her waist. In this position of mock submission, she could have broken free of his hold if she'd tried, if she'd wanted, but she allowed herself to soar even higher, fall even deeper, to a realm where the relinquishment of control did not mean surrender, but signified a gift, a freely given offering of self.

Her breath came in long, raspy groans as she released herself to the fervor, her gratification pure and explosive. She felt a pulsing in her womb and lay back breathless, her body satiated on one level, yet yearning for more on another.

Gradually her breathing returned to normal, and she looked at him and smiled. He smiled back at her tenderly. "Like I said," he teased, "you always did like a man on his knees."

She scooted down next to him, onto the floor. "But should there be all that clothing down there?" she teased back. He was still wearing his pants and shoes.

"Easily remedied," he replied. His smile was almost shy as she watched him undress. Then, barely an inch from hers, his face became solemn, his lips almost touching hers. She turned her head, inviting him to kiss the side of her face. He moved his lips across her cheek, and buried them in her neck.

He raised his head and gathered her onto his lap. In his eyes, she could see the depth of his desire. His need for her was exposed and raw, as naked as his erection.

With her legs straddled on either side of him, his hands locked on her hips, he entered her. At first they moved together tentatively, testing, feeling, searching for the harmony they had abandoned years ago. Then, as though they had been away on a long journey and were now anxious to get back home, they moved quickly, wanting, needing, demanding, until all pretense of control was abandoned and, trembling, they succumbed to the rapture.

Later, their bodies still moist with lovemaking, he lifted her onto the couch, his lips never leaving hers. Only the ticking of the grandfather clock permeated their cocoon, like a rhythmic backdrop to a song as they clung together, savoring the sweetness. And when the afterglow had faded, he reached for her again, and then again and once more, until finally, their mutual desire spent, they drifted off to sleep, wrapped in the red afghan, locked in each other's arms.

## Chapter Eight

Laura opened her eyes. Through a small opening in the curtains, a thin line of sunlight cast its glow across the walls. The red afghan prickled against her skin, and she tossed it aside. She didn't need a blanket. Contentment curled through her body, warming her like brandy.

She reached for the lamp and turned it on. Through the greens and blues of the shade, the light illuminated a layer of the dust on the side table, reminding her there was work to be done. Jake would be coming over to finish the roof, and she and Cory were going to work in the garden.

I should get moving, she thought, making no attempt to rise. In a minute, she told herself. In a minute she would get up and shower, put on something suitable for yard work and start a pot of coffee.

She stretched lazily. For the first time since she'd been back home, she felt rested. Although the upholstery had seen better days, the oversize couch, with its firm frame and feather cushions, was a lot more comfortable than her bed. More significantly, she hadn't had that awful dream. Maybe I should sleep in the living room more often, she thought. Maybe I should sleep naked more often.

Her pulse quickened. *Why* was she in the living room? *Why* was she naked? She glanced at the heap of clothes on the floor. In the kitchen, a cupboard door slammed.

*Oh, no.*

The warmth she had felt on waking suddenly dissolved, and she shivered, convinced that the temperature in the room had plummeted below zero.

She yearned for a hot shower. Should she go upstairs now or after she had faced Jake? As though paralyzed, she sat listening to the clock ticking in the hallway.

Another shiver swept through her body, this time making her teeth chatter. Where was the heat from last night? Where was the music, the dancing...the boldness?

Where was her housecoat? She couldn't let him see her like this. It didn't matter that he had seen her undressed hundreds of times before. It didn't matter that they had made love hundreds of times in the past. Last night had been a mistake. She was not going to throw away her whole life over this...incident.

She almost laughed. Some incident. What kind of person was she? Here she was engaged, rollicking around with another man. Not that she and Edward were active in *that* department. Still, she was going to be married, and women who were engaged didn't go around sleeping with their ex-husbands.

Her behavior hadn't been any better than Cynthia's.

Maybe Cynthia had been able to handle a double life, but Laura wasn't Cynthia.

So many times she had wanted to tell Jake about Cynthia's affair, hating that he was being lied to, hating that he was being betrayed. But Cynthia had been her friend and had trusted Laura with her secret.

She thought about Edward, her cheeks stinging with shame. He was caring and dependable, and he trusted her. She had a new life with him, one she intended to keep.

She had to tell Jake to leave *now*.

She jumped off the couch and found her housecoat buried under his clothes on the floor. Her performance last night replayed in her mind, how she had watched him squirm with anticipation as she slowly undressed, how his arousal had added fuel to her desire. With shaky fingers she slipped on the gown and fumbled with the buttons.

"Coffee, Squirt?" Coming from the kitchen with a tray of steaming mugs was her ex-husband, wearing nothing but his briefs. He, obviously, didn't feel the cold.

"You're still here," she said, trying to keep her eyes on his face. Dumb. Of course he was still there. How could she think straight, with him standing there practically naked? "You made coffee." Now that was a brilliant observation.

"Don't look so surprised," he said, setting the tray on the coffee table. "I managed to learn a few domestic tricks over the years." His eyes roamed over her body. "And I'm not talking about last night—you and I have *that* skill down to a science."

She felt her nipples pressing against the fabric of her housecoat. It was because of the cold, she told herself. It had nothing to do with his well-muscled chest, his broad shoulders or his powerful arms and legs. It had nothing to do with the way he had looked at her when he had alluded to their lovemaking. And it had nothing to do with the way he was looking at her now, as if he had X-ray vision.

She sat down and folded her arms across her chest. "Don't

gape at me," she said, realizing that she was staring at him in the same way.

He sat down next to her. "Why not? You've always been the most attractive in the morning, that is, whenever you managed to wake up before noon. Especially after putting on an old housecoat. And that rat's nest—" he picked up a strand of her hair "—is irresistible."

"Jake..."

"I know, I know. It's a little early for you. You like to sleep until the cows come home, and I should get back before Cory wakes up. We promised I'd bring him over, remember?" He wrapped his arms around her waist. "Although I'd much rather have a repeat performance of last night."

Her skin tingled underneath her housecoat. This was how it all got started in the first place—the tingles, the shivers, the fluttering in her stomach. She wriggled out of his hold. "About last night…"

He smiled roguishly. "Yeah, I know. No need to thank me, unless of course you want to. "

"Jake, please. You've got to leave. You've got to go before Cory realizes you're not home." *You've got to go before I ask you to stay.*

"You'd say anything to avoid drinking my coffee, but the new coffeemaker isn't half bad, considering that it's not voice activated. Go ahead, taste. I know it can't compare to your concoction, but I don't think I want to see hair growing out of your chest, not while I'm still remembering last night."

"How can you joke about this? How can you—"

He silenced her with a light touch to her lips. "Look, I know you're worried about how this will affect Cory, but he'll be fine. Trust me."

*Trust me.* Her thoughts returned to Edward, and she felt a fresh stab of guilt. What had she been thinking last night? And that was just the problem. She hadn't been thinking at all. "We made a mistake," she said firmly, as though trying to convince herself.

"Maybe just a little one," he answered. "I know we should have been more careful, but can I help it if you bring out the beast in me?" His face sobered. "Seriously, I want you to know that I wasn't completely irresponsible. I know we should have used protection, but I recently had a complete checkup, and you can rest easy. I'm, uh, clean."

"What?"

"Come on, you know what I'm talking about. I admit I haven't exactly been a monk these last few years, but I checked out fine. There's nothing to worry about. Hey, I never expected you to live in a convent, either. You even went and got yourself engaged."

The way he talked, you'd think he was expecting them to get back together again. You'd think he'd spent the past five years waiting for her to come to her senses. Not that he'd been lonely, according to his own admission. "And your point is?"

His face took on an embarrassed expression. "I hate to ask, but what about you? You're still on the pill, right? And is your, uh, health okay?"

"For your information, I haven't had the variety you claim to have had. In any case, considering the number of times I go to the clinic, I'm sure I would know if there were something wrong with me." She knew the reason behind her anger. It had nothing to do with safe sex. His casual reference to birth control was like a slap in the face, reminding her of her inability to conceive.

"I didn't mean to imply that you've been sleeping around, but how do we know where Edward's been?"

"Where Edward's *been* is none of your business." She couldn't remember the last time she'd *been* with Edward.

The corners of his lips turned up unexpectedly. "We sound like a couple of teenagers, don't we?" he said, a trace of humor in his voice.

Teenagers! Is this what kids talked about these days? Suddenly she felt old. She thought about Cynthia, wild, free-spirited Cynthia, who back in high school—and later, too—had always done exactly as she pleased.

"Seriously, Laura, protection is something we need to think about. I wouldn't want to get you pregnant."

No surprise there. It wasn't as if they were still married, not that he had wanted a child with her when they had been married. "Don't worry, there's no chance of that happening," she said with bitterness.

His voice became earnest. "I'm sorry if the subject makes you uncomfortable, but you can't shrug this off. We need to talk about it."

"Yes, I know. You're always sorry." She rose from the couch. "I'm sorry, too. I repeat, last night was a mistake. There's nothing to talk about. Protection is not an issue for us. There *is* no us."

"I didn't mean I was sorry for last night. No regrets there. Last night was no mistake, and you know it."

He tried to take her hand, but she rebuked him, stepping out of his reach. "All we had was sex," she said in a cool voice. "All we *ever* had was sex. I want to know I mean more to someone than just a strong cup of coffee and a roll in the hay. I wasn't put on this planet solely for your benefit. I want something more."

"It's the kids thing, isn't it?" He looked at her with sad eyes. "Wasn't Cory enough for you? Wasn't taking care of both of us enough?"

She wasn't just talking about having children. She wanted it all—a career, a family, a man who loved her and respected her choices. But she had no intention of telling him that having it all was no longer an option. Now that she couldn't have children, he might argue that there was nothing to stop them from getting back together.

Nothing to stop him from controlling her life once again.

"I'm back only a few days, and already you're telling me what should or should not make me happy. Things haven't changed one bit, have they?" She took a deep breath. "Where do you get off thinking that just because I had one moment of weakness, I'm going to drop everything I've worked for? Go home, Jake, and the next time you get worried about me, or Cory forgets his backpack, or whatever excuse you think of to get me into bed, take a cold shower."

"You're running scared again, Laura. Sure, I'll leave you alone. For now. But think about this. You've never done anything you didn't want to. And that includes last night." He stood up. "I'll be back later with Cory as planned. We still have an arrangement." He reached for his clothes and dressed quickly.

She looked down at the floor, feeling his stare probing through her. She knew that if she met his eyes, there would be no going back for either of them. She knew how easily his large, dark eyes could turn her to jelly. All she had to do was look up.

She didn't raise her head until she heard the sound of the front door closing.


Running scared? You bet she was.

In just one small moment, Jake had managed to turn her life upside down. When had that moment occurred? When he took her into his arms and told her he wasn't going anywhere? When he kissed her in an attempt to squelch her protests? When he started humming that sentimental tune from *An Affair to Remember?*

No, Jake had been making her dizzy ever since they were kids.

She wasn't running scared; she was terrified.

She had to get out of there before he came back. She couldn't think logically with him around, especially after last night.

She ran upstairs to get dressed. Glancing at the clock on the nightstand, she felt panic squeezing in her chest. It was after seven. Knowing Jake, she figured he'd rush right back, with Cory still half-asleep.

After quickly showering and brushing her teeth, she ran a brush through her knotted hair. A rat's nest, he'd called it. How romantic. She packed her toiletries into her carry-on, vowing never to take so much stuff with her again, no matter where she went. Back in her room, she put on the first outfit she saw hanging in the closet, a long marine-blue dress with a sailor collar. Why had she brought this atrocity to Middlewood? Why had she bought it in the first place? She'd never liked it, even though Edward said it went well with her skin tone. What did that mean? Her skin was the color of seawater? Men. It was as if they all belonged to the same secret league, the How to Tick Off Your Girlfriend or Wife without Even Trying Club.

There was no time to change. Reaching behind her to do up the zipper, her thoughts strayed from Edward to Jake and then to Cory. Cory would be disappointed that she had gone, and she felt a pang of regret. But she needed time to mull things over. Besides, now that she was planning to come back most weekends, she didn't have to feel guilty about going back to New York a few days earlier than planned.

Edward would be pleased.

Edward. How could she face him, knowing what she had done? Don't tell him, her inner voice directed. Forget about it and get on with your life.

It wasn't her inner voice talking. It was Cassie.

No, Cass, I have to tell him the truth.

The truth? What was the truth? That she had *wanted* to

sleep with Jake? That she had felt so soft and warm, she'd been convinced she was melting?

Soft and warm, just like you, he'd said the other day, referring to her makeup. The next lipstick I buy should be called My Weakness, she thought. Forget Blushing Petals. She emptied the contents of the nightstand into her carry-on. Next, she yanked the remaining outfits off their hangers in the closet and piled them into her suitcase. I can't leave anything behind, she thought. It didn't matter that she was coming back; it was as if she believed she could wipe away her offense by denying she had been here. Finally, she cleaned out the bureau drawers. The faster she got out of this place, the better. She would go home to Edward, marry him, have a slew of children and live happily ever after.

Wrong. She would never have a slew of children. But she *would* live happily ever after, even though Steady Eddy, as Cassie called him, wasn't Prince Charming.

"What, and you think Jake is?" Oh God, now she was talking to herself. "Where are my glass slippers?" she said, realizing that she had forgotten to pack her shoes. She grabbed a pair from the closet, and threw the others into the suitcase. As she was putting on the left shoe, the doorbell rang. "Go away," she muttered. "Please, please go away."

But the doorbell wouldn't stop, and hopping on one foot, trying to put on the other shoe, she made her way to the staircase.

She stood at the top of the stairs, holding her breath. Why didn't he just let himself in? Maybe he's trying to behave, she thought. Maybe he's trying to show you he's changed.

She tiptoed down the stairs, even though she knew that any noise she made could not possibly be heard outside. She looked through the peephole and, letting out a sigh of relief, pulled open the front door.

"You sure took your time answering," Cassie chastised. "What were you doing, reorganizing your wardrobe?"

"My wardrobe? What are you talking about?"

"Your shoes," Cassie said, motioning to Laura's feet. "You have on one blue, one green. Are you going blind?"

Cassie was wearing a orange sweatsuit and a purple-striped bandanna. "You're one to talk," Laura said. "Where on earth did you get that outfit? And what are you doing here?"

"Some greeting. I told you I'd come by to help you clean the house, remember?" Cassie's gaze swept over Laura's dress. "Are we cleaning or going sailing?"

"I remember you offering, but you never told me *when*." Laura stuck her head through the doorway and peered down the street. "Get inside," she said, pulling Cassie into the house. "Do you know what time it is?"

"So it's a little early. Quit griping and put me to work. But first, breakfast from The House of Wong." Cassie was holding a plastic container. "A doggy bag from last night's date. So what do you think, Chinese food for breakfast?"

"I don't want egg rolls, I want to know what time it is! When I asked you, I wasn't being rhetorical."

Cassie pointed to the grandfather clock at the end of the hallway. "It's seven-thirty. You *are* losing your sight."

"No, I'm losing my mind." Seven-thirty! She'd spent too much time getting ready. She turned and ran up the stairs.

"Slow down, girl!" Cassie hollered, following closely behind. "The dirt can wait. This old house isn't going anywhere."

Laura dashed into her room and came out again, holding her carry-on in one hand, dragging her suitcase with the other, her purse strap slung over her shoulder. "You're driving me to the station. Here, take something." She handed over the carry-on.

"Aren't you forgetting something?" Cassie asked, following Laura down the stairs, into the hallway.

"Thanks for reminding me," Laura said, pulling her raincoat off the coatrack. "Not that I'll be needing it anytime soon."

"I'm talking about the car! Didn't you rent it in the city?"

"Right. The car." Laura chewed on her lip thoughtfully. "I need to talk to you, Cass. But not here. Jake's coming over. Follow me to that little diner across from the bookstore. You know the one I mean, it's been there forever. The place where they serve eggs soaked in oil and soggy toast. Where you take your dates the morning after."

"You'd better mean the 'hypothetical' you," Cassie answered. "I, for one, wouldn't take a dog there."

Ten minutes later Laura was seated across from her friend in a booth inside the restaurant. The vinyl of the seat was torn, the table topped with a stained red oilcloth. She looked around. Sitting in the corner booth, a waitress was absorbed in a magazine. Behind the counter, a man with bushy eyebrows peeked out through a sliding window and then disappeared. Except for the four of them, the diner was empty.

"This sure is a popular place," Laura said, grimacing.

"This wasn't *my* idea. My breakfast is waiting for me, compliments of The House of Wong." Cassie scanned her friend's face. "Talk, Laura. Why are we hiding in this dive?"

Nervously Laura tapped her spoon against her cup. "I slept with Jake," she said, looking down at the table. Cassie didn't reply. "Damn it, say something. I need help here."

"You? You don't need help. You're beyond help. And you're paranoid. Do you really think he's going to come looking for you? You'd better hope not. Not the way you look, in that dress and those mismatched shoes."

"And you look any better?" Laura looked at her friend miserably. "Be serious, Cass. I'm in trouble here. How did this happen?"

"Boy meets girl. Boy marries girl's friend. Girl's friend dies. Girl marries boy. Boy screws up girl's life. Girl leaves. Girl comes back. It's an old story."

"You make it sound as if I wanted it to happen."

"Didn't you?"

"No, of course not! I have a wonderful life in New York, a wonderful man who adores me—"

"So you keep saying."

Laura raised an eyebrow. "Okay, I'm confused. I finally meet someone you approve of, and now you're implying he's not right for me?"

"I'm not implying anything. Anyway, what does it matter what I think? It's your life. I just want you to be happy. For someone who's supposed to be getting married, you sure are miserable. And you keep telling *me* I should cross that line. Forget it. I'm perfectly content to stand on the sidelines watching others ruin their lives."

"Is that what you think I'm doing?" Laura asked. "Ruining my life?"

"Isn't that why you left Jake in the first place? So you wouldn't ruin the rest of your life?"

"Wait a minute. Who are we talking about, Jake or Edward?"

"Take your pick," Cassie said. "Or is that the problem? You're having trouble choosing?"

"There is no choice," Laura answered flatly. "I'm engaged to Edward."

"And..."

"And we're going to be married and live in a castle—no, make that a condo."

"But..."

"But I slept with Jake."

"And..."

"And it was wonderful."

"But..."

"But it's history. There's no future with him. You know how controlling he can be. There's no way I could go back to that kind of life."

"And…"

It was a game she and Cassie played whenever either of them had to make a decision, and it ended only when the decision was made. "No more ands," Laura said. "No more buts. The game is over. By the time Jake realizes I'm gone, I'll be hightailing my way on the I-684, back to New York."

The car wasn't in the driveway, but he rang the doorbell a dozen times before he was satisfied she wasn't home. Just in case. He knew he was being illogical, but he wasn't taking any chances. These days, logic had become as convoluted as a maze.

Where would she be at eight o'clock on a Sunday morning? She knew he would be coming over with Cory. Whatever was going on—or *not* going on—between himself and his ex-wife had nothing to do with the arrangement.

"I guess she's gone out for a while," he said to Cory with false cheer. "I'm sure she won't mind if we wait inside." He unlocked the door, and wordlessly they made their way through the hallway, into the kitchen.

On the drive over, they had stopped to pick up bagels and cream cheese. He dumped the bag onto the counter, and several bagels rolled out. "Why don't you set the table while I cut these in half?" he said, pulling out a knife from the drawer. It was then he noticed the light on the coffeemaker. What was wrong with Laura, leaving the house without turning off the machine? For someone who liked things just so, she sure was ditsy. After the way she had been acting these past few days, not locking the front door, falling asleep in the pantry, he was surprised she hadn't burned down the house.

"We might as well start without her." He put the food onto the table and poured himself a cup of coffee. New machine or not, his coffee could never be as good as hers, but it would have to do until she got back. Maybe he could convince her to make a fresh pot.

"We're supposed to work in the garden today," Cory said, biting into a bagel, "but I don't know what to do."

"After you're done eating, clean up your dishes and then go look for your backpack. You can do homework while you wait for Laura."

"Aw, Dad! Homework? Why can't I go back to the garage?"

On the one hand, Jake had taught his son to finish what he started; on the other hand, homework was priority. He looked at Cory's long face. Just this once, homework could wait. "Okay, okay. I know you want to finish tidying up in there." *I know you want her approval.*

"Don't forget to let me know the minute she gets back."

"I won't forget." Jake didn't miss the doubting look in Cory's eyes. "I promise."

After Cory left, Jake covered the bagels with plastic wrap and put away the cream cheese. It was becoming clear that Laura was purposely staying away. Although he was disappointed, he understood. She needed a little time to clear her head, to sort things out. Didn't he relish those rare moments of solitude at home, after Cory and Rose had gone to bed? Laura probably went out to pick up a few things and would be back in no time. Why else would she have left without turning off the coffeemaker?

He had to be patient. Hadn't he always been? He knew how tough it had been for her. She'd had more bad breaks than anyone he knew. First her parents dying in that car crash, then her having to live with that horrible woman. And then her illness. But she'd pulled through it just fine. She'd pulled through it *all* just fine. Better than just fine, if last night was any indication. He felt a surge rush through him. She had become so much more than he remembered. More vibrant. More alive.

But she was still so afraid. You didn't need to be a shrink to figure that out. What was the term those books used? Fear of commitment. Yeah, that was it. And she accused *him* of pulling away. Maybe she hadn't read the same self-help books he had.

He rinsed the dishes and put them into the dishwasher. Glancing at the boxes lined up against the wall, he remembered Laura telling him that she was planning to throw them out, keeping only the boxes remaining in the pantry. The city truck came by on Monday, just before noon. He decided to take them out to the curb for tomorrow's pickup. Laura would be pleased.

He picked up the box closest to the back door. On the cardboard were the words "Tess's clothes, donate." He put it back down, realizing that Laura had not intended to throw out all the cartons she had brought into the kitchen. He made a mental note to call one of the local charities.

He picked up another box, labeled Torn Curtains & Linen, Garbage. He smiled. Laura was still as organized as ever. She even labeled the trash. The stuff in this box must be in pretty bad shape, he decided. She had never thrown out anything someone else could use. Again, so like Laura, always thinking of others. He carried the box outside.

He continued picking up boxes, taking some outside for pickup, setting others aside for charity. Laura used to say that one of her greatest pleasures was getting rid of things. She liked making a clean sweep. *A clean sweep.* She had tried to make a clean sweep of him five years ago, but there was no way he'd let her make a clean sweep of him now. He looked at his watch. It was almost nine. She'd be back any minute now, and this time he'd make damn sure she'd stay.

One last box remained, its top sliced open. It was the only box Laura hadn't labeled. He knew he had no business looking inside, but how else could he find out whether she had meant to throw it out or donate it?

He picked it up and shook it the way a child might shake a wrapped gift on Christmas Eve. An envelope flew out and he scooped it up. It was addressed to Cynthia.

Cynthia! Why would Laura have a letter addressed to Cynthia? He turned the box over, emptying the contents onto the floor. In addition to a handful of envelopes, a number of small articles flew out, mementos from another time, another life: a dried rose in a plastic baggy, a napkin from a restaurant he'd never heard of, a matchbox cover from a hotel....

Had all this belonged to Cynthia? Why had she hidden it? Sure, he'd always had a jealous streak, but the past was the past. He never would have faulted her for anything she might have done before they were married. But they had started dating in high school. When had this other life of hers taken place?

He picked up the matchbox. The name of the hotel, The Ship's Inn, clicked in his mind. She used to stay there when she went to those interior-decorating seminars in Miami.

He dropped the matchbox.

Cynthia had taken up interior decorating *after* they were married.

One by one he picked up the envelopes. They were all addressed to Cynthia, and none of them had a return address. All of them had been resealed with tape. With shaky hands, one by one he tore them open. All the letters had been signed by a man whose name meant nothing to him—until now. Although he didn't know this man, didn't want to know anything about him, he couldn't stop himself. He *had* to know.

One by one, Jake read the letters, ripped them up and threw them into the box. One by one, the strands that had held together his first marriage disintegrated before his eyes.

## Chapter Nine

Laura had known about Cynthia's affair and hadn't said a thing. There was no telling what he would do when he saw her face-to-face.

He went to the garage to get Cory. "Get your things. We're leaving."

"But Lulu's not back yet! Besides, I haven't finished cleaning up in here."

"Now, Cory. Move it."

"I still haven't found my backpack."

Jake sighed. "Why can't you remember where you put things? Think, Cory. When was the last time you saw it?"

"I haven't seen it since Tommy grabbed it and threw it across the schoolyard." Suddenly Cory's face brightened. "Now I remember! Lulu said she would fix the pocket on the outside. I think she took it upstairs."

"Go to the car," Jake said. "I'll be there in a minute." He went back to the house and ran upstairs to Laura's room. All the drawers to her bureau were open—and empty. He tore open the closet door. There was nothing inside.

Laura had gone back to New York.

He found the backpack at the foot of her bed. The pocket had been mended with a patch that read "Middlewood Varsity Football." Next to the bag was a lipstick, which she must have dropped while packing. He picked it up and put into his pocket, then slung the backpack over his shoulder and left the room.

During the drive home, Cory didn't say a word.

It was just as well. Jake didn't want to talk about Laura. He'd been wrong to think she'd learned the meaning of staying put. And they said that men had a problem with commitment! What a joke. He wasn't the one who was off and running the minute it got a little too close for comfort.

But Laura's leaving wasn't the reason for his foul mood. He knew he could forgive her for running away, as long as she came back. Hell, he had forgiven her for leaving him the first time, five years ago. As far as Laura was concerned, he could forgive her for anything.

*Almost* anything.

She had been an accomplice in Cynthia's deception.

"She took her raincoat and it's not even raining," Cory said as they walked up to their front door. "I don't think she's coming back."

Jake's heart sank. He knew he could even forgive her for the sad look on his son's face—this would disappear in time. But no matter how much time went by, he would never forgive her for being part of the betrayal.

"It sure looks that way," he said, turning the key in the lock. "But if she does come back, I think we should stop going over there."

Cory's face turned bright red. "You made her go away, didn't you? Just like the last time. Why do you always have to ruin everything?"

"Now wait just one minute, young man. There are things you don't know, things you're too young to understand."

"I'm not a little kid," Cory retorted. "I want to know the truth. Did you make her go away?"

Jake didn't answer. The truth was that Cory's real mother had found someone else and Laura had condoned it.

"Just like I thought," Cory said. He pushed by his father and ran into the house.

From the foyer Jake heard Cory slam his bedroom door. The sound of heavy metal came blasting down the stairs, as loud as if the door to Cory's room had been left wide open. Jake went upstairs, and like a warning the music exploded even louder in his ears, as if Cory had heard him approaching and had pumped up the volume.

It was Sunday in New York. Normally Laura would be spending the day working out at the gym and then painting at the loft, but right now the only thing she could think of was the peace and quiet of her apartment. She dropped off the car at the rental place and took a taxi home.

She made her way through the building's lobby, nearly tripping over a bottle that had rolled into the hallway. A remnant from a party, she thought. There was *always* a party. That was one of the best things about living in the Village, if you didn't mind the fallout in the morning. And if you were a party animal, which she wasn't.

She opened the door to her apartment and was assaulted by a wave of hot, muggy air. It was hard to believe that it was almost fall. Outside, the temperature was unseasonably high. It was funny how the unpredictability of the weather seemed to mirror her life. It was hard to believe that only a few hours ago she had felt as if she were freezing.

The apartment was small, but it suited her needs. In the center, an almond melamine counter served as the dining area, separating the combination bedroom/living room from the tiny kitchen. Her bed was a fold-up that converted into a couch, but she kept it open most of the time. A second, smaller sofa was squeezed against the wall near the door.

She didn't spend much time there, anyway. When she wasn't managing the gallery, she was at the loft or working out, or meeting Edward for dinner when he could spare the time. Her life wasn't what anyone could call exciting, but she was content. She wouldn't change it for anything, except to marry Edward. And, of course, to have children.

But there *was* something else she would change, something she had dreamed about ever since she had picked up her first crayon. She pushed the thought aside. She had to be practical. At this time in her life, supporting herself as an artist wasn't in the cards.

She switched on the air-conditioning unit next to her bed and plopped herself onto the mattress. She knew she should call Cory. She remembered the way he had looked when he'd appeared on her doorstop on Friday, so sad and lost. How could she explain to him why she had left? She couldn't tell him the truth—or could she? She wouldn't have to fill in the details. She could say that she and Jake had argued and that she needed time to work things out. It was the truth, wasn't it? But wouldn't Cory resent his father even more? She couldn't let that happen. Cory already felt enough resentment—and she above all people knew what that felt like. She had spent years resenting her aunt, and then later, Jake.

She reached for the phone—it was odd how after five years the number was still ingrained in her head—but then changed her mind. What if Jake answered? She wasn't ready to deal with him. She would have to wait until after three tomorrow, when Cory was home from school and Jake was still at work. But what if Jake called *her?*

As if on cue, the phone rang. She decided to let the machine answer.

"Laura, it's me. Call me as soon as you get in. You weren't at the house, so I called Cassie. After recovering from her initial shock of hearing my voice, she told me you had left. What's going on? I thought you—"

Laura grabbed the phone. "El! It's so good to hear your voice again." It was the calm voice of reason she had always turned to for clear, sound advice. "And don't give me that 'shock Cassie' routine. You know darn well that nothing on this planet can shock her, even hearing from *you.*"

The four of them—she, Cassie, Ellen and Cynthia—had once been inseparable. Now Ellen and Cassie rarely spoke to each other. There hadn't been a falling out; it was just a matter of two different personalities becoming more diverse over time.

Laura told Ellen she was planning to drop by the loft later that afternoon. The loft was actually an empty warehouse that Laura and four other would-be artists leased on a month-to-month basis. Its huge glass siding provided ample light, making the place an ideal studio.

"Why don't I pick up some lattes and meet you there?" Ellen suggested. "I'm not due at the hospital until six, and I want to hear all about Middlewood."

An hour later Laura and Ellen were at the loft, sitting on hard-back chairs in the middle of a clutter of tables and easels. "You look like a cat that's been caught with its paws in the fishbowl," Ellen said, sipping her latte.

"Who me?" Laura asked innocently. She started to say something else, but then stopped.

A worried look crossed Ellen's brow. "You're not sick, are you?"

"No, I'm fine. It's just that...I..."

"What is it? You're scaring me."

How many times would Laura have to say the words before they finally sank in? How many times would she hear them in her head, exactly as Cynthia had said them, the day after the Sweetheart Dance? *I slept with Jake I slept with Jake I slept with Jake...* "I slept with Jake." There. She'd said them. Again. She looked down at the floor. "You're so quiet, El. Say something."

"What do you want me to say? That I approve? That I'm happy you're intent on throwing away your life?"

Throwing away her life? This was the calm voice of reason? This was her friend Ellen talking? "Don't you think I feel bad enough, without your recrimination?" Laura shot back. "It's not as if I wanted it to happen. It just did."

"These things just don't happen. What about Edward? How could you do this to him?"

Laura regarded her friend closely. Ellen was dressed in jeans and a sleeveless T-shirt, her long auburn hair tied back in a ponytail. Unlike Cassie, Ellen never gave much thought to her appearance. Laura's two best friends were as different as night and day, but on the subject of Jake, the two of them saw eye to eye. "I'm having a hard time with this," Laura said in a plaintive voice. "I was hoping you'd be a little more understanding."

"Oh, I understand, all right. All he has to do is look at you sideways, and you go to pieces. I can't believe you're considering moving back."

"I never said anything about moving back. What are you talking about?"

Ellen uncrossed her legs and leaned forward in her chair. "I'm talking about your obsession with Jake. You've always centered your life on him. Even after he married Cynthia, you stayed in Middlewood, working at a dead-end job just to be near him." She smiled sadly. "I remember a young girl who dreamed of becoming an artist, but after you got married, you put your art aside. Now that you're so close to making that dream come true, you want to go back to him and kiss it all goodbye."

"For your information, I enjoyed teaching at the senior center," Laura said, fidgeting with the plastic cup in her hand. "In any case, what does any of this have to do with my wanting to paint full-time? I'll do it one day, when the time is right, when I can afford it."

"I have news for you. If you wanted to paint full-time, you'd find a way. Do you think my parents could afford to send me to medical school? I worked around the clock to make ends meet." Ellen's eyes were full of accusation. "You know what I think? I think you're afraid. Painting for a living is the one thing you've always wanted to do, and you're afraid to find out if you have what it takes."

Laura had always wanted to be an artist, but it hadn't been the only thing she had dreamed of. In fact, it had been second on her list. More than anything, she had wanted to marry Jake and have a family. But their marriage had ended, and chemotherapy had destroyed any hope of her ever becoming pregnant. Even adoption wasn't an option, because of her health history. Now to find out she couldn't succeed as an artist, to have that dream also go up in smoke, would be more than she could bear.

It was true. She *was* afraid. "Okay, Dr. Freud," she said. "You seem to have it all figured out. What else is wrong with me?"

Ellen pressed on. "Maybe it has to do with your upbringing, but for some reason you don't believe you have the right to be happy. Don't you see? You're using Jake. You'll do anything to circumvent your dreams."

Circumvent her dreams? The idea was ludicrous. "You're

wrong. As a matter of fact, I've decided to convert my aunt's room into a studio. The loft can get a little crowded, especially when all five of us decide to show up."

"You're keeping the house? You can't be serious!"

"I already told you, I'm not moving back," Laura said testily. "It'll be a weekend hideaway, a second home. And there's no mortgage. You know I can't afford the rent on these two places, my apartment and this loft."

"You want my opinion? Forget about Middlewood. Sell the house as fast as you can. And don't tell Edward what happened, not if you want him to marry you and back you financially."

Laura's mouth dropped open. "Back me financially! I don't want Edward's money. I can't believe what you're saying!"

"I'm saying I think it's time you woke up. You're always going on about your independence. It's time you took the steps to gain it. What does it matter where the money comes from? With your talent you'll be self-supporting in no time."

"Lie to Edward and let him take care of me? This is your advice?"

"You want advice? Look at the sketch you were working on when I came in here."

"What, this?" Laura asked. She reached behind her and snatched a rough charcoal drawing from her worktable. "This is Cory. Surely you can't fault me for caring about *him*."

"That's Cory? I don't think so."

Laura pursed her lips. "Get to the point."

"Didn't you always say that Cory looked more like his mother than his father? The picture you're holding is of Jake, the way he looked at that age." Ellen rose to her feet and tossed her empty cup into the trashcan. "The point is, you deserve to be happy, and it's time you believed it. Stop creating your own roadblocks."

"Anything else?" Laura said coldly.

"Yes. Sell the house and don't look back."

* * *

When Laura called Cory on Monday, Rose told her he was at basketball practice. "Tell him I miss him," Laura said. When she called on Tuesday, Jake picked up the phone, the sound of his voice surprising her. The deep timbre of his hello held her motionless, and feeling flushed, she could hear him breathing as he waited for a response. She remembered that he sometimes worked at home, and hung up immediately. After that, whenever she called, Cory was either at practice or a friend's house, or Jake picked up the phone and she had to hang up.

The gallery wasn't expecting her back until the following Monday. She spent the week working at the loft, trying keep busy, trying not to think about Cory…or Jake. She immersed herself in a project she'd been mulling over for a while, one that had only recently begun to take shape in her mind.

It was of Freeman's Pond in Middlewood.

By Friday she had completed her first series of drawings, having worked from memory. She put away her pencils and stepped back to examine her latest sketch. Four young girls were sitting on the sand, huddled together, sharing secrets. A large gull hovered overhead, its wings spread open like an umbrella, as if to protect them. All the drawings in the series had existed in her mind for years, but only now was she ready to release them onto paper.

Everything happened in its own time, and everything happened for a reason. Like going back to Middlewood. She was genuinely sorry her aunt had died, but why had this happened just as Laura was approaching the five-year cure mark? It was a question she had asked herself countless times in the past several days.

From nowhere the urge to do another drawing suddenly took hold. She didn't know where these inspirational bursts came from or why they appeared when they did; she only knew she couldn't ignore them. She pulled out a pencil and a large sheet of newsprint and started sketching furiously. This time what appeared across the page was a young boy standing under a large, craggy tree next to a pile of rocks. She stood back and looked at the sketch. The young boy was Jake.

She crumpled the drawing into a ball.

Enough. She had to stop thinking about Jake. She had to focus on Edward. He was her future. Yet here it was almost the weekend, and she hadn't seen him since she'd been back. When she'd called him on Sunday, he'd told her that even his lunch appointments were double booked. He would see her next Saturday at the hospital dinner.

He hadn't said, "I miss you, *darling*," or "I'm dying to see you, *darling*," or "I'm coming right over, *darling*."

He'd once told her he spent all day dealing with the physical heart and had no time for the emotional one. He also said she was as solid as oak, a quality he needed in a wife. He liked that there were no surprises about her.

Comparing her to wood was supposed to be a compliment? In any event, she wasn't solid at all; lately she'd been as malleable as wet cardboard. No surprises? Hey, Eddy, guess what? I went to bed with my ex. Surprise, surprise!

*As solid as oak.* Obviously, she no longer met Edward's criteria for a wife. Some criteria, she thought with disdain. But who was she to judge another person's needs? Were hers any more valid than his? Edward made her feel safe, which was something she had never felt before. By not investing her heart, she couldn't get hurt. But was this a reason to get married?

Maybe there was no future with Jake, but she realized with sudden clarity that there was no future with Edward, either. She supposed she had always known this, somewhere deep inside, but like her ideas for this art project, the truth had not been ready to emerge until now. Sometimes, though, truth needed more than the passage of time to make itself known; sometimes a person needed a little help, the way a writer might need a muse. And that was why she had slept with Jake. Good old-fashioned honesty hadn't been enough for her; oh no, she had to do something stupid to prove to herself that she didn't love Edward.

She pictured her ex-husband holding a tray, wearing nothing but his shorts and a self-satisfied smile, those dark, knowing eyes, that dimple in his cheek...

No muse she had seen in any book had ever looked like Jake.

"Darling, there's someone I want you to meet."

Laura turned her back on the small group of women. They were discussing the merits of living in the country, how it was just a trend and that people would eventually get tired of it and move back to the city. *Provincial* was the word they used. Middlewood's residents would get a kick out of that.

Not likely.

"If their eyebrows were any higher, they would fly off their heads," she whispered back to Edward. "What a bunch of snobs."

He laughed. "They can't all be so bad. You wouldn't have agreed to speak tonight if you believed that."

"I suppose so," she said reluctantly. She hoped she wasn't making a mistake. Talking to an audience was one thing; opening yourself up, the way she was about to do, was another.

He steered her toward a short, homely man whose forehead seemed to occupy more than half his face. "Laura, this is Martin Anshaw, the plastic surgeon I've been raving about. Martin, my fiancée, Laura."

"Well, you haven't lied, Ed," Martin said. "She's just as

lovely as you described her. I wouldn't change a thing about her."

This was Dr. Martin Anshaw? He certainly didn't look a plastic surgeon, not that she'd ever met one. "It's an honor to meet you," she said, extending her hand. "I've been reading about you in *Newsworthy*. The work you do with burn victims—"

"Turn around," Edward said. "Show him your profile."

"Excuse me?"

"Your profile, darling."

Laura looked at Edward quizzically, then turned her head.

"As you can see," he said, tilting her head upward with his fingers, "it's a relatively small procedure. How soon can you schedule the surgery?"

Laura turned her head back to Edward. "A small procedure? Schedule the surgery?"

"Don't move, darling. Let Martin look at you."

Was this some kind of joke? Were they really standing in the grand foyer of the Bolton Hotel, discussing her nose? One look at Edward's face confirmed he was serious.

She walked away stormily, toward the bar. "Whiskey," she said, pulling out a stool. "Straight up. And make it a double."

"That was rude," Edward said, coming up behind her. "And you shouldn't be drinking. You have to make a speech during dinner."

"Oh, I couldn't possibly get up there and talk," she retorted, whirling around on her bar stool. "What about my face? What would people say? Oh, wait, I know. They could hold a debate on which is the bigger smeller, my speech or my nose."

He put one hand on her waist and took away her glass with the other. "Take it easy, Laura. I know you're nervous about speaking in front of so many people, but you'll do just fine. I wouldn't have asked you to do it if I believed otherwise."

"I'm not nervous," she answered in a shrill voice. "Do I sound nervous?"

"Then what is it?" He looked at her with annoyance. "Don't tell me you're upset about my arranging a consultation with Martin! It's only the initial visit. You don't have to decide anything right away, but don't turn your nose up at the idea until you've talked to him." He smiled at his joke. "Your appointment is at nine Monday morning. Don't keep him waiting. He has a heavy schedule and he's doing me a favor."

"I'll be at the gallery at that time," she said. "I have a meeting."

"Can't you hold your meeting at ten? Your appointment is at nine."

Edward looked ridiculous, standing there with his hands on his hips, telling her what to do. He reminded her of Aunt Tess. Instead of losing her temper, Laura found herself laughing.

"People are watching," he warned.

"Oh, no! Do you think they've noticed my nose?"

Three bells rang out, signaling that dinner was being served. Edward took her by the elbow and led her to the head table in the banquet room. By the look on his face, Laura could tell that he considered the subject closed. She was to show up at Martin Anshaw's office at nine Monday morning, and that was that.

Throughout dinner, they made polite conversation with each other, as well as with the other guests at the table. Before coffee was served, she delivered her speech with dignity and calm, detailing her experience as a patient. When she was done, the crowd stood up and applauded.

"Well done, darling," Edward said, covering her hand with his.

Because she knew it was for a good cause, she hadn't minded sharing her pain. The hospital was hoping to raise enough money to build a new wing for cancer research, and Edward had asked her to speak, promising he'd be right there beside her. Although he was a director on the fund-raising committee, he rarely attended these functions—especially if they were out of his specialty, cardiology.

She looked up at his face. His eyes were shining with pride, but they were vacant of affection. She felt like a protégé, or worse, a trophy. He was nodding to the audience, as though he were showing her off.

She removed her hand from his grasp.

After dinner, there was dancing in the main ballroom. She compared Edward's style to Jake's. Even though Jake had obviously been practicing, when he had danced with her to the accompaniment of his humming, his manner had been clumsy. But still, she had felt as if she were gliding through air, just as she had felt at their wedding. Edward, on the other hand, was smooth, accomplished, and yet she felt stilted.

"Did I mention how nice you look?" Edward said, drawing her close. "I haven't seen that gown before. Is it new?"

Nice? Was that all he could say about the way she looked? The elegant black satin gown was strapless and gathered at the waist, the material coming to an upside-down V just beneath her knees.

"I bought this dress to wear tonight. I'm glad you like it."

"It kind of surprised me," he said, glancing at her legs. "It's just not you."

Why was it that everyone these days had an opinion on her identity? "Okay, so tell me. Who am I?"

He cocked his head and laughed. "I don't know, darling. Why don't we get out of here and find out?"

She stopped dancing and looked up at him. Was he flirting with her? Imagine that. She couldn't remember him ever being playful. Now he was acting frisky? Now after she had decided he was as feisty as a post? And why was she just now realizing how colorless he really was? They had been engaged for six months, and she still couldn't commit to a date—that, itself, should have told her something.

She was tired of pretending she was happy. She wanted more than just safety. It was time to tell him it was over.

"All right, let's go."

On the way out, she nodded goodbye to a few of the women she had been speaking to earlier. "Have fun at your gallery," the urologist's wife said. "And good luck with your hobby."

"What did you tell that woman about my work?" Laura said to Edward, as they waited for the attendant to bring the car around.

He didn't answer until after he had inspected the Lexus for scratches and tipped the attendant. "All I told her was that you work in a gallery and that you like to paint. You should feel flattered she was interested. Her husband is the chief of his department."

They drove off in silence. Laura looked out the window at the streets of Manhattan. Usually the lights held her captive, but tonight everything looked as dismal as she felt.

"All right, what is it?" Edward said, his eyes focused on the road ahead. "You've been acting strange all evening."

"You told her that my art was a hobby."

He sighed heavily. "Let's not have this discussion again. You know I'm behind you no matter what you do. You want to work in a gallery? Fine. You want to be an artist? Fine. Whatever you decide is all right with me."

"It doesn't matter what I do, is that what you're trying to say? Is my work so trivial compared to yours?"

"That's not what I meant at all," he said with forced patience. "Why are you so edgy? Maybe you shouldn't keep that wretched old house. Maybe that's what's making you uptight. But don't take it out on me." He reached across the front seat and patted her knee. "Look, we have the rest of the night ahead of us. Don't ruin it. I thought maybe you would come back to my place."

"Why does it always have to be your place? The whole

time I've known you, you've stayed at my place only once, and that was because the power was out in your building." She knew she was trying to pick a fight; she didn't really want him to come over. She couldn't even remember the last time she'd been to his apartment. "Silly me. I forgot that my place is a little too *provincial* for a man in your position."

"Forget I asked," he said sourly. "I can see this mood of yours isn't going to let up."

Why couldn't she just say the words and be done with it? Two simple words: it's over. She stared out the passenger window, not speaking for the duration of the ride home.

He pulled up in front of her building. "I'll call you tomorrow to remind you about the appointment. Maybe we'll have dinner."

She didn't answer.

"Did you hear me, Laura?"

She didn't move.

"Laura?"

"I slept with Jake."

This time it was Edward who didn't speak.

"Did you hear what I said? I slept with Jake." *I slept with Jake I slept with Jake I slept with Jake...* "Damn it, Edward, you look as though I told you it was going to rain."

He shrugged. "You obviously needed to get it out of your system. At least now I can understand why you're so upset."

She couldn't believe what she was hearing. Why didn't he yell at her? Why didn't he threaten to tie her to a post and shoot her with darts? "That's it? That's all you have to say?"

"What else is there to say? I'm not happy about it, but why argue over something that's already in the past? You want my forgiveness? All right, I'll say it. I forgive you."

He was so easygoing, so understanding, so...unemotional. She shook her head sadly. "It's over, Edward."

"I'm glad to hear it. Now we can get on with our lives."

"You don't understand. It's over between *us*." She looked down at her hands. "I wanted it to work, really I did. I know I behaved terribly. You deserve better than this, better than me." She twisted the ring off her finger—the ring he had given her six months ago, the ring she had taken off last week and put back on only a few hours ago—and placed it in his hand. "I'm sorry," she said softly.

"You're not being rational. Do you want to spend the rest of your life living in that rattrap?" He motioned to her building. "And what about your plans to paint full-time? How would you support yourself? By waving a tin cup? Grand Central is already filled with people like that."

"I never expected you support me," she said, the softness in her voice disappearing, leaving a sour taste in her mouth. "And in case you're interested, I'm moving out of that rattrap, as you so delicately put it. I'm going back to Middlewood to live in that wretched old house, to use another of your flattering descriptions. But you're right. I won't be able to support myself by painting, at least not for a while. Maybe I can give private art classes, or maybe I'll go back to teaching at the senior center. Either job should leave me plenty of time for my own work."

Where had *that* come from? Lately it seemed she was making all her decisions on the spur of the moment, and she was surprised at how exhilarating it felt.

"It's him, isn't it?" Edward said. "You're going back to him. How long have the two of you been planning this?"

"This has nothing to do with Jake. As for my moving back, I just decided now."

He reached across her lap and opened the door. "Get some sleep. I'll call you tomorrow, after you've had time to think."

Had he heard a word she'd said? For a minute she thought he'd say, "Take two aspirin and call me in the morning."

She ran up the stairs to her apartment, giddy with relief, giddy with the prospect of starting a new life. There's something wrong with me, she thought. She had just broken off her engagement—shouldn't she be miserable? Shouldn't she feel remorse?

Remorse for how she had treated Edward, yes. It would take her a long time before she could forgive herself for cheating on him. But miserable? No. What Ellen had said was true: Laura deserved to be happy and it was time she believed it.

Moving back had nothing to do with Jake, she told herself. It was all about her art. And Cory. She would be there for Cory.

She entered her apartment and turned on the lights. The message button on her phone was blinking. She pressed the replay button and listened as she undressed.

"Laura, it's me, Ellen. I want to apologize for what I said last Sunday. I can't stand the thought of us fighting. I can't believe we went the whole week without speaking! It's your life, and I had no business putting in my two cents. I want you to know that whatever you decide about Edward—and Jake— I'm there for you. In any case, try and have a good time at the banquet tonight. I would have gone, too, but someone has to stay at the hospital and hold down the fort. I'll call you tomorrow."

"It's your life," Ellen had said. Cassie had used that same phrase.

You're darn right, Laura thought. It *was* her life, and she was determined to live it her way. She couldn't believe she had been so wrong about Edward. What was it about the men in her life? Did they all have to be so controlling?

The next call was from Jake. "Call me as soon as you get this message." His words burned in her ears, sending a surge of heat flowing through her body. There was a long pause, as if he had needed time to compose himself. Her heart pounded erratically.

His next statement turned the surge into a numbing chill. "Cory is missing."

## Chapter Ten

With a shaky hand, Laura punched in Jake's number.

"Missing?" Her voice was so low she wasn't sure if Jake could hear her. "What do you mean, missing?" She pictured a hooded intruder climbing in through Cory's window, snatching him away.

"When I went to his room to look in on him, he was gone."

"Are you saying he's run away?" Terror stabbed at her heart. "This isn't the first time, right? He's always come back safe and sound, right? Where could he have gone?"

"I think he might have gone to your place. Your address was on the display of my electronic organizer." He paused. "He said good-night to me around ten, and now it's after midnight. He probably sneaked out two hours ago."

"You've got to call the police."

"Don't you think I already did that? The only reason I'm

calling you is to make sure you don't go anywhere. He could show up any time."

"I'm in for the night." Where did Jake think she would go at this hour?

"Good. Call me as soon as he arrives."

She realized she was listening to the dial tone and put down the receiver. Jake had been so curt with her. But what had she expected, after the disappearing act she had pulled last Sunday? It was her fault Cory had run away. She should have spoken to him. She should have made sure he understood that she would be returning. If anything happened to him... A thousand questions loomed in her mind. How did he get to the station in Middlewood? How would he get from the station to her place? She felt her face drain of color. A boy of ten riding the subway alone at this hour, walking through the streets to her apartment, was not something she wanted to think about. If she focused on that, she would go crazy.

An hour passed, then another, and another. Where was he? Should she get dressed and go out looking for him? She jumped off the sofa bed, then stopped. No. She had to stay put. What if he showed up while she was out?

She'd call Jake. Maybe by now he'd heard something. She picked up the phone, then hung up. What if someone tried to call while she was on the line? Another reason to get a cell phone, or at least call-waiting. As far as technology was concerned, she was a dinosaur. The truth was, she had never liked being so accessible. Unreachable had always been the desired state whenever she felt like disappearing.

She went to the window and peered into the night. There was nothing out there but blackness, which matched the way she felt. She began to pace.

Coffee. She'd make a fresh pot. It would be the third that night.

She was measuring the coffee for the machine when she

heard the buzzer. She dropped the cup, spilling fresh grounds onto the counter, and dashed to the door.

Cory stood in the hallway, his backpack slung over his shoulder. "You should ask who it is before you answer," he said solemnly. "New York City is full of crooks."

She didn't know whether to laugh or cry or yell at him. She pulled him to her. "Thank God," she whispered, hugging him fiercely.

He squirmed out of her hold. "You're not going to get all gushy, are you? I hate when girls cry. Can I have something to eat? I've been on the road for hours."

She placed her hands on his shoulders and looked squarely into his eyes. "Do you know how worried I've been? How could you run away like that?"

"I didn't run away. I came here. That's not running away."

"You could have been kidnapped or hurt or..." She didn't want to elaborate.

"I'm here, aren't I? I took the train. It was no big deal."

"Running away in the middle of the night is no big deal? Your father is frantic!"

A scowl crossed Cory's face. "Aw, heck. He called you, didn't he? How did he know where I was going? I wanted to surprise you."

"Oh, you surprised me all right. Where did you get the money for the train?"

"From my paper route," he answered. "I hitchhiked to the station and bought a ticket. It was easy! No one even asked my age or how come I was alone. After the train, I took the subway. Boy, was that neat! How come there are no subways back home?"

"You hitchhiked! Do you know how dangerous that is?" She shuddered, thinking about what could have happened. She peered at him closely. "You lied to me. You don't have a paper route. Now where did you get the money?"

"I saved some from my allowance, and uh, Rose gave me the rest."

"Cory..."

"Okay, so I kind of borrowed it from her. I'll pay her back, you'll see. I have some money in the bank, but I can't get it out unless Dad comes with me and signs a piece of paper. I'm going to get a job. I mean, a real job. Not just doing chores." He looked at her and pouted. "I thought you'd be happy I came."

"Don't give me that face," she said. "Why did you do it, Cory? Why did you run away?"

"You know how Dad is. He never lets me do anything. So I decided to live here with you, but if you're mad, if you don't want me, I can go somewhere else."

Even though she knew he was being manipulative, he was difficult to resist, the way he looked at her with those large, endearing eyes. "You're not going anywhere," she said, trying to sound stern. "Not tonight. But tomorrow you're going home—and not by yourself. Either your father will come get you, or I'll take you there myself. Yes, I'm mad at you. I'm mad because you stole money from Rose. I'm mad because you ran away. And I'm mad because you lied to me. If you think your father is strict, you haven't seen anything yet."

He stared at her wordlessly, his gold-flecked eyes shining with innocence.

She sighed. She'd never been anything but putty around Cory. Maybe Jake needed to lighten up a little, but she knew she had to be tougher. "Go wash up. First door on the right. When you're done, I'll fix you something to eat and we'll talk about this some more."

She waited for him to disappear into the bathroom before calling Jake. He answered before the first ring had completed. "Laura?"

"He's here," she said. "He's okay. A little dirty but none the worse for wear."

"I'm coming to get him."

"I don't think that's a good idea. We've all had a rough time tonight, and he's tired. You can get him in the morning. It's Sunday—he can sleep late."

There was a long silence. "All right," he said finally. "He'll need all his wits about him when I deal with him. I'm going to have to teach him a lesson he won't forget."

"And what is that?" she snapped, remembering how Cory had talked about being sent to correctional school. "Ship him off to a home for juvenile delinquents? Is that what you had in mind?" She immediately regretted her words. She knew that Jake would no sooner send Cory away than cut off his own arm.

"What are you talking about? I need to figure out the right punishment. Do I ground him for the rest of his life, or take him out to the woodshed?"

Even though Jake was strict, she knew he would never raise a hand to his son. "You don't have a woodshed," she said, a faint smile tugging at her lips. "But you need to find out why he does these things."

"Damn right I do. I intend to get to the bottom of this *now*. Let me talk to him."

"He's getting washed. I'll get him to call you as soon as he's done."

"On second thought, maybe I shouldn't speak to him. I'm too angry to be rational. Tell him I'll be there first thing in the morning. You can forget about sleeping late." For the second time that night, he hung up without saying goodbye.

Cory emerged from the bathroom, looking a little too cheerful for someone who had just been scolded. "I guess you talked to Dad, huh? He must have been ballistic."

"Oh, he's angry all right. He'll be here in the morning, and we'll all talk then." She looked at Cory's clothes. He had changed out of his jeans and pullover into cutoff shorts and a

Knicks T-shirt. "Didn't you pack pajamas?" she asked. "Why don't you go back to the bathroom and change while I fix some oatmeal?"

"I always sleep in my clothes," he said. "Do you have any cookies? Oatmeal's okay, but it's for breakfast. Who eats breakfast in the middle of the night?"

"The same kind of people who wear their clothes to bed." She had a lot of catching up to do. The last time she'd tucked him into bed he'd worn sky-blue pajamas patterned with airplanes and trucks. "If you want, I'll add some apple and cinnamon so that it tastes like cookies." She took out a pot from the cabinet underneath the sink. "Why don't you put together your bed? The linen is in the closet next to the bathroom. You'll have to sleep on the sofa near the door. It's not very big, but it'll have to do."

She pulled out two bowls. She'd decided to have some oatmeal, too. Good for cholesterol, Edward always said.

Ah yes, Edward. Then again, maybe she'd skip the oatmeal. She'd always hated it, no matter how hard she'd tried to disguise it. Tomorrow after Cory left, she would throw out the box. She put one bowl back into the cupboard.

She watched Cory making up his bed as she prepared his cereal, chopping up an apple, adding juice and cinnamon. He laid the sheet onto the sofa and evenly folded it in two, making sure the bottom was neatly tucked around the sofa cushion. He placed the blanket on top, smoothing it down to flatten out the wrinkles. When he was finished, he stood back to examine his work, then ripped everything off and started over.

Was this the way a ten-year-old boy behaved? At that age, Jake hadn't been concerned with hospital corners—that had always been Ellen's turf. He'd been interested in snakes and frogs and everything that went along with being rambunctious. She remembered the way Cory had set about organizing the garage. Each shelf had to have exactly the same number of cans of paint, and each can had to be arranged just so. Sure, she was happy she was getting to see some order in the place, but was this normal? What about the way he had stormed out of her kitchen in Middlewood? Because *ocho locos* hadn't been part of his ordered world, he had refused to play.

Maybe this trait came out only when something was troubling him.

Her back turned to Cory, she stirred the simmering pot on the stove. "It's ready," she called after a few minutes. She looked over the counter. Cory was sound asleep on top of the blanket.

Why had he gone through such a lengthy preparation of his bed, if he didn't intend to use the linen?

Lying there, curled up on his side, he looked so snug and content, it was hard to believe he was so troubled. His arms were folded across his chest, the palms of his hands wide open. Right from the beginning, when Cynthia had brought him home from the hospital, Cory had slept this way.

She dumped the oatmeal into the garbage and turned off the coffeemaker. She looked at the clock. It was almost four. Jake would probably be here at seven. So much for her beauty rest. These days the bags under her eyes were becoming permanent fixtures. She turned off the lights and slipped into bed.

Through the angled slats of the Venetian blinds, moonlight filtered into the apartment, lighting the living room with a cool, bright glow. She glanced over at Cory. Once again, intense relief filled her. His resiliency amazed her. Kids were like that, she supposed. Look at the way he had bounced back after she had left, five years ago.

Right. He was an insecure, mixed-up kid, and just when he was starting to trust her, she had to go and leave him again.

But soon all that would be behind them. In the morning she would tell him about her plans to move back to Middlewood.

She should have told him tonight, as soon he'd come through her door. It wasn't as if she was undecided. Lately everything seemed blurry, as if the world she had known had become an Impressionist painting, hazy and indistinct, but the one thing she was certain of was that she was going home.

It was incredible how in such a short time her whole world had turned around. Last week's events unfolded in her mind. In just a few days she had reestablished ties with her stepson, broken her engagement and decided to move back home.

And then there was Jake. It was odd that her address was in his organizer; obviously she was on his mind as much as he was on her hers. Or was it wishful thinking? She thought about last Saturday, her skin prickling with the memory. *I slept with Jake I slept with Jake I slept with Jake....*

Once again, she reminded herself that moving back had nothing to do with him. But she knew she was lying. She had always been in love with Jake, and the feeling wasn't going to go away.

Darn it all, she wanted them to try again. She wanted a reconciliation. They'd wasted too much time already. Maybe everything happened in its own time, but surely five years had been ample time for them to work out their differences!

But what if he didn't want to get back together? Could she bear to remain in Middlewood and risk running into him everywhere she went? Could she stand there in the post office, in the bank, in the grocery store, making small talk as if he were only an acquaintance? Or would she run back to New York?

She realized why she hadn't told Cory about her moving back. She hadn't decided anything at all.

She lay in bed, listening to the air conditioner's tuneless hum. A small voice came from the other side of the room, jolting her. "It was my fault, wasn't it? I told Dad it was his fault you went away, but it was mine."

In the moonlight she could make out Cory's silhouette. "No, you're wrong, sweetheart," she said. "It wasn't your fault. It wasn't anyone's fault."

"So how come you didn't tell me you were leaving?"

She hesitated. "I tried to call, but I couldn't get hold of you. I left messages with Rose. Why didn't you return my calls?" Great, Laura. Turn it around and make him the bad guy. So much for your maternal instinct.

"I guess I was scared."

"Of what?"

"I don't know exactly," he said. "It's kind of like opening a birthday present. Like, you really want your own computer, but you're too afraid to ask for one, because you know what they'll say. 'Do you think money grows on trees? What do you need your own computer for? To play those stupid games?' But then you see this box all wrapped up, and you're wishing and hoping, but you know it's probably just a new jacket or a dumb pair of pants. So you don't want to open the present, because for a while you think maybe it could be a computer, even though you know it's not since the box is way too small."

"You were afraid that if you called me, I would tell you I wasn't coming back," she said quietly.

"I was mad when you left on Sunday. You didn't even say goodbye. But then I remembered that you said you'd come back on weekends. But you didn't."

"I had to be in the city," she said. "I'd promised a...friend I'd make a speech. I'm sorry. I should have told you."

"Are you coming back next weekend?"

"I want to, but I don't think I can." She needed time to pack up her apartment and the loft, as well as sort things out at work. She normally didn't work on Saturdays, but she was planning to give three weeks' notice, and would need as much time as possible to train her assistant, who she suspected would be happy to work on the weekend if it meant taking over Laura's job. "I might have to work."

"Yeah, right," he said. "That's what Dad always says whenever he doesn't want to be with me. Like next Saturday. I want him—I want both of you—to watch me play basketball, but he says he has to go to Boston. He has to go to some kind of school. Or maybe it's a conference, I don't know for sure. He's leaving on Friday and he won't be back for a whole week."

So, Jake was going out of town. She felt a twinge of disappointment. This is silly, she chided herself; it wasn't as if she would be in Middlewood over the weekend, either. "It sounds like a seminar," she said. "These things are arranged way in advance. He probably didn't know you'd have a game when he agreed to it."

"That's not it," Cory said morosely. "I make everyone go away."

"It was my decision to go, not yours or anyone else's. I had things I needed to do." Like changing my life and reinventing myself, she thought. "I'd made these plans a long time ago. I couldn't break a promise, could I?"

"I wasn't talking about this time."

"Oh." She felt her throat tighten up. "But you were just a little boy when your father and I separated. How could you think it was your fault?"

He lay there in silence.

"Cory?"

Still no answer.

She heard him sniffle. Quietly she made her way to the other side of the room and sat down on the edge of the sofa. His head was buried in his pillow. "Sweetheart, what is it?" she asked, gently turning him around.

"I'm *bad,*" he said, covering his face with his arm. "No wonder you went away the first time. I don't blame you for going away this time, either."

"You had nothing to do with my leaving, back then or this time. And you're not bad. I think you're wonderful."

"No, I'm not! I'm always fighting and doing things, and I always make Dad mad." His voice fell into a whisper. "And I make bad things happen."

"You don't make bad things happen, unless you're some kind of wicked sorcerer. You're not, are you?" she asked, trying to lighten his mood.

"You don't understand! I shouldn't have come here. You'll probably get sick again. You'll probably die, just like her!"

"Cory, no!" She gathered him up into her arms. "My getting sick a long time ago had nothing to do with you, and I'm not going to die. Where would you get an idea like that?"

"I was at the bank with Dad," he said, his voice muffled against her shoulder. "It was after New Year's. He always makes me save my Christmas money. And I heard Tommy's grandmother talking to your aunt."

"And?" she prodded gently when he didn't continue. "What did she say?"

"She said it was my fault it happened."

"Your fault what happened?"

He jerked out of her hold. "Don't touch me!" he cried. "Keep away! I don't want you to die!"

Laura felt his panic as acutely as if it were her own. She pulled him back to her and held him tightly. "Tell me what she said. I can only help you if I know what's going on. Nothing is going to happen to me, I promise."

"My mother was holding me when she tripped on the steps," he said through his sobs. "She wouldn't let go of me, and that's why she fell backward. If she hadn't been carrying me, she wouldn't have hit her head on the concrete."

Laura felt as if she'd been punched in the stomach. Cory believed he was responsible for his mother's death. That poor, confused kid. How long had he kept this guilt bottled up inside? Suddenly she realized that he hadn't been keeping it inside at all. He'd been acting it out by getting into fights and running away. It was all beginning to make sense, even his preoccupation with orderliness. His emotional well-being was in pieces.

She felt his pain sear through her. It must have been agony for him to talk about his fears, but at least now they were out in the open. At least now the healing could begin.

"It wasn't your fault," she said, rocking him as if he were a baby. "Your mother slipped on a patch of ice and fell. She loved you very much, and that's why she didn't let go of you. She didn't want you to get hurt. She was your mother, Cory. That's what mothers do. But it was an accident, a terrible accident that shouldn't have happened, and it was nobody's fault. Not her fault, not your fault. Nobody's." She felt his tears on her cheeks as she continued to rock him. When his sobs had subsided, she said, "Promise me you'll forget everything my aunt said. She was a bitter woman with nothing better to do than gossip."

"It wasn't your aunt who said those things," Cory said, breaking away to look at her. "It was that old Mrs. Pritchard, Tommy's grandmother. Your aunt got mad at her and told her to be quiet. But Mrs. Pritchard went on and on, saying how hard it was for you, being stuck with someone else's stuff."

"What stuff?"

"You know, suitcases."

For a moment Laura was confused. "You mean baggage?"

"Yeah, that's what she said. 'Someone else's baggage.' And then your aunt called her a...you know, the *B* word. Told her to mind her own business. Told her to stop talking or she would flatten her face."

"My aunt said *that?*"

"Well, sort of. But knowing how much you didn't like

your aunt and all, I just figured Mrs. Pritchard was the one who was telling the truth."

"No, Mrs. Pritchard was the one telling the lies," Laura said. "I don't want you listening to her anymore. You got that, Cory?"

"I guess," he answered, his voice uncertain. "Lulu?"

"What, sweetheart?"

"Will you stay here until I fall asleep?"

When he was little, she used watch him even after he'd dozed off, wondering at the miracle of his being. "You bet," she said, her heart turning over. "Scoot under the covers and I'll tuck you in."

"I don't want to make any rumples."

She felt a pang of sadness. Cory was afraid to stake a claim anywhere, unsure of where he belonged. If she'd had second thoughts about living in Middlewood, they were now completely gone. Cory needed her, and she wouldn't let him down. Never again. She couldn't wait to see the look on his face when she told him she was moving back, but she decided to hold off until morning. She had to tell Jake first. It was the right thing to do; Cory was his son, after all.

Cory fell asleep almost immediately, and for a while she sat on the edge of the sofa, listening to him breathe. The air conditioner had only one setting that worked, and the room was chilly. She considered turning off the unit completely but decided against it. In only minutes the apartment would be a steam bath. She went to the closet to get another blanket, and after covering Cory and kissing him on the forehead, she went back to bed.

Her thoughts returned to Jake. Maybe they had a future together, maybe not, but she had to give it a try. If it didn't work out, she would be all right. She was a survivor. She would have her home, her art, and she would be there for Cory.

But the truth was, she didn't want to be just a survivor;

she'd lived that way too long. She loved Cory dearly, but she wanted it all—her home, her art, Cory...and Jake. In her heart they were all connected. It was like a painting. Take out one important element, whether color or texture or line, and the whole thing fell flat.

Just as she had predicted, her buzzer rang at seven o'clock sharp. She steadied herself and opened the door.

Whenever she set her eyes on Jake after not seeing him in a while, she felt a rush. This time, it hit her with full force. Last week she had made fun of him for using the phrase "struck by lightning," but today it was exactly how she felt.

He leaned against the doorjamb, staring into the living room. "Is he ready?"

"Cory's in the shower," she said a little too brightly. "Have some coffee while you're waiting. I made it the way you like it. Thick like mud. How about breakfast? I told Cory I would make him blueberry pancakes. You'll stay, won't you?"

Put a lid on it, she told herself. She knew she was babbling. She always babbled when she was anxious.

"I don't think so," he answered.

"No to coffee or no to breakfast?"

"No to both."

"Come in, anyway. Cory will be a few minutes." Jake was so cold, so distant. "I don't blame you for being angry," she said nervously. "I'm sorry I ran away like that, without an explanation. I always seem to run when the going gets tough. I know it's no excuse, but this is how I get when I'm scared. But I'm working on it." She realized she was babbling again, but couldn't seem to stop. "What I mean to say—"

"Save it," he said icily. "It's a little late for explanations."

She cringed. She knew it wasn't going to be easy, but she hadn't expected a brick wall. "If there's one thing I've learned," she pressed on, her voice shaky, "it's that it's never too late for anything, not when you really want something."

"And what is it you want?" he asked, glowering at her. "Your goals seem to change from day to day."

She drew in a deep breath. "I've decided to move back to Middlewood. I want to concentrate on my painting, and I want to be there for Cory." She waited for a reaction, but none came. She plunged forward. "And I want us to try again. I can't promise anything—you and I have a lot of issues to resolve. But I want us to at least try."

His eyes glazed as if he had retreated somewhere deep inside, somewhere he would not allow her to follow. "I'm way past the trial-and-error stage of my life, and after all you've been through, I would think you would be, too. The next time around, I'm playing for keeps. For better or for worse. Remember that, Laura? No, of course you don't."

"I thought this was what you wanted. After last Saturday—"

"I'll tell you what I want," he snarled. "I want you to stay the hell out of my life."

She stiffened as though he had struck her. "This isn't just about my leaving," she said, suddenly afraid. "What are we really talking about?"

The vacancy in his eyes gave way to something familiar, something she had seen on the night they had made love. A strange flicker of light hinted at an old scar, a wound from the past. "We're talking about trust," he said. "Something you either have little knowledge about, or little regard for."

"I…I don't understand."

"Oh, I think you do."

"Are you talking about Edward? We broke up. It's over. Did you think I could continue seeing him after what we did?"

"Congratulations," he said sarcastically. "I hope the two of you will be very happy *not* together. Just like us. Just like you and Cory."

"What do you mean, me and Cory?" she asked, panic rising in her throat.

"You're not exactly what someone would call a stable influence. I don't want you spending so much time with him."

"What about the arrangement?"

"You can call Mary. She'll schedule any work you want done in the house. Don't worry, I'll only bill you for the cost of material."

"Don't do this," she pleaded. "No matter what you feel about me, don't do this to Cory. I'll be moving back, and he'll expect—he'll *want*—to see me."

"And that's another thing. Don't tell him you're planning on moving back. I don't want him getting his hopes up. You haven't said anything, have you?"

She remembered what Cory had said about wanting a computer and getting clothes instead. "No, not yet. I wanted to tell you first."

"I know you, Laura. I know how you think. Do him a favor and don't say anything."

The bathroom door opened, and Cory came out wearing his jeans and pullover, his hair combed back and wet. By the way he was grinning, Laura could tell he hadn't heard the argument. "Dad!" he exclaimed. "You got here so quick! I guess you're pretty mad, huh?"

Laura looked at him skeptically. Why was he so happy? He was acting as if everything had gone according to some kind of plan. Had he run away just to get his father to come here? Was this a plot to get her and Jake back together? Maybe this was his way of ensuring a place in her life.

Jake approached him tentatively, then pulled him into a tight hug, just as Laura had done earlier. Then gruffly he said, "Get your stuff. We're going home. We'll talk about this later."

"What about breakfast?" Cory asked. "Lulu promised she'd make blueberry pancakes."

"Lulu should think twice before she makes a promise."

"Aw, Dad, why can't we stay?"

"You heard what I said. We'll grab breakfast at a drive-through on the way back."

Cory turned to Laura and shrugged. "I tried," he said, confirming her suspicions about his playing Cupid. He picked up his backpack and followed his father to the door.

"Have a great time at the game," Laura said, choking back tears. "Don't forget to knock their socks off."

"You're coming, aren't you?" Cory asked, his eyes filled with hope.

She looked at Jake. "I…I don't know."

"Please, Lulu? If you don't come, I'll be the only kid there without a mom or dad. Please don't go to work. Please-please-please?"

Jake let out a long, slow breath. "She told you she couldn't make it. Leave it alone."

"I didn't say any such thing," she said, staring Jake down. "In fact, I'm sure I'll be able to fit it into my schedule. Some things are worth making time for." Cory had referred to her as his mom, and she'd liked it. She'd liked it a lot. She knew she had no business going against Jake's wishes, but she thought of it as a compromise; she would hold off telling Cory about her moving back, but she would watch him play at the game. "I'll be there, Cory. I promise. I *double* promise."

Cory let out a whooping "Yes!" Jake pulled open the door and walked out.

She gave Cory a quick hug and watched him as he ran after his father. Standing by the door, she continued watching as they receded down the hallway, until they sank into the stairwell and disappeared from view.

Two weeks. It would be almost two weeks before she saw Jake again. To hell with everything happening in its own time. She'd waited long enough. If he didn't forgive her by then, she would camp out at his front door until he was ready to open his heart.

## Chapter Eleven

"Mommy! Mommy!"

Laura banged on the door, demanding to be let in. She crossed the front yard and peeked through the window. In the living room her aunt was sitting on the couch. Next to her a man was holding her hand.

Why was Aunt Tess at the house? Mommy said that Aunt Tess didn't like to visit. Whenever Laura asked why not, Mommy wouldn't answer.

Laura went back to the front door. Finally she heard footsteps. A man answered. It was Reverend Barnes. "She's home," he called to someone behind him.

Aunt Tess came into the hallway. "Where have you been?" she asked, her face creased like Mommy's whenever she got mad.

"I was at Cynthia's. Where's Mommy?"

Reverend Barnes turned to Aunt Tess. "Should I tell her?" he asked softly.

"No, I'll do it. Come here, Laura."

Laura looked at Reverend Barnes, then back at Aunt Tess. "Where's Mommy?" she asked again. "Mommy! Mommy!"

Reverend Barnes took her hand and led her into the living room. Aunt Tess followed, crying into her handkerchief. Laura saw more people, faces she recognized from the church where Mommy liked to go. Like Reverend Barnes, they all looked so sad; like Aunt Tess, all the women were crying.

She awoke to silence. It was strange how the stillness in the apartment seemed to be coming from deep inside her. As always, the dream had seemed so real, only this time it hadn't left her shaking with fear. The terror that had always chased her was gone.

She sat up suddenly in her bed. The dream hadn't been just a dream; it had been a memory. Details came flooding back. After eating supper at Cynthia's, she had walked the short block home. She'd been so proud! It was the first time her mother had allowed her to go home by herself. And why not? Laura was five years old, a big girl. Of course, it was still light outside, and she lived only three houses down the street.

As in the dream, her aunt and Reverend Barnes weren't the only ones she had seen through the window. The room had been filled with people. But where were her parents?

What else? she asked herself now. What else do you remember?

Suddenly her father's image appeared in her mind. She saw a tall, slim man wearing thick glasses. There was something wrong with his eyes.

Daddy couldn't still be at work, she'd thought on that terrible evening, over twenty-eight years ago. Her mother would have picked him up hours ago. She drove him everywhere, his sight was so bad.

As far back as Laura could remember, her father had worked in the little hardware store on Copper Hill. *As far back as she could remember.* Her heart thundered in her chest, as memories came trickling back. In the dream, she'd been standing on the landing, looking up at a specter, its dark, chilling eyes severing her with its stare. But no one could have seen her from her room in Middlewood; the overhang would have shielded her from view. And from the landing, she couldn't have seen anyone—or anything—hovering in the window.

She'd once read that everything in a dream was a symbol. Her skin went cold as understanding gripped her. When her parents died, part of her had become a specter, a mere shell of who she used to be.

"Why didn't you just let yourself in?" her aunt had said. "The door wasn't locked."

In the dream, it had been guilt that kept her outside the house. It had been guilt that had chased her, and it had been guilt that had severed her in two.

*But I was only five years old!*

*You lived and they didn't.*

*It wasn't your fault,* she'd told Cory.


Throughout the morning, traces of the dream kept running through her mind. She'd just come from a meeting, her impending resignation having created a stir. Life sure had strange twists, she thought. If she had never gone back to Middlewood, she wouldn't have had to call this meeting. She would only now be arriving at work, after returning from an appointment with the plastic surgeon.

She fingered the bump on her nose. Funny the things people get attached to, she thought. Even funnier was the way things were turning out. Although she looked to the future with anticipation and hope, part of her was sorry to leave the gallery. Her work here had been rewarding, giving her a sense of achievement, a sense of *creation,* which she had always been careful to nurture.

Had this need to create been shaped by her inability to have children? She didn't need to be a psychologist to recognize the emptiness for what it was. Jake would have a field day with *that.* "All that psycho mumbo jumbo," he'd probably say.

Thinking of Jake, she felt the emptiness inside her become an acute pain. "Stay the hell out of my life," he'd said.

Two weeks. It would be almost two weeks, eleven days, to be precise, before she would see him, before she could make him understand why she kept running, why she was so afraid. I can always call him, she thought. He won't be leaving for Boston until Friday. She quickly dismissed the idea. Jake needed time to work through his anger. Besides, she thought, we can't talk about this kind of thing on the phone.

I've got to keep busy, she told herself, or I'll go crazy. She made a pretense of going through the papers on her desk, then gave up.

Her mind drifted back to when she'd started working at the gallery. It had opened at around the same time she'd completed her treatment. Her organizational skills along with her artistic bent and education had convinced the two owners to entrust her with the day-to-day operations, and she knew she hadn't disappointed them. For more than four years she had organized exhibitions with innovation and enthusiasm, bringing in a tidy profit in subsequent sales. She had corresponded with and interviewed artists. She had written media releases and biographical sketches. She had recommended new acquisitions, overseeing the present inventory with loving care.

It would be tough leaving. Except for her assistant, Suzanne, whose pretentiousness irritated her to no end, she would miss her co-workers, and she would miss the excitement that every show brought.

Suzanne's voice came over the intercom. "You have a call on line two."

"Matheson," she answered, her voice crisp and businesslike.

"Laura, it's John Collins, Elizabeth's lawyer. Is this a bad time for you?"

"No, not at all. What can I do for you?"

"When are you planning to be back in Middlewood? I want to give you the key to your aunt's safe deposit box. Since she had no real assets, probate went through without a hitch. Normally these procedures take months, if not longer."

"If she didn't have assets, why did she need a deposit box?" Laura asked, confused.

"Paperwork. Birth certificate, social security card, the deed to the house, that sort of thing. After she paid off the mortgage, I advised her to get a box in case of fire or a break-in. It's not as if these papers can't be replaced, but it's always such a tedious procedure."

"Whoa, go back a few lines. What do you mean, 'paid off the mortgage'? I thought the house was in the clear."

"It is now, and has been for years. You should have seen your aunt's face after she made the last payment. She was beside herself with joy—and relief. She'd been determined not to lose the house."

Laura gripped the edge of her desk. "I always thought…assumed…that my parents had owned the house outright."

"Goodness, no. When they purchased the property, they took out a fifteen-year mortgage, which they couldn't afford on your father's salary. They could barely afford the premiums on their life insurance, never mind a mortgage. When they died, even though the title went to you, someone had to be responsible for the payments."

He was telling her that Aunt Tess had paid off the mortgage out of her own pocket. Laura couldn't believe it. That stingy, stern woman had never given her the time of day, never mind money for a candy bar.

"Tell me something, John. Where did all that money from the insurance go? I know it wasn't much, but I had hoped..." She knew she sounded petty, but whenever she thought about her childhood and how hard she'd had to work for any little extra thing she'd wanted, she was filled with anger. She thought about all those after-school jobs, all those Saturday nights she'd spent baby-sitting while her friends were at the movies.

"The policy was small," John answered in a tight voice. "It hardly covered the funeral expenses. But we already went over this. What are you getting at?"

"It doesn't add up. There must be something you haven't told me."

John hesitated before continuing. "As you know, your father didn't earn much at the hardware store. But what you don't know is that as his friend, I had advised him not to buy the house. He knew he was getting in over his head, but he was determined to give you and your mother what he called the good life."

"Aunt Tess never mentioned that you and my father had been friends."

"We were in the service together. After he died, your aunt hired me to take care of her affairs. She didn't want me to treat her like a charity case."

Laura didn't miss the edge in his voice. Had her father taken advantage of their friendship and not paid him for his services? "What else don't I know?" she asked.

She heard the lawyer sigh. "If your father had lived," he

said, "he wouldn't have been able to keep the house. He couldn't meet the payments. After he died, your aunt was determined not to lose it. She knew what it had meant to him, and she was determined that you would have it. Even after she paid off the mortgage, there was still the maintenance, property tax and insurance. She took on two jobs just to make ends meet."

Two jobs! No wonder Aunt Tess had never been there for her, waiting for her to come home from school. She remembered how she had envied Cynthia and Ellen. Their mothers had been home to greet them with a smile and a hug, to exchange a loving word over a plate of freshly baked cookies and a glass of milk.

*All I wanted was someone to love me. Someone who knew I existed. Aunt Tess didn't have to be a stay-at-home mom; all she had to do was love me.*

Sadness—and guilt—flowed through Laura's body. "I'll be back this weekend," she said, wanting to bring the disturbing call to an end. "But won't your office be closed?"

"Normally, yes, but I was planning to go in this Saturday to work on a trust, if you want to drop by. But you'll have to come by early. In the afternoon I'll be at my son's school, watching him play basketball. He's playing center," he added with pride.

Thinking of Cory, Laura smiled. "I'll be there, too. Why don't you bring the key to the school?"

They agreed on a time, and Laura thanked him for calling. She hung up and sat back in her chair. All this time she had believed that her aunt had been so stingy—with money as well as affection. That poor woman, having to work at two jobs, and for what? To pay off a mortgage that wasn't hers. To raise another person's child—the child of her estranged sister.

She remembered how her aunt used to go on and on about how frivolous kids were. Whenever Laura wasn't out earning spending money, her aunt had insisted she stay home and study. "Gallivanting around town won't do a thing for your future," she'd said more than once. If it hadn't been for that studying, for her aunt's constant harping, there would have been no academic scholarship.

Laura realized she had been acting like an ungrateful, spoiled child. The recrimination in John's voice had not been directed against her father; it had been aimed at *her.*

"Laura?" Suzanne stood in the doorway. "Are you all right?"

"I was just daydreaming. Did you want something?"

Her assistant sauntered into the office and sat on the maroon leather chair across from Laura's desk. She crossed her legs, making a deliberative show of smoothing her skirt. "I just want to say how sorry I am that you're leaving. I know we haven't always seen eye to eye, but I want you to know I've learned so much from you, and I've always respected your judgment. I'll miss you. We'll all miss you."

"Thank you," Laura said, studying her assistant with suspicion. The owners had hired Suzanne at the same time as Laura, and Suzanne had been after Laura's job since day one. She sure could use the raise, Laura thought, taking in the expensive Dior suit and Italian shoes. Suzanne spent every cent she earned on her wardrobe.

"This place won't be the same without you," Suzanne added. She brushed an imaginary piece of lint from her skirt, as though stalling for time. She sat a moment longer, then finally rose. At the door she turned. "Oh, I almost forgot," she said, teetering on her three-inch heels.

Laura almost laughed. Her assistant was usually so composed. "Spill it, Suzanne, before those heels drill a hole through the floor."

"I, uh, was wondering when you were going to recommend me for the job. I mean, they're not planning to bring in someone from outside, are they?"

"Don't worry, the job's yours."

Laura was afraid that Suzanne was going rush over and throw her arms around her, but the queen of coolness pulled herself together and said, "It's the right decision."

In spite of their conflicting personalities, Laura knew it *was* the right decision. Suzanne was efficient and effective, with a keen eye for what would sell. Laura had depended on her more than she liked to admit. When it came to business, Suzanne was hardboiled, whereas Laura had always leaned toward the aesthetic. But even without all that, Suzanne would do a darn good job, if ambition and confidence counted for anything.

Although the lease to her apartment wasn't up until the end of the year, Laura knew she wouldn't have a problem finding someone to take it over. This was New York. Apartments were like gold.

The week passed in a blur. Laura filled the days with work; in the evenings she packed. She was planning to keep only a few items of furniture, like her small mahogany desk and the oak chess table she used as a nightstand. Maybe the new tenant would buy the rest. She'd bought most of it at the thrift shop and didn't think it was worth taking.

Then again, maybe she would give it away. It might not have monetary value, but it had served her well. Maybe someone else could benefit.

Eventually, she would replace most of the furniture at the house in Middlewood. Except for a few pieces, she wasn't planning to keep much. She'd always liked the oversize couch, but she would reupholster it in a less ornate pattern. The exquisite Tiffany lamp, which her mother had inherited from her own mother, would remain the focal point of the living room. And, of course, there was the antique mirror, and next to it, the grandfather clock, which had stood like a sentinel in the hallway throughout the house's history.

On Tuesday Laura had dinner with Ellen at the little Chinese restaurant next to the loft. "You look tired," her friend remarked, studying Laura closely across the table.

"Stress," Laura answered, fumbling with her chopsticks. She gave up and slammed them down onto the table.

Ellen clicked her tongue. "How someone so adept with a paintbrush can be so clumsy with two little plastic sticks remains one of life's great mysteries. Take it easy before you take out someone's eyes. Are you sure you're all right?"

"You tell me. You're the doctor." Laura noticed the alarm on Ellen's face and quickly added, "I'm just tired. There's a lot I need to take care of before I move—work, the apartment, the loft. I'm not taking most of the furniture, but my art supplies can fill a barn, not to mention my dishes and linen. And what about my books? I'll have to rent a small truck." She picked up her chopsticks and made another attempt. "Don't worry," she said, watching the rice fall through the sticks, "this too shall pass."

Whenever Laura called Cassie, they talked about art, Cory's breakthrough, even Laura's moving back to Middlewood, but Jake's name was never mentioned. It was as if Cassie sensed that this time, her opinions on Jake weren't wanted.

Every night Laura called Cory, half relieved, half disappointed when Jake didn't pick up the phone. There should be a word for that, she thought. Relappointed? Disalieved? She desperately wanted to hear Jake's voice, but she knew it would be better to wait until she could see him in person. She thought about how she liked to put aside a painting before it was completely done. She reminded herself that Jake needed time—and distance—to put things into perspective.

He always said that she overanalyzed everything—art,

dreams, their marriage. Her analysis was based on instinct, she'd told him; it was the artist in her. She was right-brained. Right now instinct was telling her that spending time by himself was the right thing for him to do—as long as he didn't take *too* much time.

"Friday night and no date?"

"I had a dozen lined up," Cassie quipped. "That should tell you what kind of sacrifices I make for my friends."

"Yeah, right. But I appreciate the sentiment," Laura said, grinning. "Thanks for meeting me at the station, and for stopping at the convenience store. It didn't make sense for me to rent a car just for the weekend. Rose will be taking Cory to the game, and I can walk the two blocks to the school. I suppose I should think about buying a car, although I don't know how I'll ever afford it. I can't expect you and Rose to play chauffeur forever."

"So you're really going through with it."

In the dimness, Laura tried to read her friend's face. "Yes, Cass, I'm really going through with it. I've already found someone to sublet the apartment, starting in mid-October. I lease the loft by the month, so that's no problem—Cass! Watch out!"

Cassie swerved sharply, and in an instant was back on track. "My God, did you see that?" she shouted, her voice only a notch beneath hysteria. "Are you all right?"

"I banged my shoulder against the door, but I'm okay...I think. What about you?"

"Just a little shaky, though nothing like that poor animal must be. No matter how many times this happens, and it happens a lot, I just can't get used to it. Those poor animals darting out like that, their eyes blaring at you like headlights."

"The insurance companies advise against dodging them,"

Laura said. "They say it's not safe to try to avoid hitting them, but who would purposely hit a deer head-on?"

"I don't think I could," Cassie admitted.

Laura stared out the passenger window. Narrow and winding, the roads were as poorly lit and hazardous as when she'd left five years ago. Sometimes we know we're on a collision course, and all the logic in the world won't alter the path, she thought. Though not normally superstitious, she felt as if the incident was an omen warning her against moving back to Middlewood.

"Who'd have believed you would end up back here," Cassie said, as though privy to Laura's thoughts.

"Go ahead, ask. I know you're dying to. You haven't brought up his name once."

"Okay, so tell me. Where does Jake fit into all this?"

"I want us to get back together."

"I figured."

"That's it? What happened to 'You're throwing away your life,' or 'You're better off with Edward,' or 'Are you completely out of your tiny little mind?'"

"You must think I'm as sensitive as clay," Cassie said in a strained voice.

"Clay, at least, can be molded into something poetic. As far as Jake is concerned, you've always been a little, well, unyielding."

"Look, I don't hate Jake. I never have. He used to be my friend, too. If you're sure this is what you want, go for it."

"Sometimes I don't understand you at all. Are you now saying you approve?"

"I'm saying that circumstances have changed since you married Jake eight years ago. You weren't ready back then, and neither was he."

Uh-oh, here comes the "you got married too soon" speech, Laura thought. Suddenly she was tired of all the free advice, tired of discussing her intimate life as if it were a documentary. "At least Cory is finally making headway," she said, deliberately changing the subject. "No one, especially a child, should have to carry around so much guilt."

"Guilt does strange things," Cassie said, hunched over the steering wheel, peering into the darkness. "Sometimes a person feels guilty when someone close dies, because he's relieved it didn't happen to him. He believes relief somehow diminishes his feelings for the person who is gone."

"Are you saying that Cory's behavior is a result of his own fear of dying? That's a little farfetched."

"Isn't much of what we do and feel a result of this fear? Be honest. Didn't you feel guilty after Cynthia's accident?"

Laura sighed. They were back to the subject of Jake. "Yes, but you and I know where that guilt stemmed from," she said slowly. "I never would have married Jake if she hadn't died."

"Bull. Cynthia was planning to leave him, and everyone knew it—everyone except Jake. Look, I know she was your best friend, but she's been gone for nine years. It's time you and Jake got your act together."

"I can't believe I'm hearing this! What about all your raving about Steady Eddy? You practically threw me into his lap!"

"No, that was Ellen."

"'A match made in spic-and-span heaven,' I believe were your exact words."

"Okay, so I think you're both...retentive. But that doesn't mean you should live together. You would probably drive each other crazy."

Laura suppressed a smile. "So, you're saying you were wrong about me and Edward?"

"You're enjoying this, aren't you," Cassie accused. "Okay, you win. I'll say the words. I was wrong about you and Edward."

"And…"

"And maybe I was wrong about Jake, too. Maybe he can make you happy. He's not the same person he used to be. Neither are you, even if you're still a little retentive."

"But…"

"But when are you going to realize I never considered Jake to be the enemy? I told you, all I ever wanted was for you to be happy. Eight years ago he wasn't in a position to do that, but he's been ripe for a long time now."

"And…"

"And I think you and Jake should try again."

"And…"

"Hey, wait a minute! What happened to the next *but?*"

"There are no more buts in this game."

Cassie laughed. "Oh, I like this! We get to make the rules as we go along."

"There are no rules. Not anymore."

Cassie pulled into Laura's driveway. "Come on in," Laura said. "I'll make some coffee, and we'll talk about the lull in your love life. We can even have one of your man-bashing sessions. Except this time, I'm only going to listen, not participate."

"I'll have to take a rain check on that coffee. After that close call on the road, my nerves don't need more hype. Besides, I have a late date."

"I should have known," Laura said, shaking her head. "Will I see you at the game tomorrow?"

"Wouldn't miss it for the world. That kid deserves all the cheering he can get."

Laura waved her friend off and entered the house. She was still wobbly from the near accident, and her shoulder had begun to ache. She kept seeing the deer's wide black eyes, the way they had stared into the night as if to ask, "Why?"

Forget the coffee. Cassie wasn't the only one whose nerves

were shot. What Laura really wanted was a soothing cup of herbal tea. Either that or a stiff drink.

She left her suitcase in the hallway and went to the kitchen, carrying the small bag of groceries. She stopped in the door-way. Something felt wrong.

You're just spooked, she told herself. A hot cup of tea will fix that. She hoped so; there wasn't any alcohol in the house.

She turned on the lights. Most of the boxes were gone. One of the remaining boxes had been moved to the center of the room.

She crossed the kitchen floor. The top of the box was wide open, revealing a jumbled mass of trinkets and torn papers. No, not papers. Letters. Cynthia's letters.

Her legs threatened to give way. The weakness had noth-ing to do with the deer on the road. Only one other person had a key to the house.

Jake had found out.

## *Chapter Twelve*

No matter how many times he played it out in his head, the end came out the same. Laura had known the whole time. He could just picture her and Cynthia talking and giggling, deciding on what Cynthia would wear to her next rendezvous. "Be a doll and cover for me," he imagined his first wife saying. And Laura would happily oblige.

He opened the sliding door and stepped onto the hotel balcony. The temperature had dropped dramatically, and the night air sent a chill through his body. He looked down on the street below. From his room on the second floor, he could see couples strolling along the well-lit sidewalk. Directly below, a young woman in a bright yellow jacket threw her arms around her companion and laughed. The man picked her up and whirled her around.

He'll learn, Jake thought cynically.

This time he had been so sure it would work out with Laura. After she had left the first time, he went after her time and time again, but she kept turning him away. After a while, he gave up. But he had never stopped hoping.

And then she came back. Time, apparently, had done its healing magic—time, maturity, the letting go of old hurts and grudges. The catalyst was unimportant; he had believed their moment had finally come.

But the moment was tainted with lies. Any future would be based on a trust as illusory as smoke.

The couple below resumed their walk and disappeared from view. A teenage boy on a skateboard came whizzing by, zigzagging his way along the sidewalk, nearly colliding with an elderly woman out walking her poodle.

"Watch where you're going!" the woman shouted.

The boy skated away as though he hadn't seen her.

Jake shook his head. The only thing worse than a fool was a blind fool.

Laura didn't want to wait a whole week until next Friday. She had to talk to Jake *now*. To hell with his needing time to figure things out. That was just the problem. He *had* figured things out. The problem was not whether he could trust her to stay—she was sure that together they could work through her fears. The problem was whether he could trust her at all.

Jake was in Boston. She'd have to get the name of his hotel from Rose. But it was after ten, and she knew that Rose would be in bed. I'll call in her in the morning, Laura resolved. But in the morning Rose wasn't home. Laura knew she'd be seeing her at the game later that day. The call to Jake would just have to wait.

She spent a few hours sketching, and then after a late lunch, walked over to the school. As promised, John Collins was there with the key to the safe deposit box.

"That man's got a great butt," Cassie said after he had left to sit with his daughter. "That is, for an older man." She shot Laura an appraising look. "What is it about you? Here you are, not even moved back yet, and every eligible man is trailing after you."

"It must be the curse of the beautiful. It certainly can't be the curse of the rich and famous."

"Mark my words, Laura Matheson, one day you'll be cursed with it all. You always were a late bloomer, but your turn is coming."

"I just want a large piece. I don't want it all." Not true. How many times had she used those exact words? *I want it all.* Having it all meant health, kids, a career and, most important, a man she loved. Having it all meant having Jake.

"Okay, so you're not aiming to be rich and famous. But remember, one person's curse is another's blessing."

Laura turned to face her friend. "What on earth are you talking about?"

"I hear John is a free man again. A single father, especially one who had his kids so late in life, can always use a little unsolicited advice." Cassie peered out into the bleachers. "I think I'll get a soda from the vending machine. Do you want something?"

"Just what he needs, advice from a confirmed bachelorette. But, okay, see if there's any bottled water. It's hot in here. I don't understand why they turned off the air-conditioning."

"Maybe it has something to do with the fact that it's no longer summer," Cassie said. "It's like a freezer in here and you want air-conditioning?" She picked up her purse and stood up. "What about you, Rose? Would you like something to drink?"

Next to Laura, Rose shifted in her seat. "No, thank you.

The stuff they keep in the machines is too *old*. And if you ask me, women should stick to men their own age."

"Save my seat," Cassie said, ignoring the slur. "I'll be back in a jiff—or maybe not." She glanced back at Laura. "Are you sure you're all right? You look a little pale."

"Go," Laura answered with a wave of her hand, "and take your time. I'm fine."

"That woman is looking for trouble," Rose said after Cassie had left. "I recognize the signs. If you ask me—"

A roar erupted from the bleachers. Cory had scored a basket, the first one of the game, and the home crowd had jumped to their feet.

"He's wonderful, isn't he?" Laura said, shouting to be heard above the cheering.

Rose's face was glowing. "He sure is."

What a pair we are, Laura thought. Like a mother and grandmother, bursting with pride. "Where's your costume?" she asked, remembering Rose's penchant for dressing up.

"This is a basketball game. I'm dressed as an American."

Rose was as misfit in this world as a three-way light bulb in a two-way socket, but she was endearing. Laura regretted not having taken the time to know her better.

"Rose, I need a favor," she said.

"He's staying at the Marriott in downtown Boston. I'll call you with the number as soon as I get home."

Laura might not have known Rose, but Rose apparently knew *her*.

"I'm not one to interfere," Rose continued, "but if you ask me, I don't think you should call him. Let him stew for a bit. I know what I'm talking about. His mother and I were closer than sisters, and I've known him since the day he was born. He came into the world kicking and screaming, three weeks early, and let me tell you, he wasn't happy about it one bit. He'd cry all day and night, for nothing at all. I told his mother not to go running every time he fussed, or he'd never give her a moment's peace. But she didn't listen to me, and that's why he is the way he is. But he's not a baby anymore. You've got to let him fuss."

"I've got to talk to him, Rose. There are things you don't understand."

Rose shook her finger in Laura's face. "Maybe I don't know everything that's going on, but I'm not blind. The last time I saw him so upset was after a tiff he'd had with that first wife of his. You're still not seeing that Edward fellow, are you? I figured this is what you two were fighting about, seeing how that first wife of his ran around."

Good Lord, was there anything this woman didn't know? "Are you saying that Jake knew about Cynthia?" Laura asked. She didn't believe it. If Jake had known, wouldn't he have guessed that Cynthia had confided in her? Laura's fate would have been signed and sealed a long time ago.

*Accomplice.* The word was like a bad taste in her mouth.

"I'm saying I don't think you should call him. I know that boy like he was my own. He'll come to his own conclusions when he's good and ready. He'll come to see he's got no competition. But if you push him, you'll only drive him away."

"The argument wasn't about Edward," Laura said. "Jake is upset that I never told him about Cynthia's affair."

"That's a lot of poppycock," Rose said. "Sometimes Jake likes to pretend he doesn't know a thing, thinks it's safer that way, but as sure as that bump on your nose, he knew exactly what was happening. He couldn't admit it back then, and he can't admit it now. And he wouldn't have believed you if you'd told him. I don't know exactly what happened between the two of you, but somehow you made him confront his demons. Give him some time to get rid of them himself. After a while he'll realize that it's all water under the bridge."

Laura sighed. "How long, Rose? Another five years?"

Rose smiled at her mischievously. "When are you coming back to Middlewood?"

"Next Friday. The weekend after that, I plan to move here permanently."

"Oh, I already know that. I mean, what time next Friday?"

Laura looked at her curiously. "Why?"

"Jake's coming back Friday night. His plane lands at LaGuardia at eight. He never parks at the airport when he goes out of town for a spell, but why should he take the shuttle back to Middlewood, when you'll be driving in? You will be driving, won't you?"

Yes, Laura would be driving. She'd be in the front seat of a rented truck, with a load of her possessions crammed in the back.

She grinned. "You're a sly woman, Rose Halligan."

The storm that had been forecast finally arrived, engulfing the entire East Coast with heavy rain. Jake glanced up at the monitor and breathed a sigh of relief. His flight hadn't been delayed.

It had been a long week, filled with speeches and conferences. Normally he enjoyed these trips. They gave him a break from his normal workload, but more important, they provided an opportunity for key individuals from architectural and construction firms located all over the country to exchange ideas. But throughout the entire week his mind had been somewhere else, and now he was anxious to get back home.

He had an hour to kill. He considered going to the bar, then decided against it. His head was still pounding. Earlier that day, after the closing brunch, he'd gone to the lounge at the hotel and had, as he preferred to describe it, overstayed his visit.

The woman sitting on the bar stool next to him had reminded him of Laura, with dark-blond hair that fell to her shoulders. But it wasn't her hair that grabbed his attention when she turned to him and asked for a light; it was her eyes. Like Laura's, they were a shining blue green, and in the stranger's eyes he saw a familiar sadness, a sadness that had haunted him for five long years.

"Sorry, I don't smoke," he answered.

"Neither do I," she said. "Not usually. I just started again last night. But bad habits always seem to make a comeback. I mean, you wait and wait for something to happen, and one day you realize that what you were waiting for wasn't so important after all. But by then it's too late. That's when you start smoking again."

Jake was on his fourth gin and tonic, and feeling it. "Or maybe you realize what *is* important, but you throw it away, anyway." Damn, he was getting good at this psychology thing. Laura would be proud. "Let's trade vices. I'll smoke and you'll wallow."

"Mister, the last thing you need is someone crying on your shoulder. You have more heartache than you know what to do with." She tossed the unlit cigarette into the ashtray and stood up. "Nasty habit," she said, and with a wave of her hand, left the lounge.

People had different ways of dealing with pain, he thought now. Some drank, some smoked. Some, like Laura, hid. And some immersed themselves in work. He pulled out a folder from his briefcase, then put it back inside. Maybe he'd buy a newspaper. He'd been gone a whole week and hadn't once turned on the TV in his room to listen to the news. It was strange how easily people were able to file away the real world when they were out of town.

*Out of sight, out of mind.* That had been Cynthia's motto, not his.

Somewhere inside, he'd always known there was someone else in her life that last year. He'd tried to ignore his suspicions, hoping that the problems in his marriage would simply go away. But they hadn't. And then she had died, leaving him with no place to store his anger. Cigarettes, alcohol, working too much…these were pie compared to anger. That was another story altogether.

Was he angry with Cynthia or with Laura? Sure, he knew he was directing this anger, this mistrust, at Laura, but with good reason. She had lied to him. Her not telling him was the same as lying, as far as he was concerned.

He looked out the observation window. The plane that would be taking him home hadn't arrived. He got up and went to the newsstand. The woman he'd talked to in the hotel lounge was glancing at the magazines.

"Look at that," she said, as though continuing a previous conversation. She pointed to the cover of a fashion magazine. "Pointy shoes are in style again." She turned around and faced him. "They say that everything comes around again, if you wait long enough."

Why was she talking to him about shoes? Boy, he must have really tied one on. After four cups of coffee and a hot shower before checking out of the hotel, his head was still fuzzy. He remembered thinking that she resembled Laura.

"Like bad habits," he said. "Speaking of which, you look like my…like someone I know."

"Someone you know, or someone you knew? You have that look in your eyes. You know, lost, kind of sad. I recognized the symptoms when I asked you for a light."

"And there I was, drinking myself into a stupor, thinking the same about you."

She picked up the magazine and leafed through it. "Yup, definitely back in style," she said, studying an ad. She flipped through more pages, then looked up at him again. "My father had a heart attack." She spoke these words as if she hadn't had a break in thought, as if it were perfectly normal for her to say them, to a stranger, in the middle of an airport.

"I'm sorry," Jake said, at a loss for anything better to offer.

"The last time I saw him was five years ago. We had an argument over my choice of careers, and I haven't spoken to him since. He wanted me to go to law school, and I wanted to teach. Can you imagine anything so stupid? Five years lost, and because of what? An old hurt, an old grudge."

*The letting go of old hurts and grudges.*

"You're going to him now?" Jake asked, feeling as though he'd been socked in the gut. *Five years lost.* He and Laura had lost five years. Was he willing to throw away the next five because of something that had happened a long time ago? Was he willing to throw away the rest of his life?

"Yes, I'm flying to Hartford." She set the magazine back onto the rack. "I hate pointy shoes. Sometimes it's too late for a comeback."

Laura felt as if nature had played a cruel joke. Even though autumn had arrived and the air was cool, she felt cheated. All week, night sweats had kept her awake, and during the day she felt as if she would melt in the heat that radiated from her body. The air conditioner in her apartment had broken down once and for all, which made packing almost unbearable. Even with the window open she felt feverish, and more than once her queasy stomach had prevented her from continuing and she'd had to lie down.

She knew it was stress. Stress due to the move. Stress due to anticipation. When Friday finally rolled around, she almost canceled the plan that she and Rose had concocted. Not only was her body aching in protest, she was sick with worry. This, she believed, would be her last shot with Jake.

The traffic hadn't budged an inch in over ten minutes, and the car behind her was honking. "What do you expect me to do?" she shouted, knowing darn well the driver couldn't hear. "Ram into the truck ahead?" She turned on the radio for a traffic report and was bombarded with techno music. She switched to another station. This time country music filled the cab. I am so not in the mood for heartbreak songs, she thought, and turned off the radio.

Even with the wipers on max, she could barely see out the windshield. Damn rain. Its only saving grace was that it might delay Jake's arrival. I'm definitely getting a cell phone, she resolved, wishing she had a way to call the airline.

Two hours later she pulled into the short-term parking lot at LaGuardia. There were no vacant spots. The way things were going, why would she think there would be? Finally, after cruising up and down the lanes for nearly fifteen minutes, she spotted a man with a suitcase, and tailed him to where he was parked. Five minutes later she was standing next to the luggage carousel, out of breath and frantic.

The carousel was empty. She looked up at the monitor and burst into tears. Jake's plane had landed on time.

It had been one thing after another. *One bad omen after the other.* First the air conditioner breaking down, then the rain and the traffic, and now this. Not to mention the hot flushes she'd been having all week, which had nearly prevented her from packing and leaving in the first place. With a heavy heart she walked to the exit.

The automatic doors opened and she stepped outside. At least it's no longer pouring, she thought, standing in the drizzle. Not that it matters now. Let it hail, for all I care.

And then, farther along the curb, she saw him, about to climb into the limousine shuttle.

She had rehearsed the scene a hundred times in her head. She'd be cool, calm, as she casually approached him, and in that frame of mind she would know, as soon as he noticed her, that she hadn't made a mistake. But before she could stop herself, she found herself running toward him, calling out his name, all pretense of composure abandoned.

She stopped and looked into his face. "Hey, Squirt," he said, and smiled as if he'd been expecting her.

"Hey, yourself," she said, feeling the calmness she'd yearned for take hold. It was harmony she sought, with him and with the world, and it was harmony she found in that first instant, when he smiled.

"So what brings you out on a night like this?"

She smiled back at him. "I've come to take you home."

He put down his briefcase and pulled her against him. They stood there in the light mist, holding each other as though afraid to let go.

"You coming or what?" the shuttle driver shouted. "It's wet out here, and I'm on a schedule."

"This is an airport," Jake murmured in her ear. "You'd think they'd never seen a reunion."

She liked the sound of the word *reunion*.

He pulled out his bag from the back of the limo. "Sorry, pal," he said to the driver. "I've got my own chauffeur."

"I almost didn't make it," she said as they walked to the lot. "I was stuck in traffic. I was hoping your flight would be late, but the monitor said it arrived on time."

"It did, but we had to wait in the plane for almost an hour. It's all backed up out there because of the weather. I was sitting on that plane, trying to conjure you up, and here you are. I guess that radar between us is working after all."

Once inside the truck, Jake pulled her close to him again, and this time his mouth found hers, his tongue seeking its way between her lips. She leaned back against the window, and he moved in closer.

"Ouch, your knee!" she said.

"They sure don't make these trucks as large as they used to. That wasn't my knee."

"You've never driven one of these in your life."

"There you go again, making assumptions," he said teasingly. "There's a lot more to me than you think."

"So I recall. Are you sure that wasn't your knee? Maybe I'd better check it out. Or do you have something against fast girls?"

"Not yet, but I sure as hell plan to."

"All talk and no trousers," she said, straightening her clothes.

"The no trousers part comes later, when I get you into a not-so-cramped, not-so-public place." He looked at her closely. "You look a little tired. How about letting me drive?"

The old Jake would not have asked. He would have just taken over. Still, she was more than happy to let him take the wheel. The fatigue she had been fighting all day had finally won. She snuggled next to him, allowing herself to doze. Even in sleep she was conscious of his profile, his hands on the wheel, his eyes on the dark road ahead, but every once in a while she forced herself awake to make sure she wasn't dreaming.

Finally they pulled into his driveway. He shifted the gear into park and nudged her gently. "Laura, we're home."

"I'm awake," she said, rubbing her eyes. "What time is it?"

"It's almost two. Traffic was murder."

She looked outside the window and grimaced. It was pouring again. "What a homecoming," she said.

"Think of it as a wash. We're starting over."

"Jake…"

"Shh, don't say it. I know."

"We just can't ignore it." No matter how loath she was to bring up the subject, they had to talk about it, if they ever hoped to bury it once and for all. "I wish she had never told me about the affair. I didn't know what to do."

"She put you in a no-win situation. I shouldn't have blamed you." There was a bitter edge to his voice. "I guess part of me knew all along. I just didn't want to face it. It's not an easy thing to admit that you failed your wife."

"You didn't fail her. Sometimes things just don't work out. It's as simple as that."

"Is it?" he asked quietly, his eyes filled with pain. It was the same pain she had seen on the night he had let himself into her house, the night they had made love. "All the years Cynthia and I were married, nothing I did ever made her happy. I felt as if I'd robbed her of her dreams."

"She chose to give them up," Laura argued. "She would have succeeded if she'd gone for it. Her designs were wonderful. She could have gone back to school. She could have commuted to New York. People do it all the time. You're not the one at fault."

"No, it *was* my fault." He stared out into the darkness. "She could have done so much more with her life, but she gave it all up to stay here and be my wife."

I would have done the same, Laura thought. I *did* do the same. Ellen's words came to mind. "Even after he married Cynthia, you stayed in Middlewood, working at a dead-end job just to be near him."

"What about her interior-decoration business?" Laura asked. "She had such a natural flair. No one could have possibly guessed she got all her training from books."

"She hated it. She started the business because she was bored, not because she was interested in home decoration. It also gave her an excuse for not starting a family. She didn't want to share me with anything, not even a child of her own."

Laura shifted uneasily. The subject of having children was dangerous territory. She wasn't sure she wanted to go there.

He sighed. "But that's not all."

Nervously she bit her lip, waiting for him to continue.

"I did care for her, Laura. I wanted our marriage to work. But she knew there was something wrong. I didn't even know it myself, not consciously. I pushed it away somewhere deep inside, but it was always there. The truth is, I never did get you out of my system. And she was jealous."

"No, Jake, you're wrong—"

"Am I? She was always jealous of you, even when we were kids. Even though your house was in need of repair, it was much larger, with a huge backyard. And you're petite and dainty—you were never overweight, no matter what you say. She once told me that next to you she felt like an ostrich. But what really got her goat was that you had more talent."

"What are you talking about? She was the one with the talent. And she was so beautiful! All the girls envied her. She had it all." She had *you*.

"Being beautiful has its drawbacks. Why do you think she was so wild in high school? She thought the way she looked was the only thing she had going for her. Although," he added, his voice growing soft, "being beautiful never affected you that way."

Jake had thought she was beautiful, even back then when she had been heavier. She nestled close to him, leaning her head on his shoulder.

"I've been reading those self-help books," he continued. "Cynthia wasn't confident. She was competitive. She was in competition with you."

"Now it's you who's talking mumbo jumbo."

"No, listen to me. She knew I had a crush on you, back then in high school, but she went after me like a shark that smelled blood. You didn't seem interested in me, and I admit I was no Boy Scout. The rest is history. She knew all along how I felt about you, even if I didn't know it myself. That's why she didn't want to work in New York. She wanted to keep an eye on me. But soon even that got old, and she went looking outside the marriage. Looking for something I couldn't give her."

"Let it go, Jake," Laura said softly. "It's time to move on. You said it yourself. We're starting over."

"Not exactly," he whispered. "What you and I had is still there, in spite of everything that happened. It always was and always will be." He caressed the side of her face. "You're so warm. You know, I think that's what I missed the most. Your warm body next to mine. Curling up together in front of the fireplace, the way we used to. Not that I'd have curling on my mind." He ran his fingers along her neck. "My God, you're *too* warm. Are you feeling all right?"

"I'm fine. I'm just tired."

"Let's go inside. You need some sleep. I'll take the couch, if you're worried about Cory finding us together."

She laughed. "Since when are you concerned about my honor?"

"Laura, let me take care of you."

"As tempting as the offer sounds, I'm going home. I don't think it's a good idea for Cory to find me there in the morning, couch or no couch. It's still a little too soon for that."

His expression grew serious. "I'll give in this time, but promise me you won't unpack a thing until I get there in the morning. From now on, let me do the heavy work."

"Deal, but make that *late* in the morning."

She knew he was disappointed. So was she. She had planned on spending a few hours with him alone in his room and then sneaking out before dawn. But she was tired, more tired than she could remember.

No, that wasn't true. As clearly as though it had all happened yesterday, she recalled feeling this way before, a long time ago.

He reached for her one more time, and she pushed the memory aside. In the shelter of his embrace, she could hide from the past. And then she let him go.

He climbed out of the cab. "I'll get my stuff out of the back," he said, looking up at her from the pavement. "Drive carefully. The roads are slippery. I'll wait on the porch until you're gone."

She moved into the driver's seat. In the dim glow of the cab's dome light, she caught a glimpse of her face in the rearview mirror. Her skin was pallid, her eyelids heavy with fatigue. It's not stress, she told herself. It must be that twenty-four-hour bug that's going around. Tomorrow she would feel better. Except that twenty-four hours had already passed since she'd first started feeling sick. In fact, she'd been feeling this way for days.

A wave of nausea shook her body. She had to wait for it to pass before driving off.

*She'd tried to ignore it, hoping it was only a sign of another cold.*

A feeling of dread came over her. She had tried to ignore that as well, five years ago.

## Chapter Thirteen

The trees along the road were painted with shades of early autumn. The foliage glowed with yellow and orange, traces of purple and bronze peeking out from the leaves. Glistening through the branches, the sun cast strands of shimmering gold onto a lawn still wet with last night's rain. The storm had passed.

Laura turned away from the window, smiling. She felt like a new woman. All her aches and pains had vanished overnight. For a brief moment the words *what if* flashed through her mind, threatening to bring back the dread from last night, but she quickly dismissed them. For the first time in days, she felt rested and well.

She'd called Jake as soon as she'd awakened, and he would be arriving shortly to help her unpack the truck. Cory, he said, had too much homework, and would call when he was done.

Homework on Saturday? And why couldn't he do it here at the house? That little devil still believed he was orchestrating the whole thing. First he was allowing Jake time alone with her, and then he was planning a touching family scene to cement the whole deal.

Little did he know she was a mile ahead of him. She felt her face reddening. There were some things kids didn't need to know.

Because her suitcases were still in the truck, her choice of wardrobe was limited to what she had left behind last week. She pulled on a pair of loose-fitting jeans and her oversize Paint for Life T-shirt. She knew Jake wouldn't care what she wore, as long as she could easily slip out of it.

She had just enough time for a quick trip to the grocery store, and was back home within the hour, fixing breakfast. *He's going to need all the energy he can get,* she thought, tingling with anticipation. And she wasn't talking about his unpacking the truck. She was frying up peppers for an omelette when she heard the doorbell.

She ran to the door and flung it open. "Why didn't you use your key?" she asked, breaking into a mischievous smile.

"And risk your ire? Although I have to admit, there's something about you when you get worked up that turns me into a horn-dog." He wrapped his arms around her and nuzzled his lips on her neck. "Mmm. Something smells good."

His lips seared a path up to her ear, his tongue teasing her with gentle, probing flicks. She closed her eyes, losing herself in his slow, drugging kisses. "It's not me, it's breakfast," she murmured. "Hot and spicy, just the way you like it.... Omigosh, the peppers!"

She scooted out of his arms and dashed into the kitchen. Stirring the ingredients in the pan, she looked at him as he leaned against the wall, his eyes burning with a flame as hot as the oil sizzling on the stove. He walked over to her, slowly, a man with a purpose, and slid his hands under her T-shirt, his caress light yet demanding as he moved his fingers upward, around her rib cage. Cupping the underside of her breasts with his palms, he ran his thumbs across her nipples, at first tantalizing her with his feathery touch, then squeezing gently with his fingers.

"On second thought," she said, her voice growing husky, "breakfast can wait." She wriggled out of his reach and headed toward the hallway. With a flip of her hair, she glanced back at him from over her shoulder. "Coming?" she asked coyly.

He turned off the stove and followed her up the stairs. "Oh, I intend to."

And he did, again and again….

Later, as they lay in each other's arms, she let her mind drift lazily. She'd once felt that she'd been split in two, and that a large part of her had been ripped away. Now she was whole again, and her other half was lying next to her, in her bed. The yin and the yang—that's us, she thought, her fingers drawing little circles on his chest.

"I have a plan," he said.

"I bet you do."

"Lady, give a guy a break. I'm only human."

This was the bantering she'd missed the first time around. Even though the sex had been good, it had been missing that certain easygoing quality. Like a holiday song, her laughter now rang out her contentment.

"First I'm going to have a cup of that wonderful brew you call coffee, and then I'm going to eat. Even a man with my stamina needs to recharge his batteries. And then—"

"Ooh, I like the 'and then' part."

"And then," he repeated, planting a peck on her nose, "we unpack the truck."

"I have a better idea. Let's stay in bed all day and pretend we did those things."

"Rise and shine, woman. Feed your man."

"I thought I just did."

The phone rang while they were enjoying a second cup of coffee. "It's Cory," Laura said. "He wants you to pick him up."

Jake brought in her suitcases from the truck. "This should keep you out of trouble while I'm gone. I'll be back by the time you've unpacked."

"You forget that I have a complicated relationship with my closet. Arranging clothes could take hours."

"As long as it doesn't run into the night. I'm not done with you yet."

"And here I thought I'd have to trade you in for a younger model."

After Jake returned with Cory, the three of them set about unloading the truck. That is, Jake and Cory worked while Laura supervised. "That goes here," she said more than once with authority, and then, "No, take it back downstairs."

Cory shook his head and muttered, "Women."

Later, Laura prepared spaghetti and a salad for dinner while Jake and Cory tinkered with the furnace, and afterward they settled in front of the TV, watching one of Cory's favorite videos. During the closing credits, Jake made an exaggerated motion of stretching and said, "Boy, am I bushed. You worked me to the bone, Laura. After we rewind the film, I guess I'll take off. Get your jacket, Cory."

"Sure, Dad," Cory said, "but why don't you rewind it later, when you come back?"

Laura and Jake exchanged a startled glance, but then Cory added, "I know you two have a lot to talk about, and I don't want to be a third circle."

"Wheel," Jake said. "You mean a third wheel. You're never

a third wheel—but you're right, Laura and I have some things we need to discuss."

By the time he was back, Laura had changed into a house-coat. She'd debated putting on something a little risqué and a lot more revealing, but what was the point? It would only end up on the floor. Then why change clothes at all? she asked herself. Because Jake had a thing about housecoats—as long as she wasn't wearing anything underneath.

"So what do you want to talk about?" he asked, slowly undoing her buttons.

Her housecoat dropped to the floor, and she unzipped his jeans. "Like I said yesterday," she said, "all talk and no trousers."

"I like the part about no trousers," he said.

This time they didn't make it upstairs.

Jake left around two. In the morning the three of them were going to Ridgefield for the annual autumn fair. Each year the activities ended with a ceremony in Ballard Park, where people from all over the county gathered to watch the sunset. "It's time I took you on a proper date," he'd told her earlier. "Remember those? Me…man, you…woman."

"And Cory…child," she'd answered.

She awoke early and dressed in a hand-crocheted crewneck and a matching emerald skirt. Jake had always liked her in green, and she knew the tight-fitting pullover would start him salivating. As for him, she'd always liked his cowboy image when he was in jeans, and he knocked her socks off when he wore a suit and tie, but when she saw him standing in the doorway in navy pleated Dockers and a hand-knit wool sweater, she knew she was a goner. He looked as if he belonged on the cover of the *All-American Male*.

She tore her eyes off him and looked out onto the landing. "Where's Cory? I thought he was looking forward to this."

"He's still doing homework. I swear, I've never seen that kid work so hard. It must be your influence."

Influence, my foot. Cory was pushing this matchmaker plan to the brink. Not that she minded. Right now it was important that she and Jake spend time alone together, and somehow Cory knew this. He was one smart kid.

"You look fabulous," Jake said. "In fact, I think I want to keep you all to myself. What do you say we skip the fair and go upstairs? And let's skip the sunset, too. I hear it's the same as sunrise, only backward—not that you've ever been up at dawn."

"Nothing doing, Jake Logan. You promised me a proper date, and I intend to have one. Besides, I didn't get up this early for nothing."

"Nothing? You call what I have in store for you nothing?"

"And what would that be?"

"Everything." His expression stilled as he gathered her into his arms, and his kiss was as firm as his promise.

Before heading on to the fair, Jake decided to make a side trip. "Here it is," he said, turning off the ignition. "So what do you think? It's a great site, isn't it?"

The new community center had been in the planning phase for more than two years, ever since it had become obvious that the old building was outgrowing its capacity. Once a sleepy little town, and less affluent than other Connecticut boroughs en route to New York, Middlewood was now the latest haven for commuters. In the past five years, the population had doubled.

"It's a wonderful location," she said. And it was. On the bus route yet far enough away from town center, it was three times the size of the old site. She felt Jake's pride in having been selected for the job. "When do you start building?"

"In about six months. The designs are in the final stage. You remember Joe Sullivan, don't you? He's the architect I'm working with. He told me to thank you, by the way."

"Me? What for?"

"We're planning an outdoor winter complex with a place for kids to play in the snow, including a thirty-foot toboggan run. It was your painting that inspired him. You know the one I mean, the one hanging in my office, with the kids building a snowman."

It was only a little over three weeks ago that Jake had forbidden Cory to go tobogganing. He'd come a long way since then. And so had she.

"You're making that up," she said. "The painting wasn't that good."

"Yes, it was. You underestimate yourself. In fact, I expect to see your work plastered all over the walls of the center."

She looked at him with amusement. "I don't think you have a say on the interior design. You're a builder, not an art critic."

"I'm serious. The town council is looking for local talent. They want to meet you."

"Did you say something to them? You know I want to do this on my own. You know—"

"Hey, don't yell at me. It was Joe Sullivan who mentioned your name. He thinks your work is fantastic. Of course, I can always tell them you're not interested."

"Jake Logan, you know darn well I'm interested! Besides, they wouldn't want to see me if my work wasn't good, right?"

"Well, I do have some influence..."

She punched him lightly on his shoulder.

"I love it when you're feisty," he said, grinning. "Turns me into a horn-dog."

"Everything turns you into a horn-dog."

Laura was filled with contentment as they drove to Ridge-field. Her moving back to Middlewood, the house, their future...it was all coming together. With a little luck and a lot of hard work she might even succeed as an artist. In fact, with Jake's encouragement, she was sure of it.

The morning passed in a happy whirl. Set against a picturesque countryside, Ridgefield was a friendly place with genuine colonial atmosphere. Main Street, lined with offerings from local crafts and antique stores, had been closed to traffic. Stretching more than a mile alongside tall oak and elm, it bustled with shoppers and tourists. Even the side streets had something to offer, and after parking the car, Jake and Laura stopped to look at every display as they made their way through the town. She bargained with all the vendors, finally snagging an antique brass lamp for less than half price. He insisted on buying her a hand-painted silk scarf, its ivory fabric a canvas for splashes of turquoise.

"To go with your eyes," he said.

They were planning to join a walking tour later that afternoon, but by the time noon came around, she felt as if she were dragging.

"You'll feel better after we eat," Jake said, suggesting the Café St. Gabriel. She was surprised. She knew he didn't like French cuisine. But lately he was full of surprises.

Hand in hand they made their way through the restaurant, into the courtyard in back. It was a perfect day for outdoor dining. The sun smiled down from a cloudless sky, warming the cool autumn air, and a light breeze rustled through the trees, as gentle as a sigh.

"How are you, Michel?" Laura asked, this time not confusing the proprietor with a waiter. "And how is your wife?"

His face was beaming. "Madame had the twins. You know how it is. One sleeps, the other one cries. One cries, the other one sleeps. *Mon Dieu,* Madame and I are up all night."

No, she didn't know how it was, but she said, "And you love every minute of it."

After lunch Laura felt revived enough to continue walking, but because they had lost track of the time and stayed too long at the café, they had missed the guided tour.

"Why don't we head back home?" Jake said, looking at her suggestively. "I'm sure I can find something for us to do at the house."

"I'm sure you can, but nothing doing. It's been a long time since I've visited the historical sites, and you promised we'd see them together. Besides, you know I never sleep with a man before the first date. And our first date isn't over."

He laughed and tapped himself on the forehead. "Right, I forgot. Back at the house all we've been doing is talking."

They decided to make their own tour, starting with the Keeler Tavern. Three-quarters of a mile south of the commercial center, it had once been a gathering place for patriots of the Revolutionary War. Now it was a museum commemorating the 1777 Battle of Ridgefield, which had been fought right there on Main Street.

"Did you know that the architect Cass Gilbert lived here after the war?" he said.

Uh-oh. Once Jake started talking about architecture, there was no stopping him. But Laura didn't mind. Although he was a hands-in-the-earth kind of person, a builder, he had a deep respect for design. As an artist, she liked to hear his ideas, and as a woman, she liked when he shared his dreams.

"I remember you mentioning him," she said. "Wasn't he the architect who designed the Woolworth Building?"

Starting with the Woolworth Building, Jake went on to describe his own views on architecture. Laura was captivated not only by his words but also by the way he spoke. He had strong opinions on how he wanted to build, and his voice conveyed his convictions.

At the junction of Main and West Lane, they stopped to sit on a bench by the fountain. "You look tired," Jake said. "Maybe we should go home."

"No, just give me a few minutes. It's been a long time since I've been here. My parents grew up in Ridgefield, and I'm hoping I'll remember some of the things they told me. Maybe I'll make a psychic connection and remember more of my childhood."

"Sounds like mumbo jumbo to me," he said. "Do you remember anything?"

She sighed. "It's starting to come back, but it's so slow. I remember the way my mother wore her hair, for instance. She had long bangs that kept falling over her eyes. And I remember the way she smelled. Sometimes when I'm about to fall asleep, I can smell her perfume. And her lipstick—she always wore the same soft shade of pink."

"That reminds me." He reached into his pocket and pulled out a small pouch. "I forgot to give you this earlier. I found it on the floor in your room."

She opened the pouch and smiled. "My lipstick! I was wondering where it was. I lost it that Sunday, the day after we…the day I ran away."

He didn't speak; the look in his eyes said it all.

"Jake…"

"This moving back—are you planning to stay? I want you to be sure. I don't want to get Cory's hopes up, only to have them shattered. *Are* you sure?"

She knew he wasn't talking about Cory. "I'm sure."

He moved away from her and looked at her sternly. "You'd better be, because I've been thinking, it's time for us to make plans. Definite plans."

This was the Jake she remembered, assertive and gruff, but she now understood that his demeanor was just a veneer. "Just what kind of plans do you have in mind?" she asked, pretending to match the gravity in his voice.

"For one thing, I know how much you want to keep your parents' house, so after we renovate, we'll move in there. Besides, my place doesn't have the land to add on, and I want to build you a studio. And I don't want any argument about the cost. I figure it's an even trade—your house, my investment. The place will be worth twice its value once I'm done."

"So the original arrangement is over?" she teased. "Should we draw up a new contract?"

"The only contract I'll sign is one in which I promise you the rest of my life."

*The rest of my life.* The words had been wonderful that night at Freeman's Pond, so many years ago, but today they were magic. Except this time I'm keeping my name, she thought. Laura Logan sounds funny, always had. Okay, maybe I'll compromise. Laura Matheson-Logan. It has a nice ring.

"I'll start right away with the necessary repairs," he said, "like the plumbing. We can't live in that house in its present condition. We'll stay at my place until I'm done. And after a few months of living together, we can talk about something more permanent."

She blinked, momentarily rebuffed. He wasn't talking about remarriage; he was talking about living together. What happened to his "I'm way past the trial-and-error stage of my life" speech?

She looked at his face, and once again saw through his veneer. He was scared. With her track record, who could blame him? Before he signed that contract—and she knew he meant it metaphorically; there would be nothing in writing, no prenup, just their spoken vows—he needed to be sure. Would she run or would she stay?

"I know you're scared," he continued, as though projecting his fear onto her. "I know I wasn't exactly the best husband in the world. But I think this is the way to go. We'll get to know each other all over again. And later," he added, looking at her almost shyly, "we can think about making even more renovations."

"An office for you?"

"No, I can use one of the smaller bedrooms as a study. I

won't be working at home that much, anyway. Cory can have the bedroom next to ours, and Rose can take the room next to his. It's up to you, of course. It's your house, after all. But I'm talking about something else."

"*Our* house," she corrected. "What other renovations do you have in mind?"

His eyes were twinkling. "I'm talking about a nursery."

Whoa. She sat up straight. A nursery? As in *baby?*

The last vestige of her energy drained away in a tide of despair. She slumped forward on the bench, feeling hollow and lifeless. "You always told me you didn't want more children," she said in a small voice.

"And I didn't. But it wasn't how I always felt. I was an only child, and I grew up feeling there was something missing. I wanted a large family. Cynthia knew this, but after we were married, she said she wanted to keep it just the two of us."

All this time she had believed that Jake had never wanted kids. He just never wanted kids with *her.* "I was an only child, too," she reminded him. "I felt the same way you did."

"I know," he said, reaching for her hand. "But for me, things changed." His voice took on a wistful tone. "When Cynthia told me she was pregnant, I was so excited, I went to the Danbury Mall and bought every mobile, every stuffed animal in the whole department store. But she didn't want the baby, and said I would make a lousy father. Yeah, I know. I spent too much time at work, and I wouldn't go with her to Lamaze class. I was a crud, I admit it. But was that a reason for her to threaten to end the pregnancy? I swear I wanted him, Laura. I couldn't wait for him to be born."

"So what changed your mind about having more?" Her question was laced with bitterness.

"After Cynthia's accident, I realized how fickle life could be. I mean, one day she was here, and then suddenly, just like that, she was gone. I knew how much you wanted kids, but I thought, What if something happened to me? How could I bring another child into this world, knowing that at any time fate could step in again? I didn't want another child of mine growing up with only one parent. Look what it did to Cory."

She had grown up without a mother *or* a father, and because of that, she had wanted children more than anything in this world, to nurture them with all the love she had missed. She tried not to focus on the irony. Here she was unable to conceive, and Jake was talking about mobiles. "Cory is doing much better now," she said, trying to conceal her misery.

"No thanks to me. He's been seeing a counselor at school, and this time it's working out."

"That's great, Jake, but don't put yourself down. You're a great dad. Maybe a little too protective, but I can understand why." If she'd had children of her own, she would probably have held on to them with vise-like arms. "You're worried that something will happen to him, too. I still get chills whenever I think about him running away to New York."

"And that's what did it for me. That's what made me change my mind about having children. I was a basket case that night, waiting to hear that he was all right. If anything had happened to him, you wouldn't be talking to me now. I'd probably be locked up somewhere in a mental institution. *But he was okay.* Don't you see? I went through the worst hell a parent can go through, waiting, not knowing. And nothing happened."

"And now you want more kids," she said flatly. "You wouldn't have them with me when we were married, but now, suddenly, you've worked through your fears and you've seen the light."

"Come on, Squirt. I know it took me a while to come around, but it's not too late. I thought you'd be happy. All you ever talked about was having a baby."

It *was* too late, but she didn't have the heart—or the courage—to tell him. Life was fickle all right. It was downright cruel.

"Of course I'm happy," she said, her voice sounding tinny in her ears. "I'm just tired. It's been a long day. In fact, I'd like to skip the ceremony in Ballard Park, if that's okay."

"Hey, I wanted to skip it in the first place. Let's go back to my place. I'll throw something on the grill. How does steak sound? I'll even make fries, if you make the salad."

A raucous honking caught her attention, and she looked up. A flock of geese in a vee formation were coming from the north. They were Canada geese, she knew, and would be staying in Connecticut until January before continuing south. "I was thinking about heading back to New York," she said, watching their flight. "I know I was planning to stay the evening, but I think I overdid it today. I guess I'm not over this bug after all." She lowered her gaze, but wouldn't meet his eyes. "Would you mind just taking me home?"

A thick silence filled the air. He fingered the side of her face, turning her head toward him. "Something's bothering you, Laura. I can tell. Am I going too fast again? Talk to me."

"Nothing's wrong. I'm just tired, and I don't want to get back to the city too late." She forced a weak smile. "It's only one more week. After that, I'm here to stay."

The look on his face told her he wasn't convinced. In his eyes was written the question he had asked only moments before. *Are you sure?*

She wasn't lying when she'd told him she was tired. Whether it was because she still wasn't over this bug, as she'd told Jake, or because his words had sent her spiraling into a pit of anguish, made no difference. All she wanted to do was go back to New York and curl up in bed.

She had to drive through Ridgefield to get to the highway. Although Main Street had been reopened for traffic, a few stragglers were still browsing, as merchants and artists packed up their displays. Most of the shoppers had already gone on to Ballard Park for the sunset celebration, where there would be food and entertainment and, later, a bonfire. The old tradition had begun years back when farmers had gathered to celebrate the harvest—and to celebrate life.

Farther along Main, people were coming out of a church. They're probably going to the park, too, Laura thought. It seemed as if everyone had something to celebrate. Everyone but her. How could she celebrate life when she couldn't give any?

In Romanesque Revival style, the church was small but charming with its rounded arches and a picturesque tower. At the top the stones were smaller than the heavier blocks below, and because of the interplay between light and shadow, the sun, as it moved across the sky, played tricks on the mind.

As a child Laura would look up and see angels.

She realized that this was Reverend Barnes's church.

On a sudden impulse she parked the truck and went in. This is silly, she told herself. What did she think she would find?

She walked along a plush red carpet and sat down in the front pew. She let her mind drift, and a sense of serenity came over her. Reverend Barnes was right. He'd said she would find comfort here, and she did.

"I see you've finally decided to pay us a visit," he said, sitting down beside her. "Were you at the fair?"

"Yes, it was lovely," she said, looking at the altar. "I'm a little tired, though. I'm not going to Ballard Park. I'll go next year."

"The sunset is even more spectacular in winter. You don't have to wait a whole year, now that you're moving back. In fact, I'm hoping to see you here in church next Sunday. In case you've forgotten, Ridgefield is just a hop and skip away from Middlewood."

She turned to him in surprise. "How did you know I was...Rose told you, right? She comes to your church, too."

He smiled gently. "Word gets around. What do you say, Laura? Can I count on you to join our congregation? You know, your mother never missed a Sunday."

"I remember," she said quietly. "I remember running up and down the aisle, playing with the other kids. That's what I liked about this place. It wasn't strict or...stuffy."

"It still isn't," he said. "I believe that service should be a happy event, with lively music. I've even learned to play the guitar."

She smiled back at him. She couldn't imagine anything more incongruous than this elderly, bent-over man, in this quaint, traditional church, sitting at the pulpit, playing a guitar. "Can I ask you something, Reverend Barnes?"

The warm look on his face told her she could ask him anything.

"When you were at my house, you told me you had known my mother when she was a child. You also said that you had performed my parents' wedding ceremony. There's so little I know about them, like how they met, when they became engaged—that sort of thing."

"I'm surprised Elizabeth didn't tell you. Where should I start? I know that your aunt met your father in college, and they became friends. Your father was a constant visitor to the house, and after he joined the Navy, both she and your mother wrote to him. It was through these letters your mother and father fell in love. But she was very young, only sixteen. They decided to keep it a secret, until she turned eighteen."

Laura remembered the box she had opened in the pantry while sorting through her aunt's belongings. Containing letters written by a man in the service, it had been labeled "Navy." This was more than coincidence. The author of those letters must have been her father. "Why did he call himself Angel?" she asked, her mind reeling.

"You've heard of the Blue Angels, haven't you? They perform demonstration flights to encourage Navy and Marine recruiting. They do all kinds of stunts and aerobatics, high-precision flying. Your father dreamed of being part of the team."

"You said he was honorably discharged. Why did he leave the Navy?"

"It was his eyesight. Macular degeneration. Once it started, it progressed rapidly. And, of course, that meant the end of his flying career."

"I remember he wore thick glasses." And she remembered what he'd written in the letters to her aunt, how he'd described his love of flying. "What a tragedy for him, having to give up his dream. He must have been devastated."

"Yes, it was sad, but with the love and support of your mother, he adjusted. And he made her happy. I never saw her once without those wings on her."

"Wings?"

"His gold pin. He actually did complete the initial training, and after he graduated, he was given his wings. He didn't have much money, so instead of an engagement ring, he gave her his pin. She wore it everywhere." His face suddenly clouded. "He didn't earn much, working in the hardware store. It never bothered your mother, but he always felt guilty. He knew she had wanted to stay in Ridgefield, but on his salary they couldn't afford to live here."

True, Ridgefield was more upscale than Middlewood, but her parents had loved Middlewood, and they had loved the house they lived in. Laura knew this with a certainty she couldn't explain. And then she remembered. She remembered playing in the yard while her mother watched her from the kitchen window, smiling at her. She remembered her father coming in through the front door, singing a tune from some old movie as he hung up his hat and coat. One after another, like a dream that happens in a moment but unravels over time, the memories came back. Her parents had been happy, and so had she.

"What about Aunt Tess?" she asked, hungry for more information, the kind that memory couldn't reveal. "I know there was a rift between her and my mother. Do you know what happened?"

"I can't be sure. She never talked about it. But I do know that after your parents got married, she refused to have anything to do with them."

Laura sat quietly, reflecting on Reverend Barnes's words. Her aunt had written to Angel for two years. What if she had misconstrued the meaning in his letters? "We'll find each other again," he had written. These words were not easily forgotten; even Laura had remembered them. Angel had been offering only friendship, but what if Aunt Tess had taken these words as some kind of oath?

She rose from the pew and extended her hand. "Thank you, Reverend Barnes. You can't know how much you've helped me."

"Don't be a stranger," he said, holding her hand warmly. These were the words he'd said to her back at the house, after the funeral.

She left the church and sat for a while in the truck, trying to reconcile what she'd just been told with what she already knew. The more she thought about it, the more convinced she was that her aunt had been in love with Angel. For two years her aunt had written to him while he was in the Navy, and then the letters had stopped. Laura's mother would have been eighteen then, her secret out in the open. Had Angel stopped writing to Tess, or had Tess, brokenhearted and upset, thrown away his letters?

Years later, Tess moved into the house and cleared away all mementos of her sister's life. But she couldn't clear *me* away, Laura thought. It must have been so difficult for her, living with me. I was a daily reminder that she had been betrayed. I was a daily reminder of the love she couldn't have.

But in spite of herself, Tess had loved her niece. John Collins had said that she'd worked at two jobs to ensure that Laura would have the house. Poor Aunt Tess, Laura thought. She could have had a happy life, but she'd wasted the years resenting the past, harboring a grudge until the day she died.

Laura's hands tightened on the steering wheel as a disturbing thought occurred to her. *Am I so different?*

She knew what it was like to hold a grudge. She'd harbored anger against her aunt, and then Jake, for years. And like Aunt Tess she knew what it was like to be reminded daily of what she couldn't have. In the park, at a restaurant, in the supermarket, children were everywhere.

Jake's words echoed in her head. "I thought you'd be happy. All you ever talked about was having a baby."

Would having a baby become all *he* ever talked about?

Maybe he'd forget about this whole business. After all, his turn-about had been so sudden, and he could easily change his mind again.

But what if he didn't? Would it be fair of her to deny him his family? He was still young; he could find someone else, someone who could bear him children.

She had to tell him the truth, and she had to tell him face-to-face. When she returned next week they would sit down and talk, openly and honestly. It was about trust, which at this time for them was fragile. In her heart she knew he would tell her that it didn't matter, that being with her was what counted most. She had to trust that he'd be telling her the truth.

She turned off Main and headed for the highway. She arrived at her apartment before nine that evening, and without even bothering to change, climbed into bed.

She was exhausted. Tired in body, tired in soul.

## Chapter Fourteen

Laura woke up on Monday with a hammer in her head. Too sick to go to work, she called Suzanne and told her she would try and make it in later that day, and that if problems came up, she could be reached at home.

"Don't worry," Suzanne replied in a sugary voice. "I have everything under control. Get some rest, and I'll see you tomorrow."

On Tuesday Laura was feeling worse. This was no twenty-four-hour bug. The nausea had returned, and the night sweats had worsened. She called Suzanne, but this time her assistant was curt. "I told you, it's no sweat. We're doing fine without you."

No sweat? What a joke. Laura was bathing in it.

When Jake called that night, she told him she was feeling better. She didn't want him worrying over what she prayed was a false alarm. But what if it wasn't? What if she were out of remission? He pictured the way he'd smiled at her when she'd met him at the airport, hoping the memory would push away her fears. She fell asleep dreaming of their future, and when she awoke the next morning, after a full night's sleep, she did feel better.

Maybe she hadn't lied to Jake, after all.

She decided to fix something to eat. But once in the kitchen, she felt her knees give way and she had to sit down. Then, as if to punish her for the lie, nausea rose in her throat.

She had an appointment with the oncologist next week—the five-year milestone, she thought with anxiety. But she knew she couldn't wait until then.

She would call Ellen. In a calm and reassuring voice, her friend would tell her that she was all right, that the Hodgkin's hadn't returned, and then they would talk about the man Ellen was dating, and Jake, and life would go on.

Her body protesting with tiredness, she dressed in a fog. She called for a taxi to take her to the hospital.

"It doesn't sound serious," Ellen said, an hour later in her office.

The look on her face was unconvincing. "So what is it?" Laura asked. "I can't go on this way. I'm not sleeping well, I can't work, I can't eat… You don't think…"

"What I think is that it's the flu. I know you're worried, but by this time next week, after you've seen Dr. Waring, all your fears will have been put to rest, once and for all."

"I don't want to wait for my checkup next week. I want answers now. How can I go back to Jake if I'm sick again? It wouldn't be fair to him, and it wouldn't be fair to Cory."

"There's nothing wrong with you that some bed rest won't fix," Ellen said. She sighed. "I see there's no convincing you. Okay, roll up your sleeve. I'll do the vampire thing if it makes you happy, but I think it's a waste of time."

After Ellen had taken samples of Laura's blood, she said, "Now go home, eat a light meal, and get to bed early."

"Getting into bed is the easy part," Laura said. "It's staying asleep that's the problem."

When Jake called that evening, she kept the conversation short. What could she tell him? That she was afraid that the cancer was back? On Friday Ellen would call with the results from the blood tests, telling her that she was all right, that all her fears were unfounded. Why worry him for nothing? *For nothing,* she repeated to herself, trying to believe the words.

On Thursday she finally made it out of bed and dragged herself to the gallery. Even though her nausea had subsided, she was still so tired, and her muscles ached as though she'd spent the night at the gym.

"You look like a cat that's been hauled through a dog pen," Suzanne said in her normal delicate manner. "Go home. The exhibition's all set for next week."

"Are you sure?" Laura asked, knowing darn well what Suzanne would say.

"Of course I'm sure." Suzanne hesitated, then to Laura's surprise, added, "You did a great job with the groundwork. I don't know if I would have been able to do it all on my own. I have to admit, I'm a little scared. Would you mind if I called you from time to time for advice?"

"I wouldn't mind at all," Laura answered. "And for what it's worth, I think you're going to do just fine."

"Coming from you, it's worth a great deal," Suzanne said, surprising Laura again.

When Jake called that evening, Laura told him she had a headache and didn't want to talk. Not missing the hurt in his voice, she promised to call him in the morning. It was true about the headache—and it was a humdinger—but she knew she had used it as an excuse.

It was only a little after seven, but she was exhausted, and fell asleep within minutes. After just a few short hours, she woke up drenched. These night sweats and I are becoming old friends, she thought. Real pals. What would I do without them?

The answer was *survive*.

She lay back in bed, staring at the ceiling. Tomorrow was Friday. In the morning Ellen would call with the results, and Laura would call Jake. Of course everything's all right, she imagined herself telling him. No, I haven't been acting funny. I've just been tired. You know, that bug that's been going around. Oh yes, much better now. And then she would laugh at his jokes and make some of her own, and all this would be history.

Only that wasn't going to happen. Ellen would call and say the words she'd been dreading, four little words that had hovered above like a rain cloud for almost five years, waiting for just the right moment to burst. And just when she believed she could walk outside without an umbrella, surprise!

It's amazing how four little words could completely alter the course of someone's life. With utmost certainty, Laura knew what Ellen would say.

The cancer is back.

When she finally fell back to sleep, she dreamed she was twelve years old, back at the indoor community pool, swimming laps. Suddenly she was under the surface, gasping for air. Jake dove in after her, but he couldn't reach her. She was drowning, this time for real, and he couldn't save her.

This time, when she awoke, she was drenched not with sweat, but with tears.

A spasm of nausea shook her body. It was going to be a long night.

Jake lay in bed, staring up at the ceiling.

Earlier that evening, after he had hung up the phone, he'd

been convinced that Laura was hiding something. He didn't buy the old "not tonight honey, I have a headache" excuse for a minute. She had sounded so removed, she might have been calling from another planet. It was just like old times: one minute she was close, the next minute distant. He was certain she was having second thoughts.

Maybe he had been going too fast. Maybe he was rushing her. It had only been a few weeks since she'd come back to Middlewood. The thing was, they'd wasted too much time already. He was anxious to move ahead.

He couldn't sleep. He considered putting together the computer he'd bought for Cory's birthday. He'd also bought a hoop for the side of the house. Laura's house, he thought. *Our* house. Was he spoiling Cory? Maybe. But he'd promised his son he would shoot baskets with him, and what kid these days didn't have his own computer?

But right now Jake's mind wasn't on presents. There was something about the way Laura had sounded on the phone...

He went downstairs to fix a sandwich. Rose was sitting at the table, wearing her kimono, sipping a cup of tea. "I see you couldn't sleep, either," he said.

She looked up at him and frowned. "I have a problem."

"Don't we all," he said grimly. "So, Rosy Nosy, what's ailing you?"

"Now that Fred's retiring, he wants to move back to Iowa to be near his daughter. Last week she made him a grandpa for the fourth time. He says he wasn't around much for his own kids when they were growing up, and he doesn't want to make the same mistake with his grandchildren."

"I know you'll be sorry to see him go."

"You don't understand. He wants me to go with him."

Jake smiled. "So the no-iron lady is finally thinking about getting married again. What happened to your famous I Won't Iron Any Man's Shirts for Free motto?"

"Oh, pooh. I'll keep ironing his shirts as long as he keeps fixing things. I'm sure I'll find plenty for him to do around the house."

Jake had no doubt about it. "It sounds as if your problem is solved."

"To tell you the truth, I miss having a baby around to fuss over, seeing how I never had one of my own. Fred's daughter doesn't have a mother, and I figure she could sure use my help, with those three other little ones taking up so much of her time. Anyway, with Laura coming back, it's time for me to move out. You don't need an old busybody like me getting in the way."

"No, you're wrong," Jake said. "You're part of this family. We want you to stay." Rose's lips trembled with a sad smile, and for a moment Jake was afraid she would cry. "I'm sorry, Rose. I'm being selfish. You need a life outside this crazy, mixed-up household. And Cory is older now. We'll manage. But we'll miss you. And we'll miss your outfits. So what's in store for next month?"

"I'm thinking about Texas. That's where my parents were born and raised. My father never liked the smell of oil, or cows either, for that matter. He moved up north with my mother before I was born. How do you think I'll look in a cowboy hat? We want to go there for our honeymoon."

All those years of dreaming about exotic places and here she was planning her first trip away from home right here in the U.S.A. What was that expression? Something about finding yourself in your own backyard.

"I think you'll look great," he said. "Even better on a horse." He grinned. She'd probably dress up the poor animal, as well.

"'Course I won't even think about leaving until Laura's back for good. When do you suppose that'll be?"

"I don't know," he said honestly. "We haven't made definite plans."

"Jake Logan, do you mean to tell me you haven't set a date? I'm not one to interfere, but if you ask me, I think you should get a lasso, and rope that wife of yours home to roost before she gets away again. It's time you two settled down to business."

Jake laughed. Rose sure had a way of putting things. "Now don't you worry about us. This time she's staying. She's already moved back most of her stuff, and she'll be back this weekend, this time for good."

"You mean to tell me that you're letting her do all the moving herself? You're going to wear her out before she even puts her foot in the door. That poor little thing is as thin as a hickory stick already."

"Now, Rose, don't go off in a tailspin. Yes, of course I'm helping her."

"I certainly hope so. I've got to tell you, these days she's been looking mighty tired. Even at the game last week, I thought she was going to faint dead away, right there in the bleachers. It was as cold as a deep-freeze in that gym, and all the while she kept complaining about the heat. I'm telling you, she doesn't look well. You've got to take care of her."

He gave her a mock salute. "Yes, ma'am, I aim to."

After Rose had gone back to her room, Jake sat at the table, thinking. Taking care of Laura was one thing he'd always tried to do, but she'd kept pushing him away, insisting she didn't want help from anyone. Even last week, after they had arrived home from the airport, she had refused to come inside, although it was obvious she wasn't feeling well.

Maybe Rose was right. Maybe Jake should get a lasso.

Now that would go over well, he thought. Over the years Laura had blossomed into the woman she was meant to be, forthright and fiercely independent. But sometimes she could be so stubborn. Maybe it was because she was still afraid to trust him, just as he'd been afraid to trust her. He knew she had good cause. Throughout their marriage he'd been too absorbed in his own world, working too much, wallowing in his own mistrust. Even after she'd left him, he hadn't changed his ways. Sure, he'd gone after her, but it had been on his terms, and knowing this, she had turned him away. Although it had been her decision, the end result was the same. He hadn't been there for her when she'd needed him most, when she'd been fighting to stay alive.

*Fighting to stay alive.*

An uneasy feeling settled in the pit of his stomach. Laura hadn't been feeling well on the way home from the airport, and although she had insisted that she was all right, that she was only tired, it was obvious on Sunday that whatever bug she had wasn't going away.

"Thin as a hickory stick," Rose had said. "I thought she was going to faint dead away." The basketball game was almost two weeks ago; Laura had been sick for a while now.

Coldness gripped him as realization took over.

If she hadn't been so tired, if she hadn't been so short on the phone this past week, he might not have given the notion a second thought.

It was happening again.

No. Oh, no.

He laid his head in his hands. She was so young, so alive. Why now? Why now when they had just begun to believe they had a future? Why now when she had just begun to believe *she* had a future? His eyes filled with tears, tears he had suppressed when Cynthia had died, tears he had suppressed years later when Laura had come down with the disease the first time. He wiped them away and stared at his hand. And then, as if he were watching himself in a bad dream, he saw himself go to the refrigerator to get a beer. He saw himself reach inside and pick up the bottle, and he saw himself slamming it against the wall.

He fell back in his chair and slumped over. He wasn't a religious man, but he found himself praying, begging, *Please, God. Not now. Not ever.*

The stillness in the house screamed in his ear. He was astonished that no one else could hear it. But no one had heard the crash of the bottle, either. He was alone. Alone with his fear and grief, feeling the way Laura probably felt right now.

No. He couldn't begin to imagine what she must be going through. This wasn't about him. Not anymore. When he lost her the first time, he thought he would go out of his mind. Her disease had given him a rude awakening; he'd realized he needed her. He'd gone after her, trying to make her see that he'd changed, but she'd turned him away. And now he knew why. He hadn't been able to see beyond his own pain to be able to help her with hers.

Numb, he got up and started picking up the broken glass, not feeling the stab when a sharp jagged piece pierced his skin. Blood oozed from his hand, and he watched it with cold fascination. Let it all drain out, he thought. I deserve it.

This isn't about you, he repeated to himself. Laura needed him, and this time he wouldn't let her down. He would be there for her, for whatever time they had left, making every moment count.

But would she be coming back, now that she was sick again? He didn't think so. Whether she had decided he couldn't give her what she needed, or whether she simply wanted to spare him, was irrelevant. All that mattered was that he go to her now.

It wasn't until he was in the car, driving down Main, that he realized he had to turn around and go back. As much as he wanted to be there for her, now, tonight, he decided to wait until morning. This wasn't about him. Laura would be asleep when he arrived, and she needed her rest.

When the phone rang Friday morning, Laura stared at it, willing it to stop. Maybe if she didn't answer, this whole nightmare would disappear.

The machine came on. "Laura? Pick up. It's me, Ellen. I know you're there. I have news for you. Good news."

Laura jumped for the phone, knocking over a lamp.

"What was that?" Ellen said. "Are you okay?"

"I am now. I was so scared...so sure..."

"I know," Ellen said softly. "So was I."

Laura wiped away tears of relief. "I have to call Jake. He thinks I've been avoiding him. He thinks I'm having second thoughts."

"Look, before you hang up, I want to tell you how sorry I am for putting him down. All I ever wanted was for you to be happy."

"Thanks, El, but can we talk about this later? I need to call—"

"Yes, I know. You need to call Jake. Okay, I'll let you go, but in a minute. I also want to tell you that I wish you all the best. You deserve it, especially after all you've been through. Go back to Middlewood, marry him and raise your family. I know that the four of you—the five of you, if Rose stays on—will have a healthy, happy life."

"Thanks, El, but—" She stopped. "The five of us? What are you getting at? I don't have time for games. I already told you—"

"So you've said. You have to call Jake. When you speak to him, say hi from me, and oh, there's one more thing. Don't forget to mention that he's going to be a father. I mean, again, since he already has Cory, and—"

"What did you say?"

"You heard me the first time. Jake's going to be a father. You're pregnant, Laura."

Pregnant! Take a deep breath, Laura told herself. Steady, now. "I don't understand. How could I be pregnant?"

Ellen laughed. "If you don't know by now, you've got troubles, girl."

"But the chemotherapy! I thought…they told me…"

"They told you it was unlikely you'd ever conceive, not impossible. If you'd had radiation, your chances would have been zero. Now, let's see, you told me that you and Jake, I mean, the two of you—"

"It hasn't even been four weeks! I thought it took a lot longer than that to be sure."

"A blood test can confirm pregnancy as early as five or six days after implantation. Sometimes it comes out negative at this stage, but when it reads positive, it's time to start knitting booties."

"I didn't even consider the possibility when I missed my period. I mean, I hardly ever get it, anyway." Laura paused. "It's amazing. I go in for a cell count and I find out I'm pregnant!"

"Not so amazing. I kind of broke a few rules. You'd told me that you had slept with Jake, so I took a chance and ordered the test. I was grasping at straws. I didn't want to think about the alternative."

"I know, El. Neither did I." But Laura *had* thought about the alternative. And she had come to the wrong conclusion. "So that explains my symptoms."

"Actually, no. Other than this bug, there's nothing wrong with you except for the fact that you're pregnant. Not that being pregnant means there's something wrong, unless of course you don't want to be. You do want to be, don't you? Of course you do. Oh, heck, I'm babbling. I'm beginning to sound just like you, the way you get when you're excited. I'm just so excited for *you*."

"Are you saying that what I've been feeling has nothing to do with the pregnancy?"

"It's too early for symptoms," Ellen said. "It's just a virus— although nothing to worry about," she quickly added. "And stress. Think about all that's happened these past few weeks.

But now, as your doctor and friend, I'm ordering you to relax. You have another life to think about."

Laura hung up the phone, grinning as though she had just been made privy to a well-kept secret. And she had. Only she didn't intend to keep it a secret for long.

She called Jake's office, but Mary told her he was out. "Unless he changed his plans," his secretary said, "he's spending the day at the site. Unfortunately, I can't reach him. He forgot to turn on his cell. You know how he gets when he's preoccupied."

Laura knew too well. Jake was a workaholic. Although lately he seemed more preoccupied with *her* than with his work. And she wasn't exactly complaining.

No, she wouldn't be complaining about much anymore. She could even live with the nausea, now that she knew what it meant. Doctor or not, Ellen was wrong: it wasn't too early for symptoms. Laura had once read that some women experienced signs right from the start. Well, Laura was one of those women. She shuddered, remembering how certain she'd been that the cancer had returned. Now even the night sweats no longer scared her. Ellen had said they were because of the flu, or even stress. Whatever the cause, it wasn't Hodgkin's.

But what if, one day, the cancer did return? Because of her health history, she knew she would always have to live with this threat. Question after question assailed her. What if it happened during the pregnancy? How could she undergo chemotherapy without harming the baby? What if the doctors advised her against carrying to term? What if she got sick later, leaving her child to grow up without a mother, as she had?

"Nothing is going to happen to me," she'd assured Cory on the night he'd run away. How could she have made such a promise?

Having this baby didn't change a thing at all; it only compounded the problem.

But was there an alternative? She felt herself growing pale at the thought. All her life she'd dreamed of having a child, Jake's child, and now, against all odds, she was pregnant.

There *was* no alternative. This baby was a miracle, and she would let nothing, including her fear of dying, stand in the way. She remembered what Cassie had said. "Isn't much of what we do and feel a result of this fear?" Laura had been denying her *own* life, because of this fear of dying.

She was tired of living her life as though at any moment it could be snatched away. She thought about her parents, and about Cynthia, how they had been victims of senseless, random acts of fate. And then she thought about her aunt, who had lived in the past, alone with her grudges, without ever having lived at all. Maybe life didn't come with guarantees, but Laura was damned if she would waste another minute of her own life, another second, worrying about what could be.

Oh, yes, she would have this baby, and she would look forward to seeing her child and Cory grow up, get married and have families of their own.

Bursting with renewed energy, she resumed packing. She'd moved most of her things last week, but there were still the remaining dishes, linen and clothes. She sat back down. This is crazy, she thought. I haven't even picked up a car. She didn't need another moving truck, but there was no way she could fit it all into a taxi, never mind drag it onto a train.

She had to be in New York next week for her appointment with Dr. Waring and to hand over the key to the new tenant. She would ask Jake to go with her, and together they would clean out the apartment.

She tried Jake's office again and then she called Rose. Where was Jake? It was only nine-thirty, but she couldn't wait any longer. It was time to go home.

She packed a small suitcase and in less than ten minutes

was in a taxi, heading for Grand Central. "Can't you go faster?" she called to the driver. Even when it didn't rain, traffic was murder.

"Lady, in this mess it would take a miracle."

A miracle. She felt a stirring in her abdomen, and smiled. You're being silly, she told herself. It's just butterflies. It's far too soon for me to feel the baby. She leaned back and relaxed, thinking about the months ahead.

She'd have to change her habits, now that she had another life to consider. For one thing, there would be no strenuous workouts at the gym. Jake would go with her to prenatal class, even if it took a bulldozer. She pictured him coaching her, breathing along with her, his cheeks as puffy and red as when he'd played the trumpet. And it was time to go back to her healthy diet, which meant no coffee. Decaffeinated tea would be fine, unless there was something in those herbs she didn't know about. She'd have to ask her obstetrician. That was another thing. She'd have to find one soon.

Thinking about food suddenly made her stomach turn over. But it wasn't morning sickness that was making her uneasy. It had something to do with tea, or maybe it was coffee…

Coffee. It was the coffee. Omigosh, she'd left the machine on. She could almost hear Jake saying, "What's the matter with you? Are you trying to burn down the house?"

"Turn around!" she shouted to the driver.

"Lady, I thought you were in a hurry." He muttered something she would never repeat, and swerved the car around.

"I'll only be a minute," she told him as he pulled up in front of her building. "Don't leave." She left her suitcase in the back seat and hurried inside.

Ditsy, Jake used to call her. The new tenant wouldn't be as generous when he found the apartment in ashes. And neither would the landlord.

Anyway, who was Jake to call her ditsy? He had forgotten

to turn on his cell phone. What if there was an emergency? He always said—

She froze. A man was standing at the top of the stairwell.

He emerged from the shadows, and she felt her heart leap. She ran into his arms, relief rushing through her, blending with joy. "I tried to call you," she said, breathless, "but I couldn't reach you. No one could reach you, not even Mary. I had to—"

"I went to the gallery," Jake said, "but they said you were at home."

"I was on my way to the station. I couldn't wait. I have something to tell you—"

"I know, Laura. You don't have to say a thing."

A warm glow spread through her. Jake knew, and he had rushed right over. Suddenly she drew away from his grasp. "I'm going to kill that Ellen! She had no right to call you."

"Ellen didn't call me. No one's been able to reach me, remember? I guessed. You haven't been feeling well, and I put two and two together." He reached for her hand. "Let's go inside. You need to lie down."

"I'm fine. Just a little tired. I don't want to lie down." She looked at his face, and immediately regretted her curt words. All he wanted to do was take care of her, and without thinking, she had rebuked him. "Let's go home," she said softly.

"Soon, Laura. But first we need to talk."

He was so tense, so serious. You'd think he would be elated, after what he'd said last Sunday. What if he hadn't meant it? What if he'd only said he wanted children because he thought it was what she wanted to hear? Maybe she'd been wrong. Maybe taking care of her was the last thing on his mind.

"The taxi's waiting," she said tersely. "Can you get my bag?"

She watched him go down the stairwell, and entered the apartment. In the kitchen the coffee machine was cold. She hadn't left it on.

He had better get his act together, because she was going to have this baby come hell or high water. "Well?" she said, after he'd returned. "You wanted to talk?"

His voice was solemn and strangely sad. "I want you to know that I'm here for you and there's no use trying to send me away. If I could, I would move heaven and earth for you, but all I can do is be with you and hold you. When I think of the time I wasted, I could shoot myself."

A strand of hair had fallen down his forehead, and she smoothed it away. He looked like a teenager again, but without the happy-go-lucky facade. He was so worried, so earnest, she felt ashamed she had doubted him about wanting the baby. Ashamed she had ever doubted him at all. "It was my fault," she said. "I kept running away. I was so afraid. Afraid of losing what I might find."

"You didn't run away. I pushed you. And I want to make it up to you. I'm going to do everything in my power to make you happy. I love you, Laura. I always have."

The image of him as a teenager faded, and she saw him as if for the first time, not as the boy she'd dreamed of throughout her youth, but as the man she loved and who loved her. He was her future, her life. He and Cory and the baby.

"Let's go home," she said again. "I think we should talk to Cory. No, wait. He's at school, isn't he? But we can always meet him there for lunch, can't we? They don't have a policy against parents coming by, do they…? Darn, there I go again, babbling."

"My God, Cory. I haven't even considered how this will affect him."

It was true, she thought. Some things in life never changed. She was a babbler, and Jake was a worrywart. But were all men so anxious when they found out they were going to be fathers? It was as if he were going through it for the first time, and she was moved. "Cory will be fine," she said.

"No, he'll be just as worried as I am. Worried that something is going to happen to you. He can't lose you again. *I* can't lose you again. I said I wouldn't do this. I said I wouldn't make this about me, but I can't help myself. When you left five years ago, I was angry and hurt, but I told myself I would get over it. I thought I had, but then, after seeing you that day in the chapel, my whole world came crashing down. I knew I couldn't let you go again. And now…what if…"

Not until that moment had she realized how much her leaving him had hurt him. Blinded by self-pity, she hadn't seen that his pain had matched her own. "I'm not going anywhere," she whispered, remembering when he'd said those same words the night she had conceived his child. The mist in his eyes told her that he remembered, too. "I won't make that mistake again," she added, taking his hands in hers.

"I was the one who made the mistakes," he said. "I should have been there for you years ago, and I'm sorry. I'm so sorry. But I promise you, from now on I'm going to make every moment count, especially now that you're sick."

Sick? Why would he describe her condition as sick? "You haven't been feeling well for a while," he'd said. "I put two and two together."

And then it hit her. Jake had come to the wrong conclusion, the way she had. Before she could stop herself, she broke into laughter, realizing they were on two different tracks. "So that's what this is all about. And here I thought you were proposing."

The stunned look in his eyes told her he'd been prepared for anything she might do—cry, yell, tell him to leave—anything but laugh. "I…guess I am," he said, his forehead riddled with confusion. "But why…?"

"I'm laughing because I'm happy. Yes, I'll marry you. Yes, I want you by my side, making every moment count. But I have to warn you, you're in for a long haul. There are a lot of moments in forever."

He stared at her, unblinking.

"I'm not dying, Jake. I'm pregnant."

They arrived in Middlewood just after noon. Although they were anxious to get to the school and talk to Cory, Laura insisted on stopping at the bank. "Come in with me," she said. "I don't want to be alone."

She signed in, and she and a teller went into the safe. She wasn't expecting any surprises, like a stash of one-hundred-dollar bills or maybe a forgotten bond. Other than some legal documents—for instance, the deed to the house—she didn't know *what* she was expecting. She pulled out the deposit box, and she and Jake went into a room to view the contents in private.

She picked up a brown paper bag and emptied it onto a table. There must have been a hundred photographs, of her mother and Aunt Tess when they were kids, of her mother and father at their wedding and of their years together, of her when she was a baby. Inside a second bag were envelopes. She pulled one out, and saw that it was addressed to her mother. She didn't have to pull out another one to know what they all contained. Inside were letters of love written by her father to her mother while he was in the Navy, letters her aunt had found—and kept for Laura—after moving into the house.

And there was something else. It was a small gold brooch that had once embodied the dreams and hopes of one young, eager flier. She turned the pin around and saw that it was engraved. "Home at last, with love from your Angel," she read out loud. She smiled, and pinned the wings on Jake.

\* \* \* \* \*

*We hope you love JOURNEY OF THE HEART so much that you share it with friends and family. If you do—or if you belong to a book club—there are questions on the next page that are intended to help you start a book group discussion. We hope these questions inspire you and help you get even more out of the book.*

# JOURNEY OF THE HEART—
## Readers' Ring
## Discussion Questions:

1. From the very first page, what do you learn about Laura? What is her immediate goal? What clues on the first page tell you what the story is about?

2. What is the main theme in the story? What are some of the minor themes, and which are most prevalent in today's society?

3. The line between "right" and "wrong" is not as distinct as Jake and Laura would like to believe. Does Jake have a right to be angry with Laura for not telling him about Cynthia's affair? Was Laura justified in leaving Jake five years ago, when she was first diagnosed with her disease? What other "gray" moral areas are present in the story? Do these "gray" areas accurately reflect life?

4. It was a random act of fate that killed Laura's parents, and years later, it was a random act of fate that killed Cynthia. How much of the story depends on fate? How does the "random acts of fate" idea tie in to Laura's realization in Chapter 14?

5. Throughout the story, timing plays a major role. For example, in Chapter 12, Laura arrives at the airport after Jake's plane has landed, but fortunately, his plane has been detained on the runway. Where, on a deeper and

emotional level, is timing shown to be an important element?

6. How much of a role did Laura's upbringing have in shaping her character?

7. In Chapter 6, Jake thinks, "But there was something else about Laura...it had something to do with the way she saw the world." What does Jake mean by this?

8. Women constantly face conflict between independence and interdependence. How does Laura resolve this?

9. How does Laura change and grow throughout the story? What is she like when she first arrives in Middlewood for her aunt's funeral, and how is she different when she surprises Jake at the airport?

10. What about Jake? In Chapter 2, he angers Laura with his inappropriate sexual advances. In Chapter 14, the Jake who professes his love is a changed man. What events—external and internal—lead to this change?

11. How do the minor characters add to the story? For example, examine Suzanne's attitude toward Laura. How does it reflect how Laura is changing? In your own life, have other people's attitudes toward you served as mirrors?

12. What about Aunt Tess? What traits in Tess does Laura see in herself, and why does Laura forgive her?

13. In Chapter 12, Jake has a conversation with a stranger at his hotel, and another conversation with her later at the airport. What between them is said—or not said—that causes Jake to see his world in a different way? In your own life, has a complete stranger ever affected you in some important way? Why do you think it took a stranger to accomplish this?

14. Throughout the book, Laura's run-down colonial-style house appears as repetitive imagery. What do you think it represents? What about the overhang on the front porch? Can you find other examples of symbolism?

15. How does the constantly changing weather contribute to the overall mood in the book?

16. Laura and Jake both learn that love often requires putting the other person's needs before their own. How do they each demonstrate this? With this in mind, do you think the title portrays the message in the story?

Beloved author

# Joan Elliott Pickart

introduces the next generation
of MacAllisters in

## The Baby Bet:
### MacALLISTER'S GIFTS

with the following heartwarming romances:

**On sale September 2002**
**PLAIN JANE MacALLISTER**
Silhouette Desire #1462

**On sale December 2002**
**TALL, DARK AND IRRESISTIBLE**
Silhouette Special Edition #1507

And look for the next exciting installment
of the MacAllister family saga,
coming to Silhouette Special Edition in 2003.

*Don't miss these unforgettable romances…*
*available at your favorite retail outlet.*

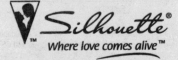

Silhouette®
*Where love comes alive™*

If you enjoyed what you just read,
then we've got an offer you can't resist!

# Take 2 bestselling love stories FREE!

# Plus get a FREE surprise gift!

**Clip this page and mail it to Silhouette Reader Service™**

| IN U.S.A. | IN CANADA |
|---|---|
| 3010 Walden Ave. | P.O. Box 609 |
| P.O. Box 1867 | Fort Erie, Ontario |
| Buffalo, N.Y. 14240-1867 | L2A 5X3 |

**YES!** Please send me 2 free Silhouette Special Edition® novels and my free surprise gift. After receiving them, if I don't wish to receive anymore, I can return the shipping statement marked cancel. If I don't cancel, I will receive 6 brand-new novels every month, before they're available in stores! In the U.S.A., bill me at the bargain price of $3.99 plus 25¢ shipping and handling per book and applicable sales tax, if any*. In Canada, bill me at the bargain price of $4.74 plus 25¢ shipping and handling per book and applicable taxes**. That's the complete price and a savings of at least 10% off the cover prices—what a great deal! I understand that accepting the 2 free books and gift places me under no obligation ever to buy any books. I can always return a shipment and cancel at any time. Even if I never buy another book from Silhouette, the 2 free books and gift are mine to keep forever.

235 SDN DNUR
335 SDN DNUS

| Name | (PLEASE PRINT) | |
|---|---|---|
| Address | Apt.# | |
| City | State/Prov. | Zip/Postal Code |

\* Terms and prices subject to change without notice. Sales tax applicable in N.Y.
\*\* Canadian residents will be charged applicable provincial taxes and GST.
All orders subject to approval. Offer limited to one per household and not valid to current Silhouette Special Edition® subscribers.
® are registered trademarks of Harlequin Books S.A., used under license.

SPED02                    ©1998 Harlequin Enterprises Limited

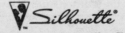

*Here I am at another airport, leaving behind another couple, brought together by mystery and the magic of a black cat detective.*

*Adios, amigos. Until we ride again!*

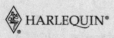

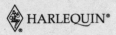

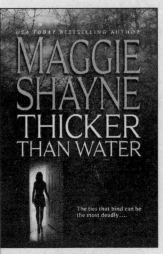

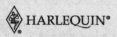

If you enjoyed what you just read,
then we've got an offer you can't resist!

# Take 2 bestselling
# love stories FREE!

# Plus get a FREE surprise gift!

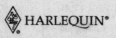

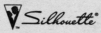

# SPECIAL EDITION™

Coming in August 2002,
from Silhouette Special Edition and

## CHRISTINE RIMMER,

the author who brought you the popular series

### *CONVENIENTLY YOURS,*

brings her new series

# THE SONS OF CAITLIN BRAVO

Starting with

## HIS EXECUTIVE SWEETHEART
### (SE #1485)...

One day she was the prim and proper executive assistant...
the next, Celia Tuttle fell hopelessly in love with her boss,
mogul Aaron Bravo, bachelor extraordinaire. It was clear he
was never going to return her feelings, so what was a girl to
do but get a makeover—and try to quit. Only suddenly,
was Aaron eyeing his assistant in a whole new light?

And coming in October 2002, MERCURY RISING,
also from Silhouette Special Edition.

**THE SONS OF CAITLIN BRAVO: Aaron, Cade and Will.**
**They thought no woman could tame them.**
**How wrong they were!**

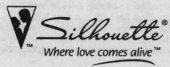

*Where love comes alive*™

# COMING NEXT MONTH

## #1507 TALL, DARK AND IRRESISTIBLE—Joan Elliott Pickart
*The Baby Bet: MacAllister's Gifts*

From the moment they met, it was magic. But Ryan Sharpe and
Carolyn St. John were both scarred by a lifetime of hurts. Then the two
met an adorable little boy who desperately needed their help, and they
realized that having the courage to face the past was their only hope for
a future…together.

## #1508 THE COWBOY'S CHRISTMAS MIRACLE—
### Anne McAllister
*Code of the West*

Deck the halls with…romance? Widowed mom Erin Jones had loved
lone wolf cowboy Deke Malone years ago, but he'd only seen her as a
friend. Suddenly, the holidays brought her back into Deke's life…and
into his arms. Would the spirit of the season teach the independent-
minded Montana man that family was the best gift of all?

## #1509 SCROOGE AND THE SINGLE GIRL—Christine Rimmer
*The Sons of Caitlin Bravo*

Bubbling bachelorette Jillian Diamond loved Christmas; legal eagle
Will Bravo hated all things ho-ho-ho. Then Will's matchmaking mom
tricked the two enemies-at-first-sight into being stuck together in an
isolated cabin during a blizzard! Could a snowbound Christmas turn
Will's bah-humbug into a declaration of love?

## #1510 THE SUMMER HOUSE—
### Susan Mallery and Teresa Southwick
*2-in-1*

Sun, sand and ocean. It was the perfect beach getaway, and best friends
Mandy Carter and Cassie Brightwell were determined to enjoy
it…alone. But summers could be full of surprises. Especially when
lovers, both old and new, showed up unexpectedly!

## #1511 FAMILY PRACTICE—Judy Duarte

High-society surgeon Michael Harper was the complete opposite of
fun-loving cocktail waitress Kara Westin. Yet, despite their differences,
Michael couldn't help proposing marriage to help Kara gain custody of
two lovable tots. Would Michael's fortune and Kara's pride get in the
way of their happily-ever-after?

## #1512 A SEASON TO BELIEVE—Elane Osborn

Jane Ashbury had been suffering from amnesia for over a year when a
Christmas tune jarred her back to reality. With so much still unknown,
private detective Matthew Sullivan was determined to help Jane piece
together the puzzle of her past. And when shocking secrets started to
surface, he offered her something better: a future filled with love!

SSECNM11